SAYING SORRY

WON'T STOP THE PAIN

ARTIE WOODINGTON

To order additional copies of this book, contact:
Bookwhip
1-855-339-3589
https://www.bookwhip.com

CONTENTS

PART 1: Chock's Family
Living in Texas

PART 3: Married Life

(For Worse, More Worse, And The Worst)

DEDICATION

This book is dedicated to my parents. They did what they had to do to the best of their ability to raise and protect eleven children.

I also dedicate this book to my children and my grandchildren. While I was writing this book, I discovered some things about myself that I wasn't aware of, and some things I thought I had forgotten.

This book is not to accuse and is not for pity. It was written to take a look back at my own life and try to understand what influenced me to make some of the choices I have made and how my choices may have affected the lives of my family.

When I began this book my intentions were to tell this story only to my family. I was encourage by some members of my family to publish this story while some of my family members felt no one ever had to know about some of the events and some of the things that happened to me.

I always told my children and grandchildren if anyone ever put their hands on them to let me know. I didn't realize I was putting them in the same situation I had been put in that kept me from telling my parents I was being molested and abused. It is still difficult for me to talk about sex and sexual abuse. I hid being molested and abused by pretending it didn't happen.

We tend to hide unpleasant things in a number of different ways. Sometimes we just hide it. Sometimes we hide. Sometimes we hide behind alcohol or drugs. I just closed my eyes and hid behind a pretense. Sometimes, I still do the same thing when I don't want to face something that maybe unpleasant. I just hide my problem and pretend that everything is fine. When I see something unpleasant or scary on TV, I just close my eyes until it goes away.

We try to raise our families by the standards our parents had set for us. When our parents are gone we forget about our own behavior because there is no one around to point them out to us.

I hope this book will help my family to understand the bad behaviors and the bad choices made by their dad and me and not hide theirs. I know our behavior was a factor in the choices they have made in their lives and is a factor in the choices they are making today.

I am proud of the distance we have come. When I look at all the generations my parents left behind, I am so proud of their accomplishments. Their potentials are endless.

Lastly, I hope this book will help the generations here today and the generations to come to remember and to appreciate the sacrifices made, and are still being made by all of our parents.

ACKNOWLEDGMENT

To God my heavenly Father, thank you for all of the blessings you have given my family and me. Thank you for preserving my memories. Thank you for giving me the desire and words to help me write this book and the perseverance to finish it.

To my children, thank you for your love and your support.

Thank you for being there, and giving me grandchildren; another chance to get it right.

PROLOGUE

When my five-year-old grandson came to visit me, he had a bump almost in the center of his forehead, the half size of an egg.

I asked, "What happened to you?"

"A boy hit me with a block."

"Grandma, I don't want you to get upset. When I get back to school, I am going to get in trouble."

"Why?"

"Because I'm going to beat him up."

"Did he mean to hit you?"

"He said he was sorry, but it didn't stop the pain."

I thought about what he had said everything I had done, and everything that had been done to me. When I said I was sorry, I felt the pain of admitting that my actions were considered unacceptable, but saying sorry exonerated me, and I was freed to go on my way.

Saying sorry lets the perpetrator off the hook, while the victim is left with the pain of the perpetrator's action. Saying sorry does not take the pain away.

PART 1

CHOCK'S FAMILY

LIVING IN TEXAS

CHAPTER 1

The Night Chock Was Reborn

Chock was born in the small Texas town her parents' families had lived in for generations. She was reborn five years later. Her rebirth took place the night the terrible, terrible, Tornadoes destroyed their house. Before the night of the tornadoes, she wasn't aware of the events that surrounded her. She didn't have any worries because her dad could fix anything, and nothing would dare to bother them as long as he was around.

Things seemed to take shape and come alive after that night. During the tornado, and days that followed, Chock became aware of the roles different members in her family played. Chock also became aware of what was going on in the world outside of their house and the power the outside world had over them. After the tornado, everything in her life changed. Their house was destroyed. They had to move in with her dad's relatives, and nothing was ever the same again.

Before the tornado, they went about their ordinary lives in an ordinary manner. They did what they had to do to get through the day. When they went home, they felt loved and wanted. They never went hungry. They knew where they belonged and felt comfortable being there.

The tornado caught them by surprise. Her daddy could always tell when a storm was brewing. They would have time to get to the storm cellar at her grandmother's. Sometimes, instead of going to the cellar, they would get on the school bus their daddy drove, and wait to see if they needed to.

They tried to avoid going down into the dark, cold, grave like room whenever possible. The cellar was dug under a hill in front of her grandmother's house and it was a haven for snakes and other poisonous creepy-crawlers. They went to the cellar when her daddy felt the cellar was necessary for their survival. There were other times when they would just sleep on the bus and wait out the storm.

The night their house was destroyed was different. The tornado seemed to come from out of the blue. Her Momma and Daddy woke them up in the middle of the night.

"Y'all, get up, get up, come on, come on, hurry up, hurry up, and get up! A storm is here." They only had time enough to get them to the room in the house that had no windows and only one outside door. That room was their bedroom—a new addition her Daddy had added to the house as the family kept increasing.

The six smaller children sat on the bed huddled together with their Momma after the storm hit. Her Daddy and eldest sister struggled to keep the door from blowing open. It had almost opened once, but they managed to get it closed again.

They could hear the moaning, howling and growling going on outside. The storm sounded as if the boogie-man had come and was mad because it couldn't get in. The noise sounded as if the boogie-man was trying to get in by tearing their house apart plank by plank. The pounding stopped as suddenly as it had started. Then it started all over again with a vengeance.

There seemed to be two boogie-men then. One was on the roof trying to get in, while the other one tried to come in the door that her Daddy and her sister were holding. The door would open a little, and then it would close. Her dad and sister held on while Momma prayed, "O Lord, come by here. O Lord, come by here," she repeated.

Her Daddy said, "You better tell him to go back cause he's already here!"

All of a sudden, it got quiet again. It was quiet for a good while, but they sat on the bed and waited. They were still afraid that it would start again as it had before. Maybe the boogie-men were just waiting for them to open the door. They sat on the bed listening while her Daddy and sister held onto the door.

After a while, it was as peaceful as if nothing had happened at all. Her Daddy opened the door to look outside and closed it with a bang. He left the room for a few seconds and disappeared through the door that led to the rest of the house. When he came back into the room, he was tying a rope around his waist.

He gathered her baby brother up in his arms and told them to take hold of the rope and not to turn it loose until he told them to.

He opened the door again and went out as they followed him blindly out into pitch-blackness holding on to the rope tied around his waist.

Silent lightning lit up the black sky. For a split second, they could see the whole countryside as if daylight had come. With the help of the lighting, they made their way safely to the bus. On this night her Daddy wasted no time in trying to get them to the storm cellar.

They were barely inside the bus when the thunder cleared its throat a few times and let out an angry, loud roar. The roars got louder and louder. The thunder boomed, rumbled, and roared until the bus shook. The sounds rolled over the bus and traveled from one end of the earth to the other.

The lighting must have seemed to think that was a pitiful performance for a thunder because it cackled loudly in an unladylike like way that hurt their ears. The black sky cracked open. Streaks of light shot through the zigzag cracks and flaming darts shot at them from every direction. When the streaks of light hit the ground, they exploded. They saw an explosion near their house and knew something had been hit.

The thunder started gargling slowly at first. Then it grew louder and louder and became angrier and angrier. Air and water spewed at the bus with such a force the front of the bus spun around slowly as if the back wheels were spiked to the road. The wind forced the bus to head back toward the house. It stalled for a little while in a gutter on the other side of the road.

The bus was no match for the tornado. The wind pushed the bus along as if it was an empty tin can in the road. Her Daddy wrestled with the steering wheel trying to keep it on the road and in the direction of the storm cellar. They didn't feel any bumps from the road, although the bus was blown off the road into the gutter.

Her Daddy got the bus headed in the right direction again. He told them to get down on the floor and stay under the seats. Her Momma refused to get on the floor. She sat behind her Daddy in case he needed a lookout and to help drive if he got hurt by something coming through the windshield.

They didn't stay under the seats either. They had to see what was going on and making all the fuss. On their way to the cellar when the lightning would light up the sky, they saw others who had also been surprised by the tornado and were trying to get to a safe place.

Some were walking all bent over, fighting against the wind and rain. Some were huddled together trying to hold onto their clothes, to one another, and trying to keep from being blown away or beat down by the rain.

Her Daddy would try to stop the bus and pick them up when the wind would permit. Sometimes they just had to leave them by the side of the road waving frantically for them to stop.

When the bus did stop, her Daddy had to throw them the rope and help them in. When they managed to get in the bus, they were so miserable, tired, and wet that all they could do was fall in a seat wailing and moaning, "Thank you, Jesus. Thank you, Lord."

There wasn't much Chock could see from under the seats. Every once in a while, they would dare to raise their heads to see what was happening. Chock could see the outline of trees and other objects gliding by them through the water and debris that was being thrown at the bus. There was a lot of ruckus going on outside, and the noise was deafening. They could hear the thumping, bumping, scraping, and scratching when objects would hit the bus or as it flew by. They were told to stay down and put their heads back under the seats. They rode around as if they were on Aladdin's rug and were sailing through the air.

Their house was less than half of a mile from the cellar, but the short trip to the cellar seemed to take forever. Once they finally reached the cellar, it was already crowded.

All through the night, they could hear the Good Lord rearranging his creations. They could also hear the creations made by man being battered, and tossed about through the air.

The rain and wind would cease, and it would get quiet outside as if the Lord was resting and thinking about what to do next. They would hear the gargling sounds of the thunder and hear the rain and wind which was accompanied by flashes of lighting fighting to get to them.

Once, they thought the tornado would surely come through the ground and the ceiling of the storm cellar. Again and again, they would hear the roaring, howling, and things being thrown about. They didn't think it would ever let up. The storms kept on for a good part of the night. They must have stopped in the wee hours of the morning. Everyone had relaxed and dozed off. Before it was light outside, they were awakened by her Daddy's voice. "I reckon we better be getting on home."

People whom they had given a ride to the cellar and others rode back with them to their homes. Everyone was still a little sleepy and groggy. They had gone a short distance when they heard her Daddy say, "Wuhu, look a yonder!"

They sat up in their seats to get a look at what he was talking about. They rubbed the fog from the windows and saw what seemed to be part of a roof blocking the road.

The men got out and looked at the obstruction. Chock's daddy got back on the bus, and with the help of the others, he used the bus to clear the road.

By the time they reached the road that lead to their house, they had dropped off the other riders.

They heard her Daddy's voice again and sat up in a hurry when they heard the horror in it. That wasn't like her Daddy at all.

"Good God from Hem!"

They hurried to get the fog off the windows. They wanted to see what had made her Daddy so upset. When they looked out to see what he was talking about, there was nothing to be seen—at first.

That was the problem.

Their house was gone. There were only planks, boards, and broken glass scattered about where their house should have been.

Everything seemed to have been torn apart piece by piece and plank by plank. The only thing that hadn't been disturbed was a little table with a kerosene lamp on it. The lamp was still lit and cast an eerie glow over the destruction of their house. The light seemed to be a beacon telling them it was dangerous for them to come any closer.

Everything that was once their home had been moved. Their house was planted in the nearby fields as a new crop of glass, singles, boards, clothes, rags, and broken furniture.

Their barn was gone. The farm animals that had survived lay in the confinements of what should have been a fence waiting for someone to come and see about them. They were heartbroken when they saw Tobey, their lovable, trusted, hardworking mule, lying dead struck by lightning.

Their smokehouse was gone. The outhouse was gone. The chicken coops were gone, and the chickens that had survived were huddled together in the spot where their coops should have been waiting for morning to come. In the field about two hundred yards away, they saw a strange little shed-like building. They wondered where it had come from. While her Daddy and her elder sisters looked after the animals, the younger kids decided to walk over and take a look at that strange little shed.

They were afraid to go inside the shed and look around when they got there. They tried to get close enough to peek through the missing door. Their curiosity got the better of them, and they finally got their courage up and went inside. Once they got inside, they discovered that it was a part of their house.

It was her momma and Daddy's bedroom—the room they had been hiding in when the first storm hit.

Everything in the room was the way they had left it. The room had been separated and moved out from the rest of the house, but nothing in the room had been destroyed. They gathered what things they could find and went back to the bus. They were on their way to live with her Daddy's folks.

CHAPTER 2

Living with Her Daddy's Family

After the storm they set out to go back to their house or to the place their house should have been. They had no home. Their home had been completely destroyed by the tornadoes the night before.

They gathered what they could and got back on the bus. They were on their way back to live with her Daddy's families.

On their way back to his family they were still in shock about losing their home. The full impact hadn't hit them of how they would be affected by this loss. When they moved in with her Daddy's family, there were too many of them for one house. They had to be split up. The six girls moved in with her aunt and her three kids. Their aunt disapproved of everything they did. When they were in her house, they were expected to wear dresses every day, stay clean, sit still, and be quiet.

While they were living with her aunt, they had to maintain their farm and do the chores at her house and her Daddy's mother's house.

During the week, they dressed as boys and did farm work.

They, as girls, did work on their farm that boys did on other farms. They did the plowing, the planting, the hoeing, and the picking. If something needed to be killed, they did the killing. They did a million other things that needed to be done to maintain a farm.

Chock can't recall one instance when her dad's family helped them with any of the chores around the house or any of the work on the farm. When everything was said and done, they got the best and first choice of everything. It was difficult trying to abide by her Daddy's family's set of rules and to also be farmers. Their farm did earn the reputation of being the worst farm in the county with the prettiest girls in Texas.

Her mom and dad and her little brother moved in with her Dad's parents. Her uncle's wife and her three kids also lived with his parents. Her aunts' husbands, her uncles, had left home to find work to their liking that would pay more money. They left their families in her Daddy's keeping.

Her momma was big at that time. Chock didn't know that she was going to have another baby. She had to sit down a lot but kept trying to do her share around both houses. Chock heard her dad say to her Mom more than once that she needed to take it easy.

When Chock got older, she realized her momma was probably as miserable as they were. She knew her Daddy's family didn't like her. They would have preferred that he had married a more sophisticated woman with light complexion. Her momma did everything and more of what was expected of her to keep the peace.

Chock didn't help her at all. They would have been better off if they had stayed in that one room left by the tornado. Living with her Daddy's family was somehow more disastrous to her than the tornado. One day, Chock saw my cousin sneak into the smokehouse where they were storing up food for the winter months. Chock knew she shouldn't have been in there. Chock snick up and locked the door behind her.

This time, she would not be able to lie and say that Chock took food from the smokehouse. And she wouldn't be able to blame one of her sisters either, as she had done before, when something came up missing. If they wanted a snack, they knew how to get it from the garden or out in the woods.

They always had dinner at noon, and suppertime was before they went to bed. Chock had locked her cousin up around three o'clock. When she didn't show up at suppertime, her aunt got worried and sent everyone out to look for her.

One of her sisters found her in the smokehouse. Her sister said she heard a suspicious sound coming from the smokehouse and decided to take a look inside. When she opened the door, there was their cousin.

Their cousin was asked how she had gotten herself locked in there. She told them Chock had pushed her in and locked the door. No one seemed to be interested in how a five-year-old had managed to open the door, push a seven-year-old in, and lock the door. The next day when they were getting ready for their Saturday's outing, they had forgotten all about the incident thinking it was over and done with.

CHAPTER 3

Her Sisters with Her

Before they had to move in with their aunt and her family, Chock never noticed anything in particular about her sisters or about their lives. Chock don't recall knowing their names. They were her sisters, and Chock had taken them for granted.

They all went their separate ways.

Before the tornado, Chock don't remember anything ever happening to her or anything she had done.

After the tornado, Chock started to notice what was happening around her. Everything changed and made a lasting impression on her as if someone was in her head taking notes. Chock also became aware of how the same people behaved in different surroundings. Chock became aware of her own surroundings and the different expectations others had of her.

At five years of age, Chock had to keep in mind of where she was, and the rules she was expected to follow. Chock learned to respect the lifestyles of others; even if their way of living wasn't to her liking. At the age of five, Chock had to learn being different wasn't bad; it was just different. And everybody had a right to be different. When they heard their Momma's voice that Saturday, before they went on their outing, they were hiding in that bedroom from their aunt. Her aunt thought everybody should be like her—the way she wanted those to be. They were tired of listening to her constant criticism and nagging. But she was their aunt, a grown-up, and they had to respect her and try to abide by her rules. She wasn't going with them on their outing, and they didn't want her to put a damper on their fun.

Sister number one, her eldest sister, whom she thought was the beauty of the family besides their mother, was lying on the bed watching the action of their two younger sisters and shaking her head when they heard the noise from outside. Chock was watching her two younger sisters in disbelief at the trouble they were going through while styling their hair and trying on clothes to make sure they would stand out and catch the boys' attentions when they went on the Saturday's trip.

Her eldest sister was also the tallest and the shapeliest of the six girls. She had polished, medium-chocolate-colored skin, and her body was sculptured from hard work. She never made an effort to impress anyone, but if she wasn't impressed, she didn't bite her tongue in saying so. It didn't matter if you didn't agree with her—just don't touch her. She had a lackadaisical motion about her. When she spoke, it rang with authority and was to the point. She was their enforcer. When someone bothered them, and they needed help and went to her, she would take care of the problem for them.

She was on the high school girls' basketball team. Some said they came to the game not to see the game but to watch her fight. They knew she would usually get in a fight during the game or after the game. Girls from other teams had heard of her reputation and would provoke her to see if they could take her down. That never happened.

She was their Daddy's main helper on the farm. She was as strong as, or stronger than, most men. She didn't have many girlfriends. Boys were intimidated by her looks and her reputation. She once told a bully, from another town, who was trying to intimidate her,

"You better get out of my way and leave me alone. I wrestle with two mules and a plow every day, and I be damned if I let one no-good-for- nothing man mess over me."

She always looked as if she didn't want to be bothered and very seldom was. She was Chock's role model because she was a female version of their Daddy. Boys would look at her and grin, but she never paid them any attention. She didn't have a boyfriend until she moved to Dallas.

Chock didn't trust her second and third sisters. They were the same in many ways. They were also pretty and had the same build as their Momma. They were partners in crime. They stuck together and were each others' alibi to keep from getting a whipping. They were her eldest sister's nemeses.

They were crowd pleasers. Usually, they had their Momma's and Daddy's approval and tried to get the approval of the adults in the community. They wanted to be liked by everyone.

They went out of their way putting on airs and trying to outdo the competition. There would be other girls too in town Saturday night trying to get the attention of the boys.

While they were trying to decide what to wear; they would be talking about the boys they hoped to see in town. Chock would know the boys by the way they had described them. Chock would already know what they liked about a certain boy or what they disliked about a boy.

One day, Chock saw one of the boys they had talked about on the street when they were in town. Chock got a slap in the mouth by one of them when she blurted out something to him she had heard them talking about.

They put a lot of effort in what they thought would make their appearances prettier and would draw more attention from the boys than the other girls would.

While the noise was going on outside, Chock's second and third sister were talking a mile a minute while pressing and curling their hair. They were trying out different styles to decide which style would be more becoming for them.

Sister number two was a homemaker. She could make the prettiest of dresses out of scraps she saved from other dresses that were no longer wearable and from the flour sacks. Her cooking was almost as good as their Momma's. She was considered a genius by their parents and her teachers. She was not in any sports nor did she work in the fields that much.

She was considered as high yellow about five feet tall. Her curves were talked about also, but she didn't have the legs my elder sister had and the easy leisured way about her. She was all business. Always busy, busy, busy, and rush, rush, rush. She wanted everyone to be busy with what she was doing and expected them to do what she wanted them to do. Her way was the right way. She was no fun to be around.

Sister number three—the organizer. She could have been Chock's second sister's twin. She liked to order them around and tell them how things should be done. Physically, her second and third sisters had the same attributes. Chock's third sister was dark chocolate. She admired her elder sister. That adoration came because of her sister's color, high yellow, a color Chock wished she had been.

Chock's third sister went to the extremes to make up for the shortcomings, she thought she had, which would make her more acceptable to others. She was business like and held herself ridiculously in high esteem. She conducted herself as the epitome of good manners, speech, impeccable cleanliness, and was intolerant of anything less— something she picked up from their Daddy's family. She expected them to behave as she did. She constantly nagged them when they were leaving the house together. She was also a pain to be around.

Sister number four and sister number five palled around together.

Their personalities were 'Yin' and 'Yang,' or the odd couple.

Chock's fourth sister would say, "Let's do it. " Her fifth sister would say, "Let's not." They were considered pretty, but they were a little young to take special care about their appearances or behavior. Chock's fourth sister, their Daddy's second helper, was very athletic. She had dark chocolate skin like their Momma's but had a flat butt like their Daddy's. She was very spontaneous and impatient. She had a big heart, was friendly to everyone she met, ready to lend a helping hand, and treated all with respect. She was the most comfortable one to be around.

When they heard the noise from the front of the house, she was lying on her bed with her dress up around her waist and her feet propped up against the wall. She was bouncing a ball off the wall and catching it when it bounced back to her.

When she heard Momma's voice, she stopped bouncing the ball long enough to say, "See, we should have been done. Y'all make me sick with all y'all messing around." Then she started back throwing the ball harder against the wall.

Chock's fourth sister participated in every sport the school had to offer and was very serious about her performances. She was good at whatever sport she participated in and was highly competitive. She was also very daring and more outgoing than her elder sisters. In fact, she was bored with them but respected them. She was always in a hurry to get where she was going so she could do whatever there was to be done and get it done. She was the fun one.

Sister number five, Chock's fifth sister, had a quiet grace about her. She was light chocolate. She didn't seem to want anyone to know she was around. She did everything that was expected of her—nothing spectacular or nothing outlandish to draw attention to her.

Sometimes when things seemed to get out of hand when their parents weren't there, she would tell them, "Y'all should stop that before we get in trouble." No one listened to her. She had a quiet disapproving manner about her. Whenever Chock was around her, she was afraid that she would do something her sister would not approve of. When she heard their Momma, she just sighed and gave everyone an "I told you so" look.

Sister number six was the youngest of the six sisters at that time and a little mixed-up. Chock tried to be like her sisters. Everyone seemed to like them. They always said how pretty that one was or how good that one was, how that one walked, or that one talked, or what that one had done that was so great.

Chock was a little bit of this one and a little bit of that one. She took what she liked best from each one of her sisters and tried to emulate that behavior. She didn't realize it took all of the things in them, the good, and the bad, to make what she thought was good and liked best about them.

It was thought by some that Chock looked a little bit different from her sisters. Their Daddy's father gave her the name 'Chocolate fox'. He said she looked like a fox and had the coloring and the eyes of a fox. He also said that Chock had the bone structure like his Indian mother.

Their mother's mother (her grandmother) said that Chock reminded her of her mother.

Chock was already dressed and ready to go into town when she heard her Momma's voice. She was on the floor playing jacks. She was also eavesdropping on her sisters. She was taking everything in. She watched how they moved when they did something. Chock listened to the way they laughed when they said something funny or mean. She listened to what they said and who they said it about. She stored everything she could in her little brain to be used later for her own little purpose.

Chock was a little mixed-up.

Chock thought she could change her personality at will. She tried to walk like her eldest sister. She tried to laugh like her second sister.

Chock tried to act sophisticated like her third sister.

She tried to be daring like her fourth sister and tried to be quiet sometimes like her fifth sister.

Chock tried to be like my sisters whenever it suited her purpose. She tried to use what she had seen them do and what she had heard them say for her own advantage or to get out of the situations she happened to get herself in. Chock was always in some situation.

Her mom said she couldn't figure out if Chock was the angel or the devil. Her Momma never considered good people could sometime do bad and bad people could sometime do good.

CHAPTER 4

Here Comes Trouble

Chock's five sisters and her were in their aunt's bedroom getting dressed to go on their Saturday's outing when they heard the awful sounding noise. "OOOOOOOOO!" The noise came from outside and sounded as if someone was being choked to death.

When they first heard the noise, they paused for a second to see what in the world was going on. When they didn't hear anything right away, they started back doing what they were doing before they heard the sound.

Aw, they thought, *their cousin and his friends are just trying to scare them.*

Then they heard the growling noise again. That time the sound was a little clearer, louder, and angrier. "OOOOOCK!" Several activities were going on among the six girls in the bedroom, but everyone stopped what they were doing when they heard the sound again. They knew their Momma's voice was making that awful sound.

The sound in her voice told them. "Uh, uh, somebody is in trou-u-u-u-ble."

They could also tell by the sound of her voice this was big trouble. Someone had really messed up.

Besides hiding from the critical eyes of their aunt, they were in that bedroom, and crowded together, getting ready for the Saturday night's outing. Some of the girls were getting dressed, some were already dressed, and some were waiting, killing time until it was time to go.

Two of her sisters had not made a decision as to how to style their hair and what dress they were going to wear, while one was lying on the bed watching them with disgust at the fuss they were making over what they should wear to attract the boys.

One of the sisters was bouncing a ball off the wall. Another was sitting in a chair watching her with a sense of doom. She was sitting as if she was in Sunday school and trying to go unnoticed in case their aunt heard the noise and came in and started screaming at all of them.

Chock was also trying to go unnoticed by my sisters. Chock was sitting on the floor playing jacks and eavesdropping. If her sisters noticed her eavesdropping, they would make her leave the room. They thought she had a big mouth.

They heard their Momma's voice again. All of them stopped doing what they were doing because the sound of her voice was a shock to all of them.

They were shocked at the angry, barking sound in their Momma's voice. Chock thought she heard—her name? Her elder sisters turned around to look at her. When Chock saw the pitying looks they gave her, she knew their Momma was calling her, and Chock knew she was in deep, deep trouble.

"CHOOOCK! You hear me calling you!" she stated. "You better get out here and see what I want!"

Chock looked around the room at her sisters hoping she would get some help.

They all distanced themselves from her. She was in this all by herself.

Their comments were: "Don't look at me."

"I ain't in this."

"You on your own this time." "Leave me outta this."

"Girl, you better hurry up and get yourself off that floor and go see what Momma wants before she come in here and get all of us!"

Chock was dumbfounded. She remained sitting on the floor. Their Momma's voice had paralyzed her. She was just getting ready to throw the ball in the air to go for her sixes. She sat there with her hand in midair, and her mouth opened trying to catch her breath.

"Chock!"

Their Momma's voice was even louder than the last time she called her. She was losing her patience.

"What I'm to do?"

"What I'm to do?"

"What I'm to do?"

"I'm gonna get a whuppin."

"I'm gonna get a whuppin."

Chock could already feel the licks from the switch already. All of a sudden, she got a chill. She closed her eyes and started shaking all over. If her momma would just stop calling her and let her think, she just might think of something to say, but she wouldn't give her a chance to think. Every time something popped into her head, her momma's yelling made it pop right out.

Chock was the youngest of the six girls in her family at that time.

She was also the one that was always in trouble.

Her mother was a Christian woman and did not let others hear her raising her voice in anger the way she had, especially while she was addressing her children. Her voice told them something had pushed her over to the other side. What had pushed her momma to the other side Christians prided themselves on staying away from? Chock sat there trying to figure out what her mom could be so angry about. Had someone seen her when she put her cousin's hair ribbons down in the outhouse? Maybe someone had seen her with her cousin's spotless, white shoes on walking over all of the chicken poop she could find.

She was going over all of her misdeeds when she heard her mom call her name again,

"Ch-o-ck!"

That time there was no mistaking what her mom was saying or to whom her anger was directed. She called out Chock's name louder and clearer, putting emphasis on each syllable. She wanted her and she wanted her then. The anger in her voice let Chock know there was no mistake about the trouble she was in, and it was getting worse by the minute.

Her momma was living with her grandmother because there was not enough room for all of them to live with her aunt. Who would go to her grandma's house and tell her Chock was being mannish?

"Chock! You hear me calling you!"

"Chock swallowed and said, "Yes, Ma'am."

Her Momma knew she could hear her. Chock did not answer because she was trying to buy time to figure out how she was going to get out of the mess she had gotten herself in.

"You better get out here and see what I want!"

Slowly, Chock got up from the floor. She walked as slowly as she dared through the house to the front porch where the calls were coming from.

While she was walking to the front porch, she had concocted a plan. She knew what she was going to tell Momma, but when she got to the porch and saw her cousin sitting there, Chock got so angry she forgot all about her plan.

Chock saw the cause of all of her troubles. There she sat—the cause of all of her miseries for the last few months. She was sitting in the porch swing with her arms folded. She was swinging her legs, and looking at Chock grinning with that nasty grin of hers.

And she was sitting there as if she was grown! She was only a year and a half older than Chock. So how come she could sit down with grown folks? Chock had another reason to not like her.

Her Mom would never let her sit in the same room listening when grown people were talking. She always made them leave. She said that children had big ears and big mouths.

When her mom saw her she said, "You come here!"

"Yes Ma'am," Chock said sweetly and as meekly as she could with a smile.

Chock continued to walk as perky as she knew how toward her Momma, smiling a smile she had learned from one of my sisters. Every step Chock took was bringing her closer to a bad end, and she walked as slowly as she dared, dreading what was to come.

As Chock walked over to where her Momma was sitting, she caught a glimpse of her aunt's face. Her aunt had her eyes locked upside of

Chock's face and was looking at her as if she was going to jump up out of her chair and slap Chock's face off.

Chock walked around her aunt's chair to where her mom sat rocking back and forth in a rocking chair. She was probably saying to herself, *I'm gonna fix her for embarrassing me like this in front of my sister-in-law.* Instead she said,

"Your cousin said that you pushed her in the smokehouse and locked the door. Is that true?"

"Yes Ma'am." It was not the whole truth, but her Momma did not give her a chance to explain. Chock was in a pickle. If Chock said yes, she was going to get a whipping. If Chock said no, she would still get a whipping. She didn't dare say, "No Ma'am," to Momma. You just didn't ever say no or disagree with parents and grown-ups.

If Chock said her cousin was telling a story, Chock would be making things worse for herself. She would be accused of telling a story on her cousin. Everybody knew her cousin was an angel and didn't tell stories.

"You get me a switch!"

Chock hesitated for a second. She wanted to try to explain. She was trying to think of what to say to get her out of the whipping that wouldn't make her Momma angrier than she already was. Her Mom's voice interrupted her thinking again.

"What are you standing there for? You better go and get that switch, and you hurry up about it."

"Yes, Ma'am."

While Chock was taking her time going to the porch to see what her Momma wanted, Chock was trying to think of what she had learned from her sisters that she could use to get herself out of the mess she was in. Her personality was deceiving. Chock was a quiet, conniving little girl. She didn't bother anyone. A lot of people then, and when she got older, took her quietness as weakness. They thought she could be taken advantage of and be controlled. When they found out they had been under the wrong impression and had misjudged her, it was too late. She had been planning my revenge on them for a long time.

Being close together made them girls notice the needs of one another and brought them closer together. They also became dependent on one another, but they were no help then. Chock was in that mess all alone by herself. She hoped her Momma wouldn't take it out on all of them by not letting them go to town.

Chock turned around and started walking slowly back through the house. She had to go to the backyard where the peach tree was located. The peach tree was designated as the official tree for them to get switches from.

As Chock was walking through the house, she could see her sisters peeking out the doors and windows that led to the front porch. They wanted to see what was going on without being seen. They were taking precautions not to be seen by their Momma at that time. They were afraid she might remember something they had done or something they had not done, and then she would start in on them.

Our parents were good at saving up stuff and bidding their time. Sometimes, when they thought they had gotten away with something, they would hear their Momma or Daddy say,

"Um-huh, Um-huh, you come here. I've been watching you, too. You've been getting a little mannish around here lately. I knew one day I was gonna haf' to give you a little touch up (a whipping) to remind you of your manners."

Today was one of those times to make one scarce and to hurry up and do all the things you should have done yesterday's ago. If they didn't mind our P and Q today, they might miss the Saturday night's trip they had been looking forward to since the last one, two weeks ago.

When Chock got to the tree, she looked at the branches. Chock had to choose carefully. If she chose a little switch, her Momma would wear it out on her and send her back to get another one. If she chose a big one, it would hurt too much.

Chock got a switch and hit the tree trunk. She tried it out to make sure that it would bend but not wrap around her. She was an old hand at choosing switches. When Chock was satisfied with her choice, she went back to the porch where her Mom sat.

Chock was in the motion of handing her Momma the switch when she grabbed her hand with one of her hands and grabbed the switch with her other hand and started in on her.

If someone had been passing by, they would have thought that her Momma was dancing with her. Chock was jumping around waving one arm in the air. The rocking chair was rocking back and forth and from side to side. They had a rhythm going. Her Momma was saying,

"You gonna mind?"

"Yes Ma'am! Yes Ma'am!"

"Your manners?"

"Yes Ma'am! Yes Ma'am!"

"When I get through?"

"Yes Ma'am! Yes Ma'am!"

"With you?"

"Yes Ma'am! Yes Ma'am!"

Chock didn't have time to cry. She had to keep up with what her momma was saying and give the right answers at the right time so she wouldn't have to repeat herself. Each lick was like an electric shock wave traveling through her body. Before Chock would get over the last shock wave, another would start some place else.

Momma sure knew how to use a switch. She used almost the same technique whipping as she used in cutting up a chicken. When she was big she would sit down to handle either task. She would firmly grab an arm or a wing and hold on.

When she wasn't big, she would let them jump around. She would start in on the arms, or wings, the legs would be next, and then the thighs. When she got to the back part, she really went to work. At times, there would be more than thirteen people for one chicken. She had to separate the back and breast into six or more parts so everyone could get a piece.

Sometimes Chock had to wait her turn to get a whipping. Chock watched her momma whip her sisters on those occasions and tried to learn how they moved their bodies to cut down on the stings from the switch.

At first, Chock would just stand there and cry when she got a whipping. After watching her sisters, she tried to move around and shimmy and shake the way they did when they got a whipping. With their Momma, they could jump around and tire her out faster.

With their Daddy, you better not move. He used a paddle or the strap he used to sharpen his shaving razor. Their Daddy was a baseball pitcher, and he had good aim. He would hit the same spot every time.

When her sisters got a whipping, watching them was almost like watching her Daddy's mother do her dance at a honky-tonk. They would be rolling their backs and hips in and out and from side to side trying to avoid the full force of the switch. Chock tried to move her body the way they had, but she was too little and uncoordinated to roll her body around the way they could.

Chock got about twenty licks in quick succession for having locked her cousin in the smokehouse. The whipping lasted for about twenty seconds. After the last lick, she was still jumping around and started crying.

Momma said, "You hush up that racket and stop that jumping around before I give you something to holler about!"

"Yes Ma'am" Chock sucked it up. She almost passed out trying to hush up.

"Now I want you to go over to your cousin and tell her you're sorry!"

Saying sorry to her cousin was worse than getting a whipping. She looked at her Momma in disbelief. She wanted me to say something that was not the truth.

Her momma was trying hard to please her sister-in-law; after all, they had to live with them.

That really made Chock stop crying. Her Momma never told them to say "sorry" to any one before. She knew that Chock was not sorry for having locked her cousin in the smokehouse, but she knew what she had done was wrong. Chock looked at her Momma, and for the first time since she had called her to the porch, she looked at Chock.

"Go on."

Her voice softened a little, and she gave Chock a little shove. "Go on over there and tell your cousin that you're sorry. Go on."

Her Momma was doing everything she could to please her sister-in-law. They had to live with them until her Daddy finished building another house for them.

Chock walked over to where her cousin sat smirking at her for getting a whipping. Chock stood there in front of her with her head down like a whipped dog. At that moment, Chock hated her more than she had before the whipping. She was going to pay.

Just because they had to move into her house when theirs was blown down by the tornado did not give her a reason to treat them like her slaves. Every day her cousin would badger her.

"Chock, do this."

"You better do this."

"You better do that."

"If you don't, I'm gonna tell on you."

"You gonna get a whipping."

Chock raised her head and looked at her. She stopped grinning and started looking at her mother. Her Momma repeated, "Now say you are sorry."

"I'm sorry," Chock growled at her.

"Now give her a hug."

What? Chock thought. When Chock reached out to give her cousin a hug, she ran to her mother screaming. Chock repeated to herself what her mom had said to her earlier. *When I finish with her, she was going to have something to scream about.*

If they missed that trip, into town today, her cousin would have more than her to worry about. Her sisters looked forward to the Saturday night trips. They had been talking about it all week and were just about ready to go.

They didn't appreciate her cousin's constant picking on her and were secretly telling Chock what she should do the next time she bullied her around. Everything Chock had done to her cousin was some of her sister's ideas.

Her aunt wasn't going to town, and she was not letting her little princess go either. She didn't feel it was a proper place for women to go at night. Chock was hoping she hadn't spoiled it for them. Her Momma was already dressed and was ready to go.

The girls and their Momma went on the Saturday night's outing. They had been looking forward to and planning for the outing for two weeks.

CHAPTER 5

Saturday Night Fever

A tornado had destroyed their house four months before Chock locked her cousin in the smokehouse. They had taken what they could find that hadn't been destroyed by the tornado and moved in with their aunt. Her five sisters and her were crowded into one little bedroom in her aunt's house.

They were getting dressed for a Saturday night out on the town. Saturday nights were big! Before they could start getting dressed for the night's outing, they had to finish all of their chores. They finished everything before dinner time, and then they were getting ready to go. They were all excited about the trip and were anticipating the treats and the fun they were going to have. They would do some shopping, just enjoy themselves messing around with others, and just have some plain old fun.

Their Daddy would take the people that could go in the school bus. Everyone went that could go. Sometimes there would not be enough room on the bus for everyone. Some would sit in the laps of others, while some would stand and hold on to the seats.

There would be buses coming to town from the surrounding communities also. That was the only time most of the people could leave their farms to get supplies and socialize with others.

The trip into town was exciting. There was a lot of laughing and joking going on. Everyone would try to talk over everyone else about what they were going to do when they got into town. The trip was noisy and confusing but fun.

When they came in sights of the town, everyone would quiet down. Chock knew by watching their faces, following their glances, and by the way they turned their heads to look at a spot that they were thinking what she was thinking. They were thinking about another trip and what had happened.

Chock noticed some of the people on the bus glancing at others. Chock knew they were thinking about what had happened to that person on one of their trips. Some were looking at the place the incident occurred. Some had vacant stare thinking about what they had to do and to watch out for to keep from being noticed and thinking of what they would do if they did get in trouble.

Some of the people, who didn't feel like walking around, stayed on the bus when they got to town. They watched the going-on in the street from the bus windows.

They looked on as if they were watching a game or a picture show. They would make comment like,

"Look at that boy."

"Look who he's trying to talk to."

"He better not let her daddy catch him."

"Her momma gonna tan her hide when she finds out that girl is being mannish like that."

"I wonder what so-and-so is saying to so-and so.

"I hope he's not trying to start a fight."

Down in their hearts, they would be hoping that a fight would start to make things more exciting and give them more to tell others when they got home.

The ones who stayed on the bus would take everything in so they would have something to gossip about later when they got home and were sitting on their porches.

It was OK if the fight was black against black. Everyone would root for their choice as if it was a game. If the fight was white against black it was an outrage.

It was a hanging offense for a black person to hit a white person. The black person had to grin and bear it and hope the beating would stop before they were dead. If another black person stepped in, and tried to stop the beating, they were dead for sure.

The little kids that were old enough to be alone would buy an ice-cream cone and just stroll up and down the streets licking their cones and looking at people.

When Chock got to town, she had to stay on the bus with her Momma as part of her punishment. They did get out of the bus long enough to go to the store. Chock got a double scoop of ice cream and her Momma got a bag of grapes. Then they went back to the bus.

She was big at the time and didn't feel like walking around. Some of the women from other communities came to the bus to keep her company. After the whipping Chock got before they left, she didn't feel like walking around either.

The married people, or farmers would talk in very small groups. Large groups of black people made white people nervous and suspicious. Their talks were about their farms and their communities.

The main topic of their conversation was usually centered on how the white people in their community were treating them.

Some of the parents hung around on the street so they could keep an eye on their children to make sure they didn't talk to someone they didn't approve of. As always, the kids always found a way to outsmart their parents.

The girls would pair up and walk up and down the street giggling while they looked over the boys. The boys would stand around talking together trying to look cool. They pretended not to look at the girls they were interested in and pretended to not notice the girls looking at them.

If there was a new picture show in town, they would get into town in plenty of time to shop and socialize before the picture show started. Some of them, who were brave enough, would try to go to the show if the show house was open, and if there was some space left in the theater after the white people got in.

The show house had a down stairs and a balcony. When it first opened, the black people sat downstairs, while the whites would sit in the balcony. That seating arrangement was soon changed when the black people stopped going.

The blacks stopped going because during the picture show the white patrons would throw their trash over the balcony on the black patrons. Sometimes the white patrons would even pee over the balcony. Whatever the accommodations were for the blacks, there would always be something a black person did that would piss off a white person!

Usually, there weren't many whites in town on Saturday nights. There seemed to be an unwritten law that Saturday nights was the black folks' nights. When there was a new show in town, the whites would be there. Some of the whites came just for the sole purpose of tormenting some black soul.

The whites that didn't have the price of a ticket resented the blacks who did. They just hung out on the street and waited for someone to come by they could harass. Others, usually young white men and boys, would hang out by the door of the show house and try to intimidate blacks and keep them from going in to see the movie.

When a new movie was in town, at least one person would get a beating before they left town. If it wasn't in the show house, it was on the streets. The beatings didn't stop them from taking their Saturday night outings or going to the movie, but when there were whites in town, it did spoil some of the fun.

When whites were in town, they had to be careful. If they saw a white person, they had to remember to stay out of his way and not look a white person in the eye. They had to remember to step off the sidewalk to let him pass when they saw him coming.

After someone was beaten, their bus trip home was different from the trip going to town. There would be a lot of confusion getting the buses loaded up. After the beating, the people would load up as fast as possible as they could.

Some would be impatient for the bus to leave. Chock's dad would make sure he didn't leave anyone. After the bus would start, everyone would be quiet. They would sit quietly and watch the light until the town disappeared.

Then someone would say,

"I'll be glad when I can get out from here." Those with the same mind would say, "I'll say Amen to that." Or, "You shoo' right 'bout that."

After a while, only a few voices could be heard throughout the bus. Everyone would seem to have fallen asleep. Chock can't recall ever staying awake for the ride home. She would wake up when they got home. Chock would hear.

"Y'all wake up. We're home!"

After church the next day, Chock went looking for her cousin. Chock headed to the porch. Before she reached it, she stopped to make sure she was alone. Chock had a vast amount of bubble gum in her mouth, and Chock was going to cover her head with a huge bubble. That's when she heard her aunt talking to her friend. She was telling her friend what that evil little nasty child had done to her angel.

She went on to say, "I'd be glad when my brother gets that house finished so he can get his black wife and his dirty, ill-mannered chulluns out from here. That wife of his, don't teach them no manners, and she 'lau them to run around here like a bunch of animals."

Chock was eavesdropping at the door. When she did an intake at what her aunt had said, she heard Chock.

She turned toward Chock. "Chock, come here!" Chock thought she was going to get another whipping. Instead, she yanked Chock's dress up over her head. She said, "See what I was talking about? She lets them run all over the place with no bloomers (panties) on."When she yanked Chock's dress up, she heard her cousin laughing.

The memory of that day, the humiliation Chock felt about not having on panties, stayed on her mind and was to get her into lots of trouble for years.

Chock attended her aunt's funeral years later. Chock was sorry that her father had lost his sister, but the only memories she had of her were how unwanted she had made Chock feel.

Chock also thought about how they had been treated when they were forced to live with her and the humiliation Chock felt when she pulled her dress up over her head to show her friend that she had no bloomers on.

Chock can't imagine what had happened to her momma while they were staying with her Daddy's family. When they grew up and left home, her momma would always send them underwear for their Birthday or Christmas. To this day, almost sixty years later, Chock always look for the prettiest underwear she can find for herself, her two daughters, and her six granddaughters.

CHAPTER 6

Their Parents and Their People

While living with her daddy's family, they still had to maintain their farm. Each day, they had chores at her grandmother's house, her aunt's house, and on their farm. They still had to tend the crops, take care of the animals, cut the wood, do all of the other things required to keep a farm going, and make sure they didn't get anything dirty when they went to her aunt's and her grandmother's house.

One cold morning, after they had moved to their own house, they were having their usual biscuit and oatmeal breakfast. Her Daddy's nephew came to tell her daddy that they were low on firewood. Then he went back home.

Her daddy told them to hurry and finish up so they could help him cut some wood for his folks. They got dressed in the warmest clothes they had. Then they went to the woods about a fourth of a mile from the back of their house.

The snow had melted, and the ground was wet and muddy. They thought they were going to freeze to death helping their Daddy cut firewood to keep his mother and his sister and the rest of his family warm. They got the firewood cut and loaded it up and took it to her grandmother's house. She saw them coming and stopped them before they could get in the kitchen to put the wood in the box. She would not let them in to get warm either because she didn't want them bringing mud in her house and tracking up her kitchen floor.

From the door they could see the roaring fire in the fireplace. They could see everyone sitting around the kitchen table. A fire was also burning in the kitchen stove. They were eating biscuits with melted cheese in them and drinking something hot out of cups.

At their house, they had to crowd around the stove in the front room to keep warm. Her Daddy had cautioned them about keeping two fires burning all day. When they left, he told her grandmother this wood would have to last them until the weather let up.

Her dad's family never helped them with anything. They got the best of everything. Her Daddy let them pick what they wanted when the crops were in. If it needed picking, they had to pick it for them. If it needed killing, they had to kill it for them, and then take it to them. When something was sold, they got their share. They got to keep what was left. They then shared what was left with those in the community who needed it.

They were taught that they were no better than anyone else because they had food on the table. But sometimes, Chock felt they were not as good as some of the other people. They had to work, when others just sat and waited for them to bring food to them. They gave them things they could have used for themselves. They didn't even get as much as a thank you.

Chock never told my kids that they should share. If they wanted to share they should. But they should not give away something they wanted that would make them sad to make someone else happy.

They lived on a farm in the black community of a small Texas town. Her daddy's mother had raised them to think they were better than her momma's family and on a higher level than the other people in our community.

Her daddy was an exception. He didn't agree with their way of thinking. He didn't sit around his mother the way his brother did, but he made sure she had what she needed and did everything he could to see that she was well cared for.

Her daddy's mother was a petite, light-skinned woman with long reddish-brown hair. Chock don't recall if she ever smiled.

Every once in a while, she would go to one of the little honky-tonks, run by her Daddy's cousins, and do a dance with her skirt pulled up around her knees.

Everyone at the honky-tonk would sit down and watch her dance. She would dance until she got tired of dancing or until a family member would make her stop and take her home.

When she was home, she would often take a drink from a bottle she kept hidden somewhere around the house.

Her grandparents, her Daddy's parents, seemed to have a rocky marriage. Her Daddy told them once that his mother had left her grandfather and them: he, his brother, and their little baby sister.

When her grandmother left, her grandfather had different women to come to live with them. These women didn't take care of him, his brother, and their baby sister.

One day he got fed up with how his daddy's women were treating them. He decided to go and look for his mother. He took his little brother by the hand and carried his baby sister and set out to look for her. He was only a little boy himself.

He said they had gone a long way from home. A man in a wagon, who knew his family, saw him walking down the road carrying his baby sister. He gave them a ride to where his mother was staying with some of her friends. His mother came back home with them, but she didn't seem happy after that.

Her momma's family was devout Christian, whereas her daddy's family was not. Chock heard her Daddy say once when her momma asked him to go to church with them.

"I ain't gonna go in that church."

"And I ain't gonna' try to stop you from goin'."

"You could go to hell listening to them folks in that church. All they do is talk."

"When somebody needs help, they just go home and shut their doe' and talk about 'em." Her daddy's family consisted of mostly light-skinned people, while her Momma's family consisted mostly of dark-skinned people.

Her Momma's family came from slaves.

Her Daddy's family had never been slaves.

Her Daddy's family didn't accept the white man's unfair treatment quietly.

Angry white men were always coming around looking for her Daddy's father.

He was a tall, handsome, red-skinned man. He was always dressed up like a cowboy and rode on a black stallion named Star. He would wear the suit, hat, boots, and two big pearl-handled pistols around his hips.

He thought he was like the cowboys they saw at the picture show. When he got on his horse and got ready to leave, he would impress everyone by taking his hat off and waving it in the air. His horse (Star) would rare up and paw the air. Chock doesn't ever remember him helping with anything around the farm either, except helping to make white lighting and peach brandy.

One time, he came home after being gone for a couple of days. Her grandmother was as angry as a setting hen.

When he came in, a fight started. Her grandmother picked up a piece of wood burning in the fireplace and hit him over the head with it.

Her grandpa took off running.

He ran out the door, jumping up and down, and hollering as if he had the Holy Ghost.

Smoke was coming out of his clothes, and he was patting them as he ran.

He ran to the little pond in the back of the house and jumped in with gun, boots, and all of his clothes on. His big black hat with the silver band floated for a while and finally disappeared underwater.

Those of them who remember still laugh about it when they get together and reminisce about their experiences while growing up.

Once her grandpa and his buddies, including her daddy, buried moonshine liquor in the field in front of their house. Just before dark, the ground started shaking, and then the ground just exploded showering dirt, rocks, and bits of glass everywhere. That was her closest experience to what could be called fireworks.

Years later, Chock was to recall that experience when she felt the ground rumble a number of times. Chock was to feel the rumbling of the ground before the earthquake of 1968 reached them in California. She felt the rumbling when the Teton Dam gave away in Idaho. She felt the rumbling once again when the volcano, Mount Saint Helena, exploded in Seattle. Maybe, everything that happened in her life was just to get her ready for things that were yet to come.

Her Daddy's grandmother was a full-blooded Cherokee Indian. It was said that her great-grandfather found her one day tangled up in the barbed wire fence. He later found out she was running away from the men that had killed her parents and captured her.

She had managed to get away until she tried to cross the barbwire fence. She gotten her hair and clothes caught. When she tried to get untangled, she had fallen. She became more tangled and was unable to get up. She would have probably come to a bad end if my great-grandfather hadn't come along.

Her great-grandfather found her and got her untangled. He took her home with him and hid her in his barn. After a while, they were married.

They would run when my great-grandmother (her Daddy's grandmother) came around. They didn't understand anything she said, and they thought she wore the strangest clothes. Her hair was completely white. She wore it in one braid that hung almost to the floor. Chock doesn't think she ever left the grounds that surrounded her grandparents' house.

Chock doesn't know where her grandmother (her Daddy's mother) came from. Chock knew her grandmother's sister, and she was just as mean as her sister. They also knew her brother. They all thought something was wrong with her grandmother's brother. But they never talked about him until they left home and had children of their own.

He always seemed to show up when they were bathing outside in the washtubs. Her daddy had built a wash bench on the side of the smokehouse where the well and the big iron wash pot were located. On wash days, they had to draw water from the well and fill up four tubs for washing. The fifth tub was for taking the clothes to be hung on the line to dry.

After they finished washing, they always filled the tubs up, and to take their Saturday baths. They would play in the water while they were bathing.

Sometimes the wash day was changed, but her grandmother's brother (her Daddy's uncle) always knew when to show up. He seemed to come out from nowhere and would start singing or whistling when he got right up on them.

The bigger girls would jump out of the tubs, run, and hide when they heard him coming, but they were always too late. Even when they had lookouts posted, he would somehow manage to sneak up on them. They came to the conclusion that he would hide out and wait for them to get in the tubs so he could see them when they jumped out and tried to hide. They had to stop bathing outside.

They were not sure where her grandfather (her Momma's daddy) came from. They said he came from across the water. He always had a smile on his face, but he seldom talked. When he did talk, his voice sounded like soft thunder, and it was hard to understand what he was saying. He was very tall, very dark, and very skinny.

When they visited their mother's parents, there were always one of her brothers and their kids living with them. Her mom had two sisters and six brothers.

Her grandpa would always go to his big steamer trunk where he kept all of his belongings locked up to get them a treat. Chock felt sad that he had to keep his things locked up in that big old trunk and hide his money in his pants from his children and the grand kids he was staying with.

He had to put his money in socks and hide it in his pants. Chock knew he had a lot of money. He always had money to buy them treats, and Chock could see the big bulges in his pants. He had to wear big pants, big enough so he could hide his money. When he got ready to sit down, he would always have to move the money out of the way. (When Chock got older, her Momma's dad stayed with them one summer.

Chock found out by accident that it was not money he kept hidden in them big ole, ugly fitting pants he wore.)

Her mother's grandmother was a slave. When she was freed, she took her daughter (her Momma's mother) and found work in the home of a former slave owner.

Her great-grandmother said, "The man was constantly complaining that my daughter wouldn't do what she was told to do. I got mad and whipped her for disobeying the boss man. I told her she had better mind the boss and do whatever he wanted her to do." When she found out what the boss man wanted her daughter to do, her daughter was pregnant.

Chock's mother's mother was a typical grandmother. They couldn't wait to visit her. She would have tea cakes ready for them. And she would always cook them something special. Her Momma told her one day when she was making her specialty "poke salad" for them, "They won't eat that." Her grandmother said, "Don't ever say what your chulluns will or will not do. They will make a fool of you every time."

At one time, both families were big landholders. Her daddy's family lost their land because her great-great-grandpa was a player. He was too busy having fun to take care of the land. As a consequence, my great-great-grandmother had to sell off small portions of land a little at a time for money to hire others to work the land and for money to live on. Chock's mother's family was forced to sign over their land to an unscrupulous white man. During that time, if the whites didn't get what they wanted, someone would come up missing. Any white person could do anything to punish any black person for anything or for nothing.

One day, Chock came upon what could happen to a black man when a white person was displeased by a black man, or didn't like what a black man had done. At the time of Chock's discovery, she didn't know what she had discovered.

Later on that week, Chock heard that one of Jack's girls had found the man who had been missing for about a week hanging in a tree, and he had been burned as black as coal. That was the last time Chock went alone for a walk in the woods. When she went with others, she was still afraid of what she might see. They always had food on the table at meal time, but if they wanted a snack, they had to find it, dig it up, pick it, or get it out of a tree. Chock always liked walking in the woods. She liked being alone, collecting nuts, berries, fruits, rocks, or anything she thought was unusual looking.

On the day of her awful discovery, Chock went in the woods looking for a snack. When she entered the woods, she didn't like the smell. The smell seemed to get stronger as she went further into the woods. Animals were always dying in the woods, so Chock kept walking.

Chock came upon the ugliest, most horrific looking thing she had ever seen in her life hanging from my favorite tree. Chock stopped in her tracks. Chock stood there transfixed too afraid to move. She wasn't close enough to see what was hanging in the tree, and she was not going any closer.

Finally, Chock came to her senses and slowly started to step backward. Her movement must have alerted the birds. They flew away making angry noises. The animals around the tree turned toward her and started growling. They stood their ground and didn't run away. Chock had a big stick for her protection, but there were too many animals under that tree. Chock backed up and started running.

Her Daddy was working in a nearby field. When he saw Chock running, he called,

"Hey, Chock! Chock! What you running from?"

Chock told him she had seen something in that big old hickory tree in the pasture, and the animals had started growling at her.

"Come on, I'll walk back to the house with you." When they got home, he told them to go in the house and stay until he got back.

They didn't go to town for the next few Saturday nights. At church that next Sunday, after Chock had seen that horrible sight, everyone was talking about one of Jack's girls finding the missing man and what had happened to him.

Chock heard someone say one of Jack's girls had found him hanging in a tree in their pasture, and he had been burned to a crisp.

People were standing around in groups at church and talking in whispers.

When Chock would happen to walk by, they would stop talking and look at her.

Chock knew they were talking about her.

They were giving her the same look her sisters had given me the day she got a whipping for locking her cousin in the smokehouse. Chock was guilty of something, but she didn't quite know what it was.

Chock was the guilty culprit. She had brought trouble upon everyone. She had found something. They would have been better off if it had not been found.

No one knew what to do about what Chock had found. They knew something should be done. What could they do? The only thing they could do was to help the family of the dead man.

Everyone was afraid to do anything. In their hearts, they knew nothing could be done and nothing would be done. They were ashamed to face the dead man's family.

Everyone had to deal with the hanging quietly. They had to carefully guard everything they said and to whom they said it. Too much said to the wrong person could be their death if it should fall on the wrong ears. The next hanging would be theirs.

My parents' families seemed to have come from opposite poles. They didn't approve of each other, but they had one thing in common.

They hated white people.

They, the children of those two families, were caught in the middle. They tried to fit in with both sides. They were her Daddy's girls and Momma's daughters, her Daddy's boys and Momma's sons. They were neither completely accepted, nor fitted in on either side, but that didn't bother them too much. Whatever they thought about them, they kept their opinions to themselves, but there was always one.

One of her Momma's nieces always wanted to be the center of attention.

Whenever they visited her mother's mom, she would be there. She would make sure that she was always the center of attention. She tried everything she could think of to keep their grandmother from spending time with them or giving them praise for the things they had accomplished.

Her cousin would always find something bad to say about the person to distract their grandmother. She was mean to them and just as mean to all of her other cousins.

She always tried to cause a fight. She knew if we got into a fight with her, Chock's Momma would send them home, and they would miss out on the good food and fun. Then she would be the center of everyone's attention again. They always tried to wait until after dinner to get into a fight with her. After dinner she was dead meat. Chock's eldest sister would always beat the holy crap out of her. They stuck together, and they did not want to mess with their Daddy.

Everyone in their community loved and respected their Daddy. Those who knew him didn't want to cross him. He was the smartest, strongest, bravest, and the biggest man in the world.

His shoulders were as wide as he was tall. He was all muscles from working so hard. He had trouble buying shoes large enough and usually had to cut out the toes of the shoes so he could wear them.

He had a way of fixing things with words or with tools. He didn't boast, and he didn't brag, but he made everyone he came in contact with feel everything was going to be all right because he was there. He said he should have been taller, but his legs decided to grow into feet. He was five feet six inches tall.

When Chock was growing up, black men and women who stayed home and took care of their families were the role models. They grew up wanting to be like their parents. They were proud when they said their names.

When they were around people who didn't know them, they would oftentimes ask,

"Who's your daddy or, who's your momma?"

Chock and her sisters were proud to tell them the name of their daddy or the name of their momma. They thought everyone knew their parents because their parents were worth something.

The men and women their parents went to school with wouldn't be caught sitting around in the middle of the day, in the middle of the week, doing nothing.

When the schools were integrated, black kids had white teachers. After a while, black kids no longer considered their parents as role models.

Everything that black parents tried to teach their children was devalued. White teachers would sometime treat black kids as if they were worth nothing. Pretty soon, black kids started to feel as if they were worth nothing.

Black kids were praised only if they were outstanding athletes or if they had the ability to entertain. Their academic abilities were discouraged and overlooked.

The values Chock's parents had taught them, the values they had fought for to be treated like they were worth something were felt as a threat to what others felt about themselves.

Others were threatened when they discovered that color didn't give anyone a monopoly on having the ability to achieve and be successful in fields other than athletics or entertainment.

The values and expectations Chock's parents expected for them to strive for were forgotten and replaced by values that were easy to obtain. They started listening to and believing in others. The values of their parents were left behind and ignored whenever it suited their purpose or the purposes of others. They put the blame on one another as an excuse for their failures.

Their role models were replaced by role models created by others. They had been made to feel they need to emulate the role models created by the news media and others, for greed and personal gains, to feel they were worth something.

Chock's role model was her dad. Chock was mostly interested in everything he did. When the crops were in and the canning done, Chock would follow him around while he was working on things around the house or when he went hunting. Chock didn't like sitting home doing nothing trying to be cute like her cousin.

Chock learned how to be devious. She would follow her Daddy around asking questions about what he was doing and why.

Chock noticed how he set things up to get the animals to do what he wanted them to do. Chock watched him set traps for the wild game they needed for food. She watched as he sat patiently and waited for the game he was looking for to come and take the bait.

Chock watched and listened to her elder sisters' plan and scheme. They thought Chock was too little to understand what was going on. She just smiled and waited until she could use what she had learned.

Their mother was a beautiful, dark chocolate woman built like the proverbial brick house. All of the girls were built like her momma but had skin tones from light yellow to dark brown.

All of the children resembled both of their parents in some ways. Anyone could tell who their parents were if they had seen them. Their parents were their role models.

Their mom could have been the first Martha Stewart. The things Martha Stewart got rich doing, her momma had done them a long time ago out of necessity. She could go in a kitchen and make a delicious meal out of whatever was there. There was not always a whole lot of choices for her to work with.

She could make anything taste like a delicious feast from boiled potatoes and cornbread to the wild game her Daddy was lucky enough to bring home. On Sundays, their house would be the first house the visiting preachers would choose to go to for dinner. They used to be devastated on seeing the preacher come home with her momma.

Her dad didn't go to church, but when the preacher came to their house her dad would always sit at the table, in his chair, with the preacher. Her daddy would always sit in his chair at the head of the table regardless of who came to dinner.

Their momma designed their clothes and made them out of whatever materials were on hand, which usually consisted of flour sacks, feed sacks, and cotton sacks. When the cotton season was over, she would take the sacks and bleach them in the old, black iron wash pod. Then she would dye them blue. She would make pants and jackets for the children that needed them.

Their momma taught them how to sew, cook, can food, and other things women did on a farm. And every Sunday, she took them with her to church. Chock was told that she had a good voice and got to sing in the choir with grown people. At church, Chock was considered an angel. There were eleven of them when her momma stopped having babies. There were five kids older than her and five younger. That was my lot—odd man out. They resembled one another, but our skin or hair had different coloring.

Chock was considered a little bit different from her sisters and brothers.

When the sun shone directly on her, her hair turned copper red, and her skin took on a reddish coloring.

Her eyes were shaped like a cat's and were a deep dark blue with a thick black ring around the iris.

Her eyebrows were high and arched as if they were ready to take flight. Her cheekbones were high like her Indian great-grandmother. Some folks said that Chock looked like her daddy when his Injun came out. Some said Chock looked like a Chinaman. Others said she just looked mean and evil like the devil.

Chock's mom would often say, "When Chock was born, she couldn't tell if she was going to be an angel or the devil." Before she died, she said she still hadn't figured it out.

Chock had a tendency to react to the actions others made that was directed at her without thinking. Those actions caused her to get into situations she had a hard time getting out of.

Everyone saw a different side of Chock. When she came in contact with a person, she knew exactly which sister that person liked. She would then behave toward them the way that sister would behave.

They would then say, "Oh ain't she cute? She's just like her sister." When someone smiled at her, Chock smiled back. When someone frowned, Chock frowned back. If they were happy, she was happy. Her eyes would change to match her true mood.

There were seven girls and four boys in their family. The boys were younger than the girls, and they were spoiled rotten.

When they went out on the weekend, they dressed in their Sunday's best. Men would look and make remarks, but someone would be quick to put an end to the remarks by saying,

"Man, them Jacks women, you don't want to mess wit' 'em." Their Momma and Daddy never told them that they were pretty.

Their Momma said they didn't want to give them a big head. Their Daddy went to the extremes to make them look as ugly as possible.

Later, he said he dressed them in boys' clothes so when he left them alone on the farm, they wouldn't be too noticeable. He didn't want men to know there were eight women on the farm and for them to start hanging around when he was away. The way he dressed them then, became a fashion statement later.

Sometimes their Daddy had to leave home to work for others to earn money for things they needed and couldn't raise on the farm. He always left instructions about what he wanted them to do for the day.

Usually, they did what he wanted them to do, but sometimes, they looked for loopholes to get around some of his rules. When they did find a loophole, they ended up in a bunch of trouble.

CHAPTER 7

June Nineteenth Celebration

The biggest event of the year was on June nineteenth. This was the day they found a loophole and decided to get creative with what their Daddy had told them to do. He was hired out to work on another farm. He told them they had to plant the cornfield before they went to the June nineteenth Celebration.

The celebration was the biggest celebration of the year for them. Everybody was going to be there from miles around. They had been talking and getting ready for the event for weeks. Their momma had made them little cute outfits to wear.

When their daddy told them they had to work on that day, they were crushed, but they didn't let on. They got everything ready and set out to do what he told them to do.

They took the seedling corn to the field about half of a mile from home. Their daddy had already plowed the field and made it ready for planting. When they got to the field, they knew it would take them all day to do the planting.

They sat on the pile of rocks that had been piled, by them, to the side of the field when they had cleared it. They sat there with their chins in their hands and just looked at the field for a while before the arguments started.

They started arguing about the best and quickest way to plant the corn. Someone said, "I wish we could just hide it and go home."

That sounded like a good idea.

They thought about it, and then started talking about where would be a good place to hide the seeds.

Someone said, "Why don't we just put them in these rocks?" We looked around and decided that the rocks would be the best place to hide the seeds.

They could come back another day and plant them.

That's just what they did.

They put the bags in the rocks, waited a while, and then went home. When they got home, they were surprised to see that their Daddy was home. He was surprised to see they had finished so early.

"Wuhu! Y'all finished already?" "Yes, sir."

"I took off early to give y'all a hand so you wouldn't miss out on any of the fun."

He gave them a whole dollar to spend. The only time they got a whole dollar was for something extra special like the Dallas fair.

That was a lot of money.

Chock was able to buy bottles of soda for a nickel, watermelon was free, and huge fried fish sandwich a dime. Two pieces of fried chicken was a dime. There were pigs roasting over a pit and ever so often some would swab it with barbecue sauce. You could pick out the part you wanted to be put in your sandwich, and it was only two dimes. Some of the women made old-fashioned ice cream. Man, all that stuff was good! There was group singing and group dancing. There were card games, dominoes, checkers, and horseshoe throwing. There were a number of other things going on too. Some people just sat and looked, while others walked around and looked.

The highlight of the evening was a baseball game. The baseball team that their Daddy played on was playing a team from another town. He was pitching. Their Daddy was ambidextrous and would use either arm for pitching. He could pitch, and he could bat. When he got up to bat, he always hit a home run. Most of the time, they would walk him.

The won the game when one of their Momma's brothers slid home for the winning run. He broke his leg, but when he was carried off the field, he was grinning from ear to ear.

After the game, there was a big dance at the school gym. They should have enjoyed themselves more. They had a guilty conscious about lying to their Daddy. They also were worried about what was going to happen when he found out that they lied about planting the cornfield.

He kept them so busy they didn't have time to go back and do the planting. In a few days, he started checking on the corn. When their Momma would ask him how it was coming, he would say,

"It's not up yet."

One morning, when she asked him how the corn was coming, he said, "Oh, its way up. I never seen corn like it 'fo now."

"Man, you otta see it. It's a sight for sore eyes!" "Come on, y'all. Y'all should see it!"

"It's really somepin' to see. You won't believe your eyes!"

They were flabbergasted at what he was saying. When they got to the field, they saw no corn. Then they looked to where the pile of rocks should have been, but there were no rocks, just corn. Stalks of corn grew from everywhere and in every direction.

He pulled off his belt, lined them up, and wore them out. That winter their animals and chickens went kind of hungry.

They seldom got a whipping from their Dad. He would give them a whipping when they did something that could become serious later on. Or he would give them a whipping when they didn't tell what they had done, and he couldn't fix it before it became a problem.

Their Momma did most of the whippings. When they were into something together, they should not have been in, she would say,

"Just wait till your daddy gets home." Sometimes they would beg her, "Don't tell Daddy. I'll be good."

He would line them up and whip them in order so he wouldn't leave anyone out. He would line them up and start with the eldest or the youngest. He would always start with the youngest if no one 'fessed up. They all loved their cute little baby sister so much that the guilty party would confess to keep her from getting a whipping.

Doing something to get their Daddy upset enough to whip them hurt more than the whipping itself.

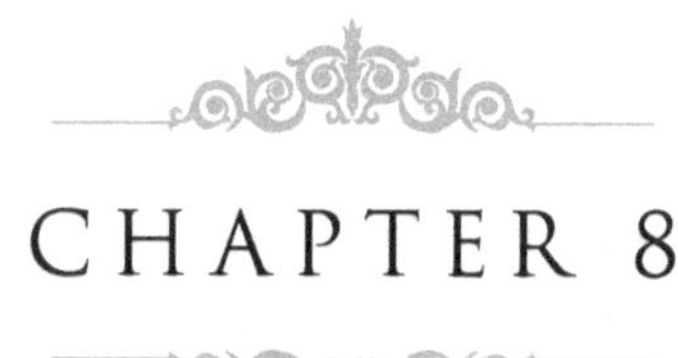

CHAPTER 8

Free atlast! Free atlast!

They had been living with their aunt all spring and on into the summer before their house was finally finished. It was the grandest house in their community. They had five whole rooms to themselves. There were three bedrooms. One of the bedrooms was also used as the living room. There was a kitchen and a dining room. Their house wasn't painted. The floors were not covered with linoleum, but it was theirs.

Trying to adjust to the lifestyles of their Daddy's family had been very tiring. When they finally moved into their own house, they were like starving, wild animals that had been pinned up in a cage. They didn't know what to do first. They could run, jump, sing, laugh as loud as they wanted, talk as loud as they wanted, wrestle, play ball, or just sit in the dirt and play.

Their friends started coming back around to visit on the weekend. It was nice having friends visit again, but we had learned to enjoy themselves without having company.

Their daddy's father would come to visit, and their daddy's brother came to visit when he was in town. His mother and sister never came to visit them. They would stop by if they wanted something, but they never took a seat.

Sometimes their aunt had to come to get her eldest son. He had become attached to them. He spent most of his time at their house just hanging out and getting in trouble with them.

They moved into their new house the summer Chock was to start first grade. Chock was five years old. She didn't care how others felt about her as long as she got things her way. Chock was more than ready for first grade, but first grade wasn't ready for her.

Chock had learned too much from listening and watching her elder sisters and following her Daddy around. Chock was considered too cute and too smart for her own good. Chock was bold and outspoken. She got at least two whippings a day. She earned the name "Ms. Smarty-pants" from her teacher in the first week of school.

Chock knew all the answers to the questions and to the math problems. She had listened to her dad help her sisters with their schoolwork every night for almost five years.

At recess, Chock was teased and called, "Ms. Smarty-pants, Ms. Smarty-pants." Chock thought if she beat up enough kids, they would stop teasing her. Chock got a whipping for fighting and got another whipping for fighting when they laughed at her for getting a whipping. Chock got another whipping for being bad in school when she got home. Chock didn't stop to think how she could keep from getting all of those whippings, and no one tried to explain it to her. She was just bad. After about two weeks in first grade, she was put in second grade.

While Chock was in second grade, she stopped being the center of attention.

The parents of a girl in her class had deserted the seven children in that family. It soon became apparent to all that those children could not take care of themselves. They were split up and placed in different families of those who could take care of them or who wanted a child.

Luzine, one of the girls and Chock's classmate, was placed in the home of a couple that wanted children and could afford to care for them. The couple was childless, and they doted on Luzine.

They bought her ruffled dresses. She had ribbons in her hair. She wore shoes to school every day! She had bloomers of different colors, and they had ruffles on them! She had good stuff for lunch in her sack, and everybody followed her around so they could get a taste.

Luzine was the leader of the pack, and Chock was out. She didn't like Chock. Everyone stopped being Chock's friend. They stopped playing with her, because Luzine had told them to. If they played with Chock, she wouldn't give them any of her lunch.

Things came to an end one day when she sat down to play jacks. She hiked her dress up over her knees so everyone could see her bloomers. Either Chock saw red or she had a panty phobia. Chock said, "Luzine, put your dress down. Everybody knows you got on new panties!"

You didn't say panties then, you said bloomers. Chock had used a bad word. Her least favorite teacher heard her. She came over and jerked Chock up and pulled her into the cloakroom. She gave her a whipping.

Then she said,

"You need that smart mouth of yours washed out!" She put some ole green soap in her mouth that made her sick.

"I guess this will teach you to keep your mouth shut!" she said. Chock was so mad, and she hated her.

Chock said, "You should put some of this nasty soap in your husband's mouth to stop him from being on Lucy Lee!"

"What did you say? You smart mouth little witch!"

"Everybody knows he kisses Lucy Lee when she's in here."Chock knew because she had heard her sisters laughing about it.

Chock also knew because he gave her money to take a note to the senior class to Lucy Lee. They didn't think Chock could read, because she had only started school a few weeks ago.

Luzine didn't pull her dress up when she squatted down to play jacks anymore. She found another way to show off her new bloomers.

The next time she got new bloomers, she got on our homemade monkey bar. She was hanging upside down and had the other children count 1 . . . 2 . . . to see how long she could stay up there.

Chock was not going to be outdone by her. She got on the bar, and everybody started laughing. Chock thought they were laughing, because Luzine had fallen off at twenty-five.

By the time Chock got to fifty, everything got quiet. She couldn't see what was going on at first hanging there upside down. Then she saw a skirt in front of me.

"Chock, get down!" That was her eldest sister.

When she got home, she got a whipping. She told their Momma one of her cousins (from their Momma's side) had come to tell her Chock was on the monkey bar hanging upside down with no bloomers on.

After the whipping, her Momma decided she should wear bloomers to school every day until she learned to keep my dress down.

Chock hated those homemade bloomers. They were too hard to untie when she had to use the bathroom and too hard to tie back to keep them from falling off.

One day, Luzine's family just up and left everything. No one knew why they left or where they had gone. Their leaving was a mystery, but Chock was happy she was gone.

CHAPTER 9

Third Grade

Chock enjoyed the first part of her second year in school. Chock was in the third grade. She had a nice teacher, and she enjoyed school. She was the leader of the rhythm band one of her sisters and her friend had started.

Everyone loved to see Chock strut her stuff. They went to other schools marching and dancing. They performed at school functions, such as basketball games, programs, and assemblies.

Sometimes the people in the white community would hear about the outstanding performances of their teams. They would come to their school to see a game or to see them perform.

A special section would be roped off for them. Which meant no black people were allowed in that section of our facility while whites were present.

Those were usually the quietest and the scariest times. They would even challenge their teams. Their team had to make sure they would not come in contact (touch a white player) during the game. They had to figure out a way to look like idiots and make sure the white team won. In the spring, while Chock was in the third grade she caught whooping cough and almost died. Everyone at school started coughing.

By the time the county nurse came to their school, a number of children had already died.

The kids in Chock's family that were still in grade school caught it, but got over it. Chock had it bad. She would cough and cough until she couldn't breathe. Everything she ate would come up. She became so sick and weak she could barely move.

Each spring her Momma would raise chickens. They had about two hundred chickens roaming around the yard. Chock was like a dinner call to those chickens.

When they saw Chock, they would come running. The chickens would get impatient. They didn't have the patience to wait for her food to come up. They would start jumping on her until they would knock her down. When Chock fell they would continue their attack on her, especially pecking at her mouth, trying to take food from her.

Someone had to be with her when she went to the outhouse to keep the chickens from killing her. Chock hated those chickens, which is ironic, today chicken is her favorite food.

Chock was not expected to live.

When someone came by, they would remark, "Is she still here?"

Or, "I didn't think she would hang on this long."

Chock's mom would say, "I'm surprised she made it through the night." Or, "I don't think she will make it much longer or another day."

Chock's Daddy would make her eat, but nothing stayed down. He would also make sure that she would go out and get some sun.

Everyone avoided her, and when she went around they would get up and leave. Most of the time, Chock was alone.

No one wanted to be around her. They were afraid she would throw up on them when she started coughing or drop dead. Chock was just skin and bones, and they were afraid she would die.

Chock was crying when her Daddy came home for dinner one day. "Gurl, what you crying 'bout?"

"They said I am going to die."

"Don't listen to them folks. They don't know what they talking 'bout. If you gonna die, you wudda died a long time by now. Now you hush up and come on in here and eat something."

Little by little, Chock got strong enough to go back to school.

When Chock returned to school, it was all a buzz. A girl and boy in the senior class were caught standing up outside back of the gym doing something nasty. She had no idea of what nasty was. Words relating to the human reproductive system were never talked about. They didn't know about words, or the slang words, pertaining to sex, penis, vagina, or pregnancy.

After supper that night, her Daddy told her Momma he wanted to talk to the girls.

Her Momma took her and her younger brothers and sisters to the front room.

When they got to the room, Chock told her Momma she had to go to the toilet. Chock went around back, and looked in the hole that should have had a doorknob in it, to see what was going on.

Chock's Daddy had lost his mind! He told Chock's sisters to pull down their bloomers and hold their dress up. They looked at him for a second or two, but did what they were told.

Chock's Daddy said, "See that hair between your legs? That's called a rabbit."

He went on to say, "Boys have hair 'tween they legs, but they have a worm.

"Don't ever let a boy pull your dress up and pull your bloomers down." "He will put his worm in your rabbit, and a baby will grow in your belly."

"When y'all leave home, I want y'all to stay together.

Make sho' them boys keep their hands off y'all, and leave y'all 'lone." That was the extent of their sex education.

One day, Chock heard the kids at school giggling about her Momma. They said she was going to have a baby. Chock got mad and had a fight. Chock knew they were telling a story on her momma. Her Momma would never let a boy do to her what Chock's Daddy said boys would do.

When Chock got home, she asked her Momma if she was going to have a baby. She was so angry, she slapped her face. She said she didn't want to hear that kind of talk coming from her.

That was the first and last time Chock heard her parents disagree about something the other had said or done. Her Daddy said to her

Momma she was never to hit them with her bare hands. If the chulluns needed a whipping, she should get a switch or a belt and whip them.

Chock watched Momma closely after that. She got bigger.One night, they were gotten out of bed and sent to her grandmother's. The next morning, they were told they had a new little baby brother.

When they went out to any function, they left home together and came home together. Sometimes a boy would walk with her elder sisters to where they couldn't be seen from their house. This was their way of getting around what their Daddy told them to do.

When they got ready to come home one night after a school function, they could not find one of their sisters. They looked everywhere. The lights were being turned off in the school buildings.

From their house, their Daddy could see that they should be on their way. He would be on the porch waiting, and sometimes he would meet them.

They decided that they better go on home and tell their Daddy. On the way home, when they came to the field in front of their house, their sister who prided herself on being immaculate was lying on the ground crying. Her clothes were torn and dirty. They ran over to her and asked her what had happened to her.

She said her boyfriend had told her they were waiting for her in the field. He said he would walk with her to the spot where they usually waited. She said when they got to the field, he tried to take off her bloomers, and they got into a fight.

She begged them not to tell their Daddy. They didn't tell him. She, however, had to tell him later when she found out she was going to have a baby.

He didn't say anything when she gave him the news. He just got in his truck and went to the boy's house. When he came back, he said that the boy was going to marry their sister. He never asked my sister if she wanted to get married. That was just the right thing to do under that circumstance. The next day, they heard the boy's mother, unbeknown to the father, had sent him to live with his sister in California. After hearing about the baby's daddy, my sister never left the yard again. Also, she never talked to anyone outside of the family in their community.

Chock's sister left town when the baby was born. She left the baby with them and went to Dallas to live with another sister. Her mother said she was never the same after that.

CHAPTER 10

Fourth Grade

Chock started the fourth grade under a big cloud. Her sister was pregnant. At that time, getting pregnant was the worst thing that could happen to an unmarried girl. When Chock Started fourth grade she was about two years younger than the other fourth graders. Everyone thought her being in the fourth grade at her age was something of a miracle. Chock was miserable.

Chock had no problem with keeping up with the class academically, but at recess, Chock had no friends. Everyone thought Chock was cute, but she was too young for them to spend any time with. Chock was treated like a little sister you were nice to, but you didn't want to play the games she wanted to play.

No one ever considered what the impact of her being exposed to older kids at her age would have on her psychological growth later on in life. Chock missed out on peer interactions that would help with her social development. Socially, Chock was a misfit. Chock just sat and watched others have fun. Watching and listening to others became a habit with her—outside looking in.

One of her Momma's nephews came by to see her sister before she told their Momma and Daddy she was going to have a baby. They sat in the truck talking.

Chock was playing with her younger brother in the pickup bed and eavesdropping. Chock heard her tell him about what had happened to her the night she had a fight with her boyfriend.

He said, "I ought to get my gun and shoot him."

Chock' sister remarked, "That's all right. When I see him again, I am going to shoot him myself."

Chock doesn't think she ever saw him again.

When the baby was born, she went away and left the baby with them. The baby's other grandfather came to visit the baby a number of times.

The grandmother wanted to see the baby, but she would never come to their house. They had to take the baby to her house and wait outside during the visit.

When Chock's sister's pregnancy became common knowledge to the community, she never went to the front of the house or to the front porch. When visitors came by, she would go to her room and stay there until they left.

She put a blanket over the window to keep nosey neighbors from getting a look at her when they came to visit and passed by the window to her room. At school, when Chock walked by, the kids would giggle and make obscene gestures at me. It made me boiling mad, but she had learned to hide her feelings and ignore them. They tried to egg her on by pointing at our house. Their house could be seen from the school. Sometimes they would point to their house and make the obscene gestures and laugh.

Chock's first savior was a boy in her class. He came to her rescue. His family was usually the one that was talked about and was the butt of the community's disapproval and criticism. He told the kids that were teasing her; if they didn't leave her alone, he would make them sorry. He started being nice to her. Chock started talking to him. She had a boyfriend.

Their limited sex education session didn't warn them that sometimes they may want a boy to bother them or be nice to them. They weren't equipped on what to do in such situations and still keep the boy as a friend.

One day at recess time, Chock saw her boyfriend talking and holding hands with an older girl in her class. Chock wouldn't have dared to let him hold her hands even if she wanted him to. Chock got angry and would not speak to him for the rest of the day.

Another the boy didn't like Chock talking to the boy who had rescued her from the mean kids, because he wanted her to talk to him. Every time he saw her talking to that boy, he would beat her up. Almost every day they had a fight.

Chock's eldest sister had graduated, and Chock was on her own. Chock didn't have a protector anymore. The boy she liked wouldn't help with the bully.

The boy that was bullying her was older and bigger and had two big brothers. The bully was also her friend's cousin.

Chock's bully and his brothers hung around the school yard like a pack of hyenas. They walked around the grounds giggling, making obscene gestures, and picking on everyone they felt like picking on. They came to school to make someone's life miserable. Chock doesn't recall ever seeing them inside a classroom.

After school, that boy and his pack would chase her home. Chock could outrun the younger two. When the older one, the leader, caught her, he would try to feel on her and kiss her. Chock always managed to get away from him, because he needed both hands to hold her.

All day long, Chock had to watch out for them when they came to school. When school was over, Chock had to watch for them so she could make her getaway and have a head start. When she thought they weren't looking, she would make a mad dash for home.

Chock was relieved when they didn't come to school. Chock thought they had stayed home one day, but she was wrong. They were waiting for her in the ravine halfway from school to their house.

The three boys jumped her when she went into the ravine between her house and the school. Chock was unable to fight them off. They finally got her on the ground and were trying to take off her bloomers. Chock heard a noise that was made when someone got hit on the head with a rock or a big stick.

Then Chock heard her Momma.

"Y'all, get up from there, and get out from here!" When the boys ran away, Chock saw her Momma standing there with an ax handle in her hand.

Her Momma said later that she had seen the boys pass by and wondered why they were hurrying toward school after school was out. She watched them go to the ravine. When she didn't see them come out, she got curious as to what they were doing there for so long.

When she saw Chock coming, she had an idea of what they were up to.

When she popped the eldest boy upside his head with the ax handle, they jumped up and took off running. Chock lay on the ground crying. Her Momma picked her up and started hugging her. Her Momma wasn't big on hugs. When her Daddy got home; she told him what the boys were trying to do to her. Her Daddy took her to the boys' house and told her to tell their parents what they had been up to.

When Chock finished telling the parents about their boys, her Daddy told the father,

"If these boys put their hands on any one of my girls again, someone is going to come up hurt."

They never bothered Chock after the visit to their house.

That year, when Chock was in fourth grade, she also found out something about her Daddy that troubled her. After school, an elder sister, an eldest brother (although he was younger than her) and Chock decided to hide in the school bus and go with their Daddy to take the school kids home.

They hid behind the backseat of the bus. Their intentions were to hide there and surprise their Daddy when all the kids got off. They knew their Dadd would be happy to see them. He was always happy to see them. But he wasn't that day. When he got to the last stop, of an absentee father, he got off with the kids.

He was in there so long that they got cold and tired of hiding. When their Daddy finally came out, they were sitting in the front seat waiting for him.

He was surprised to see them, but he was not happy. He was upset with them and told them to never do it again. When they got home, their Momma asked where they had been for so long. Somehow, they felt that they should not mention their Daddy's visit at the last stop.

One of the kids that lived in the house where her Dad had made his last stop was a girl in her class. Chock picked a fight with her the next day. She started crying and said, "You just mad at me because your dad likes my mom!" Chock didn't like her anymore until they went back home years later to visit. Chock spent a couple of nights at her house.

CHAPTER 11

Doing Battle

There wasn't much contact between the black and white people in their community. They only came in contact with the white people usually for business reasons only. When they did come in contact with them, they tried to stay out of their way.

They would step off the sidewalk when they met a white person on the street. They had to give them enough room so they could pass to make sure they wouldn't touch them. They smiled and said, "Yes, sir" and "Yes, ma'am" when they were spoken to. They kept their heads down and didn't dare look them in the eye.

If their jobs or crops didn't take them into town, they stayed in their community. They didn't go to town on weekdays to hang out on the streets or to pass time with neighbors. If they gave them the wrong change, they didn't let them know or tell them they had made a mistake. That was the way things were in that town and many other small towns in some southern states.

Her Daddy was probably in contact with the whites more than anyone. He took whatever job he could find as long as he could come home at night. Once when he had gone to work on the river, a hurricane came in. The water rose, and the waves flooded the work site.

He didn't think he would ever see any of his family again. He said he pledged that if he ever got home to his family, he would never leave home again.

He drove the school bus and was respected by the teachers and the students at the school. Occasionally, he would stop by the school, when asked, and help the teachers solve complicated math problems in trigonometry or calculus. Once in a while, some of the teachers would come and sit on the porch while he helped them solve math equations. He worked hard at keeping eleven children fed. He cut all types of wood, worked on his own farm, and on the farm of others. Sometimes he would even doctor on animals. He was really a jack-of-all-trades. Maybe that was how he got his nickname.

When her Daddy went into town that awful day, her Momma went along with him. It was a Saturday, and her Momma wanted to do a little grocery shopping. Sometimes they couldn't go on their Saturday night outings and her Momma had to do her shopping in their little town.

Her Momma got dressed in one of her church dresses. They told them what they wanted them to do while they were gone, and they took off. Chock think they wanted to get away from them for a while. As usual, they did what they always did when they were gone, they fought. They never dared to fight or argue with each other when their parents were around. When they went out, they presented a united front. If you mess with one, all of them would mess with you.

They would leave them sitting on the porch, waving to them, and watching the bus go about a quarter of a mile up the lane to the turnoff. Then they watched as it turned to the right and started to disappear down the hill. They could see the bus slowly disappear as if it was being driven into a lake and was being slowly submerged in the water. When it had completely disappeared, the fight was on!

One Saturday, after their parents left them home as always, Chock's second and third sisters began fighting with her eldest sister. Her eldest sister was here Daddy's helper. Her second sister was her Momma's helper. Her third sister was her second sister's helper. When their Momma and Daddy left, there was an argument as to who was in charge. Chock usually sided with her eldest sister.

Chock was too little to go one-on-one, but she could throw a mean rock, or could clobber someone over the head when they came close to where she was hiding.

They used everything they could find as a weapon or as a shield. They used knives, hoes, rakes, rocks, stick, plates, pans and one another. During one fight, her second sister got the drop on her first sister.

Her third sister came out of hiding so she could help, but she was following too close.

When her second sister swung the plank back over her head; it went back and hit the sister who was standing behind her. Instead of hitting the sister the lick was intended for, she knocked her helper out.

The fight came to a screeching halt. Everyone came out from where they were hiding. Their sister was lying on the ground, *dead*, they thought.

They started screaming and crying; "She's dead!

"She's dead!" "You killed her!"

The sister that had hit her, and the sister the lick was meant for, were hugging and kissing the sister they thought was dead and pleading with her,

"Please don't be dead, get up."

That went on until their sister sat up.

The sister that had hit her dragged her behind the stack or tires they were hiding behind. The fight was back on!

The house and yard would be in shambles when they fought. Chairs were overturned, cooking utensils would be strewn about, and debris would be everywhere. They fought with everything they could get their hands on.

They thought that everyone had enough sense to duck and look out for himself, and no one would ever get hurt.

Their Daddy had loaded guns in his and their Momma's room. They never ever thought of or even dared going into their room under any circumstance. They never thought of touching his guns unless someone in the family was in danger from something, or someone outside of the family, when he was away from home.

They would fight until they heard someone say, "Here they come!"

The smaller children were usually the watch out. They would get out of the way of the fight and just watch from the ladder placed by the side of the house. From the ladder they could also get a good view of the bus a longer way off. The warning would give them plenty of time to put everything back in place before they reached home.

CHAPTER 12

Driving Reckless

On this faithful Saturday morning, when their parents went into town, a fight broke out between her fourth sister and her eldest brother. That was the last trip their parents would ever take together to that town, and the last fight they would ever have among their kids at that house and in that yard.

Chock's eldest brother was only nine. He was the eldest male in the house, so he thought he should be the boss. When their parents were away, he would proclaim himself man of the house and would expect everyone to obey him.

Their fourth sister, the eldest person still living at home, told him he was not the boss and he couldn't tell them what to do. She went on to tell him she was the eldest, and their Momma and Daddy had left her in charge. The fight started. He picked up a broom and swung it at her. She grabbed Chock and held her in front of her for a shield. She was standing too close to the wall. The broom hit the wall and the handle broke.

Chock's sister took off running. Her brother then grabbed a knife and threw it at her. She ducked and the knife stuck in the wall behind her.

The fight was on. They squared off and found cover. They called the place they hid behind and fought from a fort.

Chock sided with her sister. Her brother's partner was his younger brother. Her three younger siblings went up on the ladder as look-outs and to watch the fight from a safe distance. Her fifth sister went around trying to stop them.

When one side found out where the other side's fort was located, they would attack. The other side would counterattack. The side that was attacked would pick up whatever had been thrown at them and throw it right back.

The hiding places, the fort, were bombarded with sticks, rocks, or whatever was lying around. When they ran out of ammunition, hand-to-hand combat would start.

If one side thought the other side was too strong, the weaker side would retreat back to the fort to regroup. The fight would last until they got the warning from the look-outs that their parents were coming home. They had been fighting for about an hour before they got the warning.

"Here they come! Here they come!"

That was a relief! No one had to give in. The fight was a draw. They were tired of fighting and were running out of ideas on how to get the upper hand on one another. When they heard the warning, they quickly threw down their rocks, sticks, planks, skillets, or whatever they had in their hands and quickly came out of hiding.

They were going to the yard to look at the mess they had made. They had to get it cleaned up before their parents got home. They had always managed to get the house, yard, and themselves cleaned up before they got home, but that day was different.

They looked to see how far away the bus was so they could judge how much time they had to get themselves and everything cleaned up before they came home.

Usually, their Daddy would give someone a ride from town. He loved to talk.

He would take his time dropping them off before he came home.

They would track their progress. They would watch as the bus slowly came into view. Then the lookout would watch it go from house to house dropping people off. The lookout would say,

"Y'all, better hurry up, they at so-and-so's house now and they gonna be here in a minute."

On this Saturday, all of their lookouts were sounding the alarm. They were having their hands frantically and were yelling over and over.

"They coming! They coming! They coming!"

They all rushed to the front of the house to see why they were making such a ruckus out of seeing the bus come home. When they saw it they knew why the lookout was raising such a ruckus.

Boy, were they ever!

We saw a yellow streak come into view. They stood there with their mouths open looking at it. They didn't think that it was coming home first but was going straight down the road to drop someone off.

They were more shocked when the bus started turning. Their heads jerked back, and they twisted their necks around, following the bus to help it make the turn. We could hear the brakes squealing all the way to where they were standing.

They all stood frozen while they watched the bus speed down the lane toward the house. They stood there with dirt all over them, their clothes torn, and their hair messed up.

The mess they had made of themselves, the house, and the yard was forgotten. They stood there transfixed watching the bus racing toward them and leaving a huge cloud of dust trailing behind.

What was their Daddy trying to do driving like that? Was he trying to kill himself and their Momma? It was outrunning the dust it made until it turned the last corner by the house. The dust caught up with it, and the bus was lost in the dust. It finally came to a stop, in an unusual place, as close to the side of the house as it could get. Their parents got out before the dust settled and were almost running toward the house. They had no packages.

They started toward them to help with the groceries. Before they reached the bus, their Daddy started calling out to them,

"Y'all go back, and get in the house! Y'all get in the house."

He didn't notice the mess they had made. Their Momma didn't say anything either and they forgot all about it.

They knew it was not a time to talk. Their Daddy went to the back of the house to their bedroom. He came back with all of his guns and put them on the bed by the front door. He checked to see if they were loaded.

He always kept his guns loaded and under no circumstances would they ever dare to touch them unless they were told. They had been taught how to handle the guns and knew they could kill.

Their daddy had a gun for big game, little game, birds, things close, and things far away. He also had the two pistols his father had worn all the time while he was living and had jumped in the creek with them on. He got the Winchester from behind the door. He then put some ammunition in his shirt pockets and went to the front porch and sat down.

O Lord! Lord! Chock thought.

They went to the windows to see what kind of animal Daddy was looking for. They couldn't see anything. Their Daddy sat by the corner post with the gun across his lap and his hand close to the trigger.

Chock had seen him like that a number of times when he went hunting. He would just sit there waiting not seeing anything but could feel something coming and could tell from what direction it was coming. Her Daddy was never one to let others know how he felt. His only emotion was to say "Wuhu" and smiles to show he was happy or surprised. If he said

"Wuhu" and didn't smile when he talked, they knew that something was wrong. And they had better stop what they were doing and walk light.

A stranger would think that he had no feelings at all. This Saturday there was something different about the way he looked and acted while he sat on the porch. At the time they didn't know her Daddy wasn't looking for an animal, but animals were looking for her Daddy.

Some would say his Injun had come out. All he needed was war paint. He sat there, his jaws clenched so tightly Chock could see his cheekbones moving up and down. His eyes looked as if they were closed. He just sat there staring off in a distance, just waiting for something to come.

The whole community seemed to be waiting for something. Their community had come to a sudden halt. Everything and everyone was dead quiet. Everything seemed to come to a standstill. The sun just hung there in the sky. When they went inside and closed the doors and pulled down the shades, the chickens went to roost.

The animals could feel what seemed like a storm coming. They stopped grazing and stood still with their heads up listening. Their dogs moved from the shade tree and went under the house.

They craned their necks to look out the windows and around outside to see what was happening. They heard it coming. They could hear the rattling noises, the droning, and moaning sounds coming their way before they saw what was making the sounds. It didn't sound good. A storm was coming. The sun was shining and there was not a cloud in the sky, but we could hear what sounded like a storm coming. They could hear the sounds getting louder and coming closer and closer. Then three trucks came into view. They came up the same incline their Daddy had come up a few minutes ago.

When they saw the trucks, we knew these trucks belonged to white men. This was our storm. Men were standing, crowded together, in the back of the truck, and there were poles sticking up over their heads. The trucks were going up and down the dusty road of their little community that ran about a quarter of a mile in front of their house.

The trucks kept going up and down the road—the same road their Daddy had just come down before he turned into the lane that led to their house. They were looking for someone.

No one was in sight. The people in their little black community went inside and closed their doors when they saw the trucks loaded with white men. White men carrying guns was a very bad sign. They knew it was not a time to be seen.

The word had spread.

There were no sounds even from the animals or the birds. All they could hear was the droning sound and the noise made by the trucks.

All they could see were the three trucks, that seemed to be lost, chasing one another on the dusty road.

They watched the trucks go up the road again, at this time, when the first truck got to the turn off to the lane that led to their house, it turned in, and the others followed. Chock's heart sank.

Chock knew they were looking for their daddy. The poles sticking up were guns.

White men with guns were looking for her Daddy! "Y'all keep quiet now."

They were sitting on the same bed they had sat on during the storm that had demolished their other house. The storm that was coming toward them on this day was a different kind of storm and it was not a surprise. They all watched the storm come closer and closer to them. Their Daddy sat on the porch watching the cloud of dust bring the storm to their door. He knew when it got there, it would come with a vengeance and before the dust cleared lives could be lost. There was nowhere to go and nowhere to hide from this storm. He just had to wait it out.

Usually, no one survived this storm. The kind of storm coming toward them on this day was deadlier than the storm that had destroyed their house. This storm would leave no one to rebuild and only hate as a foundation to build on for the generations to come.

This storm would leave its streak of devastation in their minds and in their hearts. They were familiar with this storm. They have witnessed it or have heard about it many times. And they all knew this storm by its name. The name of this storm is "Racism." It was not brewing. They stood in their house and looked out the windows and watched it come. It was coming down the lane to their house. Then, it was there. And it was there for their dad.

They knew what this storm would do. It would destroy everything in its path. And it would kill anyone that tried to stop it.

They were in the path of this storm. They were alone, but they would do everything they could to keep it from leaving its path of destruction at their door.

The sun was still shining, and it was quiet outside, too quiet.

Their Momma wasn't sitting on the bed praying with them for this storm. But this time when she prayed, she was sitting in a chair by the door. She was sitting where she couldn't be seen by anyone from outside. While she sat there praying she held a twelve-gauge pump shot gun on her lap and her finger close to the trigger.

After their Daddy told them to be quiet, Chock saw him raise his rifle and take aim. He fired a shot across the last truck when it turned in their lane. The resound from the shot was deafening, and it went on forever.

Chock guessed that shot let everyone in their community know the fight had started.

And they knew at that point of time, their Daddy was in a fight for his life.

They also knew their Momma and some of the children would be fighting for his life and some of them could also die. There could be no one left who could tell about this storm.

The shot their Daddy fired brought them to attention. This was not the time to feel sorry for themselves. This was also not the time to cry.

They had to be alert. Their faith was in God's hands. They had to listen and watch closely to what was going to happen right here on earth at their house.

No one, and nothing, in the community reacted to the shot. Usually, when a shot was fired, everyone would come out in their yards to get a look to see what was going on. The animals would take off running. The chickens would start flapping and clucking and the dogs would have a barking fit. Everyone and everything remained quiet and still. Even the trucks froze in their tracks.

Chock wanted to go out there and stand by her Daddy, but he told them to stay inside and be quiet. Chock knew the other kids wanted to go out and stand by him, too.

He was sitting there on the porch all by himself. Chock wanted to cry. But this was not the time to cry. They had to be brave and do all they could to help their Daddy. Chock knew their neighbors and friends heard the shot. No one came. Where were all the people her Daddy had helped?

Chock remembered what her Daddy had said to her momma when she asked him to go to church with her. "Emma, you can stop asking me because I ain't going. I ain't going to sit in that church all day and mess around with them folks. You'll go to hell listening to 'em talk all day. When somebody needs help all they do is talk about 'em and go home and close their doe."

Chock didn't understand what he was saying then, but that day, everything became quite clear. Chock lost that deep warm feeling she had about the people in their community.

Their Daddy told them to stay in the house and be quiet.

He had said that to her many times when she had gone hunting with him. He would tell me,

"If you go, you got to sit still and be quiet. The least little thing could frighten it."

"You need to be ready. Think about what you gonna do when it get here. What's coming may not be what you been looking for."

He needed to concentrate, and they needed to concentrate. He needed to concentrate on what was coming, and they needed to concentrate on him. He couldn't worry about any sudden movements, or noises from them that would distract him or give someone the wrong signal.

They needed to do just what he told them to do and listen in case they had to do something else. They knew how to use a gun. And if they had to, they would.

The men in the trucks heard the shot. The trucks came to a screeching halt.

There was a lot of yelling going on between the men for a moment. Then, they came on.

They got to the house and pulled up in the front yard. Their dogs didn't even bark. They parked in the flower beds. Those flowers were her Momma's pride and joy, but they meant nothing to the men.

When they got out of the trucks, they finished trampling down the flowers the trucks had missed.

While they were getting out of the trucks, her Daddy said, "Wuhu! I almost shot y'all."

Her Daddy had two languages. He used the one that whites expected from a black person.

"I had my sights on a lion just crossin the road 'fore y'all turned into come down here. I almost had 'em."

"I wanted to get after it, but I was 'fraid to leave the wife and chulluns here by thyself case it double back on me."

Her Daddy kept talking. While he talked, he kept his gun barrel aimed at the man in front. He was watching for any movement, that would alert him to shoot, from the men that were coming toward him. He made his voice sound apologetic about the mishap of almost shooting someone, and at the same time he sounded distraught about letting the lion get away.

The men continued to get out of the trucks and started walking closer toward the house. They came to a standstill when the man in front was about ten feet in front of her Daddy and put his hands up. He knew if they kept moving, he would die. Her Daddy had a reputation for his shooting.

Her Daddy continued to talk about the lion and the destruction it had caused among the farmers in their community. Another man asked,

"Which way did it go?"

"It went over yonder," said her Daddy, keeping his eyes on the man in front while he pointed in the direction the men had come from.

They all looked in the direction her Daddy was pointing. He was pointing to the part of the town where they lived.

They seemed to get a little anxious about the news. They started talking about their families and the animals on their farms they had left unprotected.

Earlier that week, they had been warned about a lion that was killing farm animals in their part of the community. They had seen it cross the road, late one evening. Before her Daddy could get his rifle, it had disappeared in the woods her Daddy was pointing to.

"Hey, load up! Load up! Let's get us a lion!"

They couldn't get loaded fast enough for the man that was standing in front of the pack—the culprit that seemed to have brought the trouble to their house.

He kept insisting, "Come on, y'all. Hurry up, load up, and let's go! Letgo!"

The men got loaded up and drove out of the yard—one following the other. When they had gone a little distance from the house her Daddy called her Momma and asked, "Emma, Y'all, all right in there?" Her Momma put the gun she was holding down and went to the porch. They followed her out to the porch and stood by their Daddy. They watched silently as the trucks drove up the lane away from their house, followed by a cloud of dust that shielded them from view until they got to the corner. They kept watching as they turned the corner and disappeared down the incline.

When they were out of sight, without saying a word, they cleaned up the debris from their fight and the mess the men, and the trucks had made. Her Momma and Daddy went on about their work as usual.

More than sixty years have gone by since the day white men came for their Dad. Chock can still see them coming down the lane to their house. Chock can see her Daddy sitting there all alone on their porch waiting for them. Chock can see him as he faced all these men with guns all by himself. Now, when Chock think about that day, she still feels the same pain, and she cries the tears she denied herself to cry.

CHAPTER 13

Their Daddy Hit a White Man

After the men had gone they went about their chores without being told or reminded. They didn't know why the men had come to their house with guns, looking for their Daddy. They didn't dare to ask. That was grown folks' business.

Later that night after the white men had gone they found out what had happened to their Daddy and Momma while they were in town. Their Daddy lost his temper and hit a white man.

In the summer of 1951, their Daddy hit a white man!

Before Rosa Parks was arrested in 1955; before Emmitt Till was murdered in 1955; before John F. Kennedy was shot in 1963; before Dr. Martin Luther King Jr. was shot in 1968; before Medgar W. Evers was shot in 1963; before the Mississippi Burning Trial in 1967 about the civil rights workers murdered in 1964, their Daddy hit a white man!

Black men were being burned, shot, dragged, drowned, hung, and killed in unspeakable ways for a little of nothing, and sometimes for nothing at all. Black people were being put to death all over the south. While all of that was going on, her Daddy hit a white man.

They were in deep, deep, shit.

After the white men had gone, some of their neighbors were brave enough to sneak through the woods to see if they were still alive. Before the night was over, they heard different versions of what had happened in town. They put the bits and pieces of their stories together, but the facts and endings were the same. Their *Daddy had hit a white man.*

Her Momma and Daddy had gone into town that Saturday morning to sell the vegetables they had picked earlier that morning. Her Momma decided to go with him and pick up a few things. They couldn't go, because they had to finish up work they had not been able to do because of rain.

The weighing scales were located in a shed in the back of the store. Her Daddy went to the back of the building where the scales were located to get the produce weighed. Her Momma went to the little mercantile to do her shopping.

The owner of the store had a reputation with women and seemed to take a liking to her Momma. He was struggling with her. Her Momma was trying to keep her dress closed with one hand and was trying to push him away with the other.

Her Momma's resistance seemed to irritate the store owner. He got rough with her because she dared to resist him. Her Daddy heard a commotion coming from the front of the store. Men were stumping and clapping, talking loud, laughing, and egging the storekeeper on.

Her Daddy decided to see what was going on. When he got to the front of the store, he saw their Momma struggling with the owner of the store. Her dress was ripped open, and he had his hand inside her dress. He didn't hesitate when he saw what was happening to their Momma. He knocked the man out cold. He grabbed their Momma, and they ran to get on the bus before the man came too. That's how they got a chance to make it home.

They knew they had to come home. Chock's Daddy could have run like a lot of others had. They knew men would be looking for her Daddy. There were eight kids at home. They didn't even want to think about what would happen when the men came to their house, and they couldn't find her Daddy.

They would come—the way they had come to so many houses, and call for her Daddy to come out. If he didn't come out, they would burn the house down, not caring if children were inside or not, thinking he was hiding inside.

Chock's Daddy waited on the porch so they wouldn't have any reason to think he was in the house, or give them a reason to come in the house and bother his family. We would still be in danger whether they found him or not.

They made it through the night, but they didn't sleep very much. They all stayed awake listening for any sound. They were afraid they would come back for their Daddy any moment.

When Chock did fall asleep, she dreamed about the awful sight she had seen hanging on the tree the day she had gone for a walk. She dreamed; as she walked through the woods, a nice breeze was blowing. The branches were swaying. When Chock looked up at the tree she saw the awful sight hanging there. The breeze made it turn toward her. When the horrific looking thing hanging in the tree turned toward her. Chock saw a face. She saw the face of her Dad. Chock woke up screaming.

CHAPTER 14

Days of Torment and Terror

Chock's Momma and Daddy knew their troubles were not over, because the men left. The day after the men left was Sunday. Sunday was the only day her Momma got out of bed before Daddy.

Morning finally came. On this Sunday morning Chock heard her Daddy get up before her Momma and go outside. Chock got up and followed him outside. When she got outside she sat quietly on the steps and watched him doing the chores they usually did before they got ready for church. While he did their chores he was talking to God. Chock wondered what he was saying. What could he have said to God that had given him the courage to face three truck loads of white men with guns without showing an ounce of fear?

They didn't go to church that Sunday, but their Momma got up and made a feast any preacher would appreciate. No preacher came to their house that Sunday and no one else did either.

There were agitators from both sides. People, black and white, like to talk and keep things going.

Blacks and whites had seen what had happened in the store. People from both sides exaggerated about it, and some laughed about it. People from both sides, black and white, thought something should be done about it.

Some whites said that if nothing was done, then niggers would think that they could walk in there any time and act like they owned the place.

Some of the whites had witnessed the man putting his hands on her Momma. He had a reputation of being a ladies' man. He had been known to bother their women, but he was still white.

The blacks said if nothing was done, the white men would keep on grabbing their womenfolk. It wasn't safe for black women to stay home or go to town.

People from both races started showing up in their little community. They didn't know what their motives were. They didn't know those who would help or those who would hurt.

They were told to stay away from them, to keep close to the house, and not to trust anybody. Some of the visitors wanted to get a look at the man that had hit a white man and lived. Others wanted to see the woman, they said, that had caused the trouble.

Chock's Daddy knew going to town wasn't safe after that, but they had no choice. He still had to make a living. A day after her Daddy hit the man, the white man rounded up all of the men from town he could and came looking for her Daddy again.

They usually came when Chock's Daddy wasn't home. They would drive around the community asking everyone they saw if they knew where her Daddy was. They would give her Momma messages to give her Daddy.

They would take whatever they saw or wanted: watermelons, sacks of cucumbers, corn, peanuts, and chickens. They would take whatever they wanted from anyone that had something they wanted. They were reminded to keep their eyes down and remember what they should do when white people were around. They were also told to let the white men have whatever they wanted and not to say a word about it. Don't give them any excuse to hurt you. When they came around, Chock's Momma would stand in the door and tell us to stay inside and be quiet.

They were harassed at least twice a day. Chock's Daddy thought that it would be a good idea if they took turns watching for them. When they saw them coming, they would run and hide in the woods.

They hid out in the woods a few times before they started harassing the other people in the community. They thought people in the community were helping Chock's Daddy and hiding him.

When they could no longer find him or them at home, they began harassing him when he was working and on the job.

They would block the road when they saw the school bus coming with a load of children. That scared the school children and their parents half to death. Their Daddy got someone to drive the bus for him.

Things finally came to a head one day when the men went to the field where Chock's Daddy was plowing. The same three trucks filled with white men came.

This time, they had a sheriff with them. They pulled their guns and demanded, "Get down off that tractor with your hands up!"

Chock's Daddy told them later that getting down off the tractor without the use of his hands was a pretty hard fete to accomplish. When he managed to get down—flat on his face, they then took him with them and put him in jail.

They had no knowledge about her Daddy's arrest until another white man from town, whom he had worked for, came and told them what happened. For three days, they didn't know if he was dead or alive. They didn't know if they would ever see him again or ever know what had happened to him.

After a week had gone by, their father came home and the harassment resumed. Chock's Daddy decided that it would be better if they left town and found some other place to live. He knew they were not safe any longer and that the harassment would continue until someone, or he, was dead.

Where would he take eight children? My three elder sisters were in Dallas living with her uncle. That left eight children at home that were in danger.

That still possessed a problem of what could be done to keep them out of harm.

When Chock's Daddy heard that migrant workers were needed in Arizona and Idaho, he felt that was the answer to their problem and started making plans for them to leave.

CHAPTER 15

Leaving Home

Months before the white men came to their house, Chock's Daddy came home with a huge, yellow flat bed truck. Unknown to anyone, this truck was to be their passage out of Texas to their new home.

When Chock's Daddy bought that truck, everyone thought he had lost his mind. What was he going to use a big truck like that for? Her Daddy found that he could use the truck for a number of things. Everyone then wanted to borrow it or asked him to haul something.

Her Daddy started getting the truck ready for their trip. He put the sideboards up and covered them with tarps. When he finished, the truck resembled a covered wagon.

When he bought the truck this wasn't what he had in mind. He had no inkling this truck would literally become a life saver.

Chock's Momma cooked for days. She fried up as many of their chickens as she could. She made fried fruit pies and sweet potato pies. She made batches of biscuits, cakes, tea cakes, and cookies. They also took canned peaches, pears, and pickles. They took with them any other food that wouldn't have to be cooked or heated up.

They packed up things they would need for bedding and a few personal items. They packed things they would need for the trip and things they would need once they got to where they were going.

Finally, they were ready for their journey. They had no choice. They had to leave. They had to leave before people started talking too much.

They had to go before word spread about their leaving and got back to the wrong people.

The day they left home was a bittersweet day for them and for some of the people in the community. They were glad to leave all of the turmoil behind. They were not happy about leaving their home, their friends, and people they had known all of their lives.

Their family had lived in the community for generations. They were not just leaving their land, their home, their schools, or the things they had collected through the years. They were leaving a way of life— the way they had learned to live and interact with their friends and neighbors.

They had to tear themselves away from their roots. They had to tear themselves away from where they belonged. They had to find another place where they would be safe and start a new life.

They were leaving their sense of belonging and acceptance. The only things they could take with them to help them to survive that move were in their hearts and in their minds.

No one would ever be able to measure the effect the storm would have on them. No one would be able to measure how that storm would affect their families for generations to come. They just had to ride it out and see.

Some of the people realized their leaving would put a big hole in the community. They had a big family. They were involved in every aspect of the community. When something went wrong, Chock's Daddy was the first person sought out to help fix it, and they all would tag along to help.

Chock's Daddy was always putting his neck on the chopping block for the people in the little community. Once, a family sought his help when their son who was considered slow or not too bright or (touched) in the head had gotten into trouble in town.

The boy was just trying to help a white woman who was having trouble getting over a fence. He put his hands on her arm to help her across. Her teenage brother saw him and started beating him for putting his hands on his sister. By the time Chock's Daddy got to town, it was a mob scene. No black person would be safe in town during that time. Her Daddy went. He went to town to try to convince the white girl's family that the boy meant no harm to the girl. He was just trying to help her get across the fence. He had to make them understand that the boy didn't know it was wrong to touch a white person.

They believed Chock's Daddy, and he brought the boy home. The boy was almost dead. They were just waiting to hang him. He had been beaten, dragged around town, and tied up. They were just waiting for night to come.

Chock's Daddy had put his life in jeopardy many times for the community. Where were they when he needed their help? They knew what had happened to them wouldn't stop happening. It had been going on for years, and people kept on leaving.

Some were relieved. Some had already distanced themselves from them. They were hoping that staying away from them would keep them from being targeted. The kids at school said that the white men were going to hang Chock's Daddy. They said they couldn't be their friend because they would get killed, too.

Chock's Daddy knew and everyone in their community knew it was a matter of time before someone died. The man her Daddy hit would keep harassing them until he got his revenge. Black men just didn't go around hitting white men at that point in time and lived to tell about it. An example had to be made; the niggers had to be kept in their place. Her Daddy was liked by some of the whites also. His reputation with some with these influential whites was keeping him alive, but the father of the man her Daddy hit was also influential. It was a miracle any of them was still alive and unharmed-physically that is.

Some of the people in their community believed that their leaving would let things get back to normal. They felt if they left, the white men would stop coming around. Strangers would leave them alone, and things would get back to normal and they would be safe again.

The day they left, only one of Chock's Momma's nephews and Daddy's nephew were there to see them off. A few single men and one of her Daddy's cousins and his family went with them.

Chock's Momma's nephew had become so attached to her Daddy that he ran after the truck begging to be taken along. He chased after the truck as long as he could. People were standing in their doors watching them and waving as we drove slowly by.

They watched their cousin running after the truck until he couldn't keep up and disappeared from sight. Then they picked up speed. Their little community disappeared. When they could no longer see the place where they had lived, everyone got quiet. They looked back as long as they could before they fell asleep.

The farthest they had ever been in the daytime was a little town about thirty miles away from home. They had been to Dallas a few times for the fair, but they hadn't seen anything along the way. They had gone at night and had returned during the next night.

They hadn't seen any of the sights they saw before darkness set in. The only body of water they had seen was a creek about ten feet wide. They thought this creek was huge. That creek divided their little community from the white community.

The bridge was originally made from wood and would not hold the weight of a bus full of people.

Before the bridge over the creek was repaired, they had to get off the bus or truck and walk across. The bridge was too weak. After they unloaded, the bus would cross. They were afraid it would fall in. Then, they had to walk across the bridge to get back on the bus. When they walked across, they had to be careful where they stepped.

The bridge was reconstructed, but they were still afraid when they crossed it. They would lift their feet off the floor of the bus and hold on to something until they made it across.

The men, who left their homes and went with them, took turns driving. They didn't think they should stop to rest. It was safer that way. They didn't know if they would be followed or not. Black people had to be careful where they stopped when they traveled. They only stopped where they saw other black people to buy gas. A few times we stopped to buy bread and bologna.

They didn't have that much money and every cent counted. Everyone put their money together to buy gas and other things needed for their trip. The food, her Momma had cooked for the trip, came in handy and had to be shared with everyone on the truck.

The afternoon of the fourth day they spent their last cent on gas, and there was not much food left. They were scared, hungry, and tired. They were going to a little town about fifty miles from Parker. When someone saw the sign "fifteen miles to go" a shout went up.

Everyone started talking again. But the truck was getting low on gas. They were almost there. They could see the campsite. They could see little buildings with a backdrop of tall, flat top mountains out in the middle of nowhere. They saw strange-looking plants and trees and funny-looking little animals running about.

They had their necks stretched as if that would help the truck in reaching their destination. The truck started stalling. They sat there in the truck for awhile hoping against hope that the truck would start up again. Her Daddy kept trying to get the truck to go just a little further. It would start up and go a few yards, and then the motor would die again. Finally, the motor just wouldn't turn over again. They ran out of gas about a mile from the campsite just before sundown. They were devastated. Chock couldn't remember the last time they had seen a gas station. It didn't matter if they were close to a gas station or not. They didn't have any money.

They sat there looking at the vast landscape. They were hoping to catch a glimpse of another vehicle, a horse, or tractor, or truck, anything moving. They gave up hoping.

"Well, I guess that's that," Chock's Daddy said and got out of the truck.

"I don't think we're that far from the camp. They could probably get there before dark. Chock guess they gonna haft to start pushing or they just haft to leave the truck here until they can get some help."

Everyone got out of the truck. The women and children started walking, and the men started pushing the truck while her Daddy steered.

The going was slow. At first, they were a little scared being out in the middle of nowhere with the strange-looking trees and strange-looking little animals running around. Chock was glad the men had brought their guns along.

After they had walked for a few minutes, everyone seemed to relax and started to enjoy themselves. They had not been out of the truck for days. Walking and looking at all of the different plants and animals was interesting and help them to forget about their dilemma.

About twenty minutes or so had passed when someone spotted houses about a quarter of a mile away. They started hollering, jumping around, and waving things in the air. They must have attracted someone's attention.

When the people in the camp saw them, they came running and driving whatever vehicles they had to meet them. Shouting and laughing, they pulled the truck on into the camp.

They made it.
Their new home!

PART 2

LIVING IN NEW PLACES

("OUT FROM HERE")

CHAPTER 16

Arizona Labor Camp

Before they reached their destination they had run out of gas, money, and were almost out of food. They were about a mile from the labor camp in Arizona before the truck came to a complete stop. Everyone was disappointed but determined to get to where they were going. We got out of the truck. Some started walking, and some started pushing the truck until they got close enough to be spotted by people in the camp. They came running to give them a hand.

Their truck was pulled to their new home, a labor camp, by another truck from that camp.

When they got to the camp, it was almost dark. They didn't have time to look around the campsite, but they could see several buildings in the camp. They had to find the building in which they were going to live.

The contractor, or overseer, or manager, whatever he was, took them to one of the long buildings. The buildings were divided into individual living quarters. Each family was given a large-sized room. Each dwelling came with beds, a table, and a stove. That was to be their new home.

There was no bathroom or running water in their dwelling, which was nothing new to them, but they were a little surprised to find the kitchen and beds in the same room. They helped with unpacking the truck.

After they finished unpacking, they had to get themselves cleaned up from the long trip. The women in the camp brought food to their dwellings.

The kids went right to bed when they finished eating. It felt good to stretch out on a bed. They had not slept in a bed for three nights.

They could hear the celebration going on all around them when they got into bed. The men talked and laughed about the trip way over in the middle of the night. They went to sleep with the sound of laughing and joking. It was a pleasant change.

The next morning, they couldn't wait to go outside to take a look around at their new home. Besides the long houses, there were also a few small houses made out of wood.

There was a long building of concrete that contained the camp's washroom and the bathrooms for the whole camp. That area caused a few altercations among the farm workers.

The building housed the men's bathroom at one end. The washing area was located in the middle, and the women's showers and toilets were on the other end.

Sometimes the men would accidentally, on purpose, wander into the women's area. They claimed they had come in the wrong door by mistake-right. They solved their problem by going back to the wash tubs to bathe in and using the night pans after dark.

There was one building off to the end of the camp. Chock's first thought was it was a church. When they went inside, they saw it was a common meeting hall used for a honky-tonk.

The man that ran that honky-tonk was called Fats. He was nice. When they had money, they would go there to buy food and other goodies. When they didn't have money to buy a snack, he would give them something to share.

There was also a juke box in that building. At night and on the weekends, that joint would come alive. People in the camp would go there to drink and dance. They would hear music until they fell asleep. The man who ran the camp "honky-tonk" told them the camp had been used as a prison before it had been turned in to a labor camp for farm workers to live. He said the government had rounded up all the Japanese families during the war and brought them there to keep an eye on 'em.

They were in the middle of a desert. There were no sidewalks, there was no grass, and there were no other houses except for the ones in the camp and no trees anywhere.

The sun shone so hot on the sand in the middle of the day it made the sand too hot to walk on without shoes and the sand was too deep to walk in with shoes.

Chock kept going from one end of the camp to the other just looking. As far as the eyes could see in any direction, there were only tumbleweeds, sage brush, cactus plants, lizards, snakes, and insects dashing from one place to another trying to avoid the hot sand, the hot sun, and their predators. There was nothing at the camp but the huts, a few broken down vehicles, and the people who lived there.

When the newness and the novelty of the camp wore off little by little, the camp became a dismal place to live. One could say the camp was similar to a prison for them who were living there now.

As they walked through the camp the next morning, they saw people from different states. They also noticed that people of different colors were living there. They thought they had left all of their worries and fears behind, but there they were staring back at them—right smack-dab in their faces. *White people*!

They were surprised to see white people living in the same place they were going to live. When they looked at them, they could see in their eyes what they thought they had left behind in Texas.

They could see it in those eyes and see it in those faces what they didn't have to bring with them. Fear and hatred had gotten a ride with someone else. They were already there, long before Chock's family got there, just waiting.

Everyone in the camp shared a common bond. They were all there to get away from some kind of storm that had threatened their survival. Some came to avoid the law. Some came to avoid their wives, their families, and their husbands. Some came because they felt there was nowhere else to go. And some came to take advantage of others, in any way they could, to satisfy their own selfish or unhealthy needs. They were to learn that everyone was there, because they had to get away from something, or were there to get something any way they could and from anyone they could. They were all there trying to survive to make a new life for themselves and their families. Yet, some still brought with them the belief that they were still better than others and entitled to make others do their bidding.

Chock's parents and their kids also brought along their beliefs. They believed, and they were taught to believe, if you were nice to people, they would be nice to you. They believed that black people could be trusted to keep their word and they could depend on them.

Chock's parents also believed when a person sat at their table they were their friends and could be trusted. And they assured the people they considered their friends were also their friends.

They were faced with a different breed of people than they had been accustomed to in Texas. A good majority of the people at the camp were hustlers, pimps, prostitutes, gamblers, thieves, abusers, and child molesters. Some were takers and some were predators.

These were the kind of people Chock's parents had been careful to keep them away from. They tried to protect them from anything that was unpleasant. If they happened to see a dead animal by the roadside, they would tell them not to look at it.

Chock is sure her Daddy was acquainted with people who were considered to have unhealthy or unsavory characters. There were a sprinkling of members in his family who had lifestyles some considered unsavory, but they had been kept at a distance.

Before they left home, sometimes they would accidentally come upon someone hiding out in the woods drinking or gambling. There were also those going on in the honky-tonks in their community.

When underage kids would come upon the people caught in the act of those activities, they would stop what they were doing and wait for them to leave before they continued doing what they thought they shouldn't see.

Chock's Daddy took a drink every once in a while. When he did, he had to sleep in the bus or truck so they couldn't smell the alcohol. They were not equipped to handle their hip talk and smooth manners.

The contractor was paid by the number of people he recruited to work the crops. He went all over and brought anyone he could find back to the camp whether they would work the crops or not. Some of those people were smoother and a little more hip than what her Daddy had been accustomed to.

They were overwhelmed and taken in by the praise and attention they gave them. To think everyone was sincere and could be trusted was their worst downfall.

Their little dwelling became the center of attraction. Everyone was welcome.

There was always something going on at their house.

They weren't allowed to sit around doing nothing on the weekend or when there was no work to be done. When they were inside, they were singing, dancing, wrestling, or playing other games. When the sun cooled, they went outside to play ball, race, or any other game her parents had concocted to keep them busy.

There was always food at their house for those who came to their lodging. There was food for those who didn't want to spend their money to buy food for whatever reasons. And there was food for those that didn't want to work and for the free loaders. Some of the single men brought food to their quarters for her Momma to prepare for them also. There they were way out there in the middle of nowhere; some people were trying to put on the dog and trying to act like something they were not. Their house was full of others children. Some of the men came to their house because there were females there. Some of the females came because there were females and males there. Her Momma was still a beauty. She was about forty at the time. Chock's two eldest sisters that were with them were fourteen and sixteen.

They had been away from Texas for about a year when the eldest sister that came with them ran away and married the camp's live-in playboy.

After they had been there for a while, and after everyone had satisfied their curiosity about them or about what they could get from them, they went back into their little groups.

Some put on the pretense that they were better than the rest of them and said they were there by choice and would be leaving any day. Some gave themselves airs and tried to impress others by segregating themselves from different groups.

Most of the residents at the camp were black people. There were a few white families, and there were some families who talked too fast to be understood. They knew they were not white, but they didn't know what they were. That was Chock's first time seeing Mexican People.

There was segregation between races and also within the black population. Some of those people, from different races, tried to prevent their kids from playing with them.

Chock's Daddy told them, "Don't mind 'dem folks. Their just trying to make their self feel worth something. 'Side, you got enough chulluns already here to play with."

The road they came into camp on was the only road leading out of camp. There were no buses, no trains, no horses, no wagons, and only a very few run-down vehicles that were dependable enough to get them to and from work.

Whoever came up with the plan for the camp made sure it was far enough away to keep everyone in they wanted in, and everyone out they wanted to stay out.

CHAPTER 17

School in Arizona

The labor camp, that was Chock's new home, was owned by a cotton grower. When they got there, they were not only scared, confused, and lost, but they were also broke.

They had been out of school for almost a week. They helped their Momma and Daddy in the cotton field for the rest of the week. They needed money.

Chock's parents were strong believers in education. When Monday came, they had the five kids ready to get on the bus and ready to go to school.

They went to the bus stop and waited for the bus. When the bus came, they got on and got right back off. They thought they had gotten on the wrong bus. There were only white kids on this bus. The driver told them it was their bus, so they got back on and went to school. All the way to school the white kids called them names and threw things at them. They drove for over an hour before they reached a little, one-room red school house.

Needless to say, they were not welcome at that school. The skinny, blonde, curly-headed teacher almost fainted when they went inside. That was Little Rock before they ever heard of Little Rock. They were faced with twenty-five white kids. Chock heard a kid say, "What you niggers doing in here? Y'all better get yawls asses out of here before you find out what's good fer ya!"

They started throwing everything they could get their hands on at them when they didn't leave. They were five scared little black kids.

They weren't ready for all that. Going to school with white kids?

They left Texas to get away from white people. They weren't even allowed to speak to white kids in Texas. Something horrible had happened to them. They were closed up in a room with loud, bad- mannered, mean white kids all around them. *What was going to happen to them? Were those white kids like thewhite men that had come to their house?*

Chock was surprised that some of them were not beaten to death that first day in school. There was no one to stop the kids from doing whatever they wanted to do to them. We were hit, kicked, knocked down, spit on, and abused and harassed in every way they could think of.

The teacher just looked at them the way they looked at the maggots in their outhouse. In the school they came from in Texas, some of the kids were mean and some of the teachers too, but most of the teachers were proud to have they in their room.

The only thing good about that day and the days they attended that school in Arizona was the lunch. Every day they looked forward to the school lunch. The food was delicious! Whoever cooked the lunch could cook!

The food tasted just as good as their Momma's. There was food there they didn't have at home. They could eat as much as they wanted. The cook was nice and made sure they got as much as they wanted, which was their good fortune, because food was hard to come by at their camp, and very costly at the camp store.

They told their parents about how they were being treated by the white kids at school. They said they just had to put up with it for a while. They didn't want them to fight back. They knew what hitting a white person would get them.

They felt they were too far from school and couldn't be around to protect them from the parents who might drag them off the bus and do something horrible to them for hitting a white kid. Chock guessed they were still traumatized by what had happened to them in Texas.

Chock was ten years old. The teacher didn't believe her when she told her that she was in the fifth grade. She gave Chock a third grade test. Chock finished the test so fast that she accused her of cheating. She said that Chock copied from the girl sitting next to her. But the girl sitting next to her hadn't even finished her test.

She made Chock take the same test over all by herself. Chock finished it faster than before. She continued to give her tests for each grade level. Chock completed each one with a 100 percent. She said Chock could work in the group with the two sixth graders.

The two, big, sixth graders were the two boys who were giving them the most trouble.

The two boys were repeating sixth grade. They eased up on her a little when they discovered that she could help them with their school work, but sometimes they became angry when they didn't know something, and Chock did.

Chock's brother caught the brunt of their attacks. They got angry at him if he beat them at anything. They got angry if he got them out during a game, or beat them in a race, or caught their ball when they thought they had hit a home run. My brother didn't stop getting them out, or winning the races and they didn't stop beating on him. Chock think this was her brother's way of getting back at them. Their parents reminded them to not fight back.

The bus driver was a nice guy. He always seemed to know what field her parents were working in. After school, he would drop them off at that field so they could help their folks out until quitting time.

One Friday, when he let them off at the field, her parents were working in, Chock heard a window being let down. She looked up as a boy stuck his head out of the window, hawked, and spat right in her hair just above her forehead. Before Chock could react to that insult, the bus had driven off. Until the bus got out of hearing distance, Chock could hear the kids laughing and taunting her.

Chock stood there with that yellowish, foamy, slime, that had the consistency of a half beaten egg white, running down her face. Chock had to put her hand in it to wipe that slime away to keep it from running in her eyes and getting into her mouth.

Chock didn't know a kid could have that much slime in their mouth. Chock sat on the ground crying with slime running down her face and watched the bus drive out of sight.

Chock couldn't stop crying. She had taken all the licks, the name-calling, the kicking, and the sticking with pencils without crying. This slime running down in her face was much, much worse than all of the other harassment and insults put together. She had never felt so helpless. They had beaten her down. All she could do then was cry.

Her Daddy came over to see what Chock was crying about. He saw the messy glob on her. She told him what had happened to her.

He said, "When you get back on that bus you kill that boy!"

There was no water to wash that glop of spit off her. Her Momma took off her head rag and cleaned her as best as she could. Chock had to go for almost four hours before they could go to camp and wash that smelly sticky stuff off her.

All Chock could think about was the grump of mess on her for the remainder of the day. When Chock got back to camp, she went to the shower house to take a shower. She stood under the showers with all of her clothes on, washing her hair and scrubbing her face, until she got as wrinkly as a raisin. It didn't seem to Chock that she would ever get her hair and face clean again or make the smell go away.

All weekend all Chock could think of was that disgusting, horrible glob of gunk running down her face. The more she thought about it the more consumed with anger she became.

On Monday, Chock got up early and got dressed and went out in the cold and waited for the bus. When Chock got on the bus, the kids started pointing at her and laughing.

Her Daddy didn't mean for her to literally kill the boy, but that's what she almost did. Chock got on the bus and walked directly to where the boy sat and grabbed him around the neck with both hands. Chock locked her hands together and started squeezing with all of her might. Chock didn't seem to have enough strength.

He was hitting and kicking Chock, but she held on. He started turning red, and then he started turning blue. Chock still held on. He started clawing her hand trying to pry her fingers away. Blood started running from her hands and down her arms. Chock saw the blood, but she didn't feel any pain.

The bus driver looked back in his mirror and saw what was happening. He stopped the bus and tried to pull Chock away, but she held on. He started to talk to her and pleaded with her to let the boy go. Chock came to her senses and let him go. He fell out on the floor holding his neck and gasping for air. The driver made her sit in the seat in back of him and told them not to move until they got to school.

He said if they moved, he would put them off the bus right in the middle of the desert. Chock caught his face in the mirror after he started the bus; he was looking at her and grinning.

When Chock got to school, she didn't know what was going to happen to her. She thought the other kids at school would kill her for what she did to one of them, but no one said a thing to her. They looked at her in an odd manner. That was all they did that day to any of them. That day was the beginning to the end of their torment. The kids weren't so quick to abuse them after that day, and when they did, they let them know they didn't like it.

CHAPTER 18

Leaving Arizona

The bullying at school had toned down somewhat, but troubles had started at the camp. The workers were upset with the cotton growers and the contractors, because they were not making enough money for the work they were doing.

The contractor would recruit people and bring them to the camp to live and to work for him and the owner. He used his discretion as to how much he would charge, and who he would charge.

He got some kind of a fee from each person in the camp. That money was taken from their weekly wages. The contractor was also charging the workers for taking them to the fields. He was getting a hefty fee from everyone, especially from us Chock's family.

The workers were also complaining about the costs of food at the camp store. Sometimes things had to be charged until payday. When payday came, all of their wages were put toward their bills. Some thought their bills had been tampered with, and they owed more than they thought. They were always trying to catch up with their charges and had no money to spend.

Cesar Shavaz heard about the problems and came to the camp to talk to the workers and try to organize them (Chock didn't know who Cesar Chavez was until years later.) His efforts were unsuccessful, because there was no other way for the people to earn a living. They had to work or leave the camp.

Chock's Daddy decided to leave.

The man told her Daddy about a camp in Nevada that needed workers. Chock's Daddy decided to go there. When the word got out that they were going to a town in Nevada, close to Las Vegas, everyone wanted to go with them. They started paying her Daddy to save them a space on their truck.

They had lots of help getting the truck ready for the trip that time. The headed out for Nevada. They left Arizona one Friday evening after work so they would be where they were going by Monday and not miss any work. The camp they left was close to the California border. The truck was overcrowded and the going was very slow—just like when they left Texas. The grown-ups sat, and also slept, on their belongings around the bed of the truck. A pallet was made in the middle of the truck at night for the little kids to sleep. If there was space, adults would take turns sleeping on the pallet with the kids.

When they left the labor camp in Arizona, there were about ten to twelve kids sleeping on the floor. Late that night, Chock felt a hand on her body where she didn't want it to be. She went to move the hand thinking it was one of the other kid's just turning over.

When Chock tried to move the hand that was touching her, another hand went over her mouth, and the body of a man pinned her down. Chock could feel the stubble of his face.

While Chock was stifled and pinned down, a hand continued to rove over her body and probe between her legs.

His hand suddenly stopped, and his grip tightened on Chock. Chock thought he was going to smother her to death.

He remained still for a few minutes before he stopped pinning her down and took his hand from over her mouth.

Chock lay there scared and trying to catch her breath. Chock was afraid to move. She pulled all herself inside as tightly as she could and curled into a tight ball. She wrapped her arms around her body and lay still.

It was too dark in the truck to see if he was still there close to her or if he had gone to sit with the other adults.

She couldn't tell who the person was. She couldn't see in what direction he had disappeared.

When Chock felt safe enough to move, Chock got up and went to sit by her Momma and her elder sister. Chock sat with them and kept awake for the rest of the night.

Everyone in the truck seemed to be sleeping. The only sounds Chock could hear were the sound of the truck engine and the sounds people made when they were sleeping. The only movements Chock felt were the movements made by the truck.

Chock felt someone else was also awake watching her. Chock was afraid that at any moment, she would feel his hand over her mouth. Chock stayed awake, staring into the blackness of the truck, trying to see the hand she thought would be coming for her. When light started to filter in through the holes in the canvas of the truck, she fell asleep. Chock continued to wake up startled when she heard the least bit sound at night. Later, when she got older, she would hide some type of weapon under her pillow.

Her personality took on a drastic change overnight. Everything Chock had out there, she had taken and put inside of herself. She kept all of her feelings to herself and avoided doing anything that would require her to make contact with anyone, or anyone to make contact with her. Chock stayed as far away from others, besides her family, as she could get. How could they act as if nothing had happened? Can't they see what had happened to her?

The next day, Chock refused to talk to the men folk on the truck. If anyone touched her the next day, she would jump as they had stuck her with a hot poker. She would move or shrug out of the way. Her Momma saw her behavior and gave her a warning look to remind her of her manners.

For the rest of the trip, Chock avoided the men on the truck. She watched them closely. She was trying to find something that would tell her who had been on the pallet touching her under my underwear. Chock refused to sleep on the pallet the next night. Everyone thought she was putting on arrogance and trying to be like a grown-up.

They arrived in Vegas after midnight the next night. Everyone was so excited.

They had never seen so many people or so many lights in one place. Some left the truck and came back bragging about a place they had seen which had a floor made of silver dollars. Imagine that! A floor made of silver dollars!

They had to see that. Her Daddy went in and came back out. He said,

"He sho' was telling the truth."

As far as he could see, the floor was covered with silver dollars, and the silver dollars were sealed under something like glass to keep people from taking them.

When they left Vegas, the truck was not so crowded. Some of the people stayed in Vegas to look for work. They had about thirty-five miles left to go before they made it to their new camp. They arrived at the campsite in Nevada at about mid-morning.

CHAPTER 19

Labor Camp in Nevada

The labor camp in Nevada was much better equipped than the one in Arizona. The camp had different apartments, and each apartment had its own bath and washroom.

There was a long shed that contained a convey table used for sorting different produce plants and produce that was ready for marketing.

School was almost out. Chock's folks didn't insist that they go to school. They didn't mind. They still remembered what they had been through at the school in Arizona.

They could see the school from the campsite. They saw kids at recess playing, and they saw the band practicing. There was not a black face among them. They didn't feel like going through another Arizona. They went to the fields to help their folks.

When they got to the fields, they saw a whole group of people that reminded her of her dad's Indian grandmother. The women wore colorful clothes decorated with beads the same as her great-grandmother had. The men were dressed as cowboys. They worked without saying a word. Chock couldn't keep from staring at them.

When they looked at them, they could see they were not pleased with seeing them working in the same field with them.

The Indian people they were with were not pleased with them in the field. The people they were with told them to stay away from the other people. They were dirty and had head lice. Some said they would probably eat them if they caught them alone.

The Indian people worked on one side of the field, and they worked on the opposite side. After work, they would disappear.

Chock's curiosity got the better of her. Chock wanted to see where they disappeared to when they left the field for the day. Chock followed the young girl whom she thought was the prettiest girl she had ever seen, of course, besides her mom and sisters.

She seemed different from the other Indian women she was with. She wore her hair loose, and it hung to her waist. She was dressed differently from the rest of the Indian women. She wore a little straight dress that came above her knees. Sometimes she would wear Western clothes like her husband, while the other women wore long, full skirts, and long-sleeved blouses.

When Chock followed the girl, she found out where they were disappearing to. Chock saw where they lived. They had a camp about a quarter of a mile from the campsite down by a little stream.

They had tents and campfires everywhere, and everyone seemed to be busy doing something.

They would sit around the fires cooking and eating.

Some of the children would be playing in the water while some of the adults fished.

Chock would hide in the bushes and watch them for hours.

Chock thought she was hiding as she watched them, but they were watching her, too. The girl came up to Chock one day and started a conversation. She was very friendly, and Chock was amazed that she could understand what she was saying. Chock thought she would speak the way her great-grandmother had.

She told Chock her name was Mary. She was married to one of the men in the group. She laughed when she said that her husband was the tall, good-looking fellow.

Her tall, good-looking husband didn't seem to like her talking to Chock, and Chock was a little afraid of him. Chock told her how she felt about her husband.

She laughed and said, "You don't have to be afraid of him. He won't bother you."

She was only fourteen. Chock told her about her great-grandmother. She said she was also a Cherokee. Chock asked her why she didn't dress like the other women. She said the other women were Navajo.

Later, she told Chock that the government had taken her people's land a long time ago and wanted them to live in a place they didn't like. Her parents had refused to live on the land and had hid out in the mountains. They had to travel from place to place to find work. That's how she had met her husband.

Chock told her about them having to leave their land and why they were traveling around from place to place trying to find work and another place to live—just like Mary's family had.

She said, "White people!"

Chock chimed in, "Yeh, white people!"

Mary didn't seem to have to work as hard as the other Indian people. They seemed to have about the same responsibilities—looking after the younger children and going for water or whatever the field-workers needed.

Chock's family's stay in Nevada was pretty nice but short. Chock's friend from Texas and her family decided to return to Texas. Her mother was going to have a baby and wanted to be in her own home when the new baby came. She was tired of moving around.

Chock's family left Nevada with only their family in the truck. It seemed that their work was taking them farther and farther away from Texas, and the people they knew were getting fewer and fewer. Their next job was in Idaho.

CHAPTER 20

Idaho

Chock's family headed for Idaho when they left Nevada. They were going to live in a labor camp that needed workers for sugar beets. They left Nevada on Friday evening, and the next day they were in Utah. Chock can't recall ever hearing of any of those states before they left Texas.

On the way to Idaho, they went across a lake made out of salt. Chock had never heard of The Great Salt Lake or Salt Lake City before. The lake was an amazing sight to see—all of that salt. They crossed the lake and drove for an hour before they reached the labor camp. They got to the camp around noon on Saturday.

When they got to the camp, they were surprised to see her sister who had run off and married the playboy. A number of the other people they had left in Arizona and Vegas were there as well. They had another big celebration.

The camp was right by a sugar plant. The sugar beets were brought there and sugar was made from the beets. Chock always thought beets were red. Chock was a little puzzled about how they got the sugar to turn white.

Chock was surprised to see white beets. When Chock tasted them, they were not hot like the red beets. They were very sweet.

The camp was basically designed as the camp in Arizona. It was situated in better surroundings. There were sidewalks, grass, trees, and a little store within walking distance.

Chock's family had access to a town. The town was about five miles away. There were dress shops, grocery stores, and a movie theater. There was also a place they could drive up to the window and order hamburgers, chicken, ice cream, and other foods and eat it in the car.

On Monday, the whole family would to go to the beet field. They were given a hoe with a handle about a foot long. The blade of the hoe was about six inches wide. They had to bend over all day long and thin the beets and pull weeds that had grown with the plants.

The work was back breaking. They were paid by the number of rows they thinned. They worked from sun up to sun down only taking a short break for lunch or to get a drink.

Again, their dwelling was the center of attraction during the day. It was there, in Idaho, where Chock discovered who the man was that had been feeling on her on their way to Nevada.

That man, Mr. TC, was considered a close friend of their family. He was always around doing whatever he could to help any of them. When her Momma and Daddy tried to show their appreciation, he would say he was happy to give them a hand.

He was around when they were in Arizona. Since her Daddy's cousin had gone back to Texas, Mr. TC began to come around more often.

He was invited to eat with them whenever he showed up. He would get involved in every activity that was going on, whether it was playing catch, giving them a ride to the store, or helping her Daddy with the truck. He would never show up empty-handed. He always had something for her Momma to cook or treats for the kids.

Sunday was always their free time. There were no churches for them to go to.

They would dress and do whatever they wanted on Sunday. It was a day of rest.

That Sunday evening, Chock decided to walk to the little store for a treat. The store was about half of a mile from the camp.

Chock was out of sight of the camp when a car stopped Chock looked to see who was in the car, it was our trusted friend. He asked

Chock if she wanted a ride, but she told him she just wanted to walk and look at things.

Chock really did want to walk, but he was so persuasive. He said he was going down by the lake to do a little fishing. Chock had heard about the lake, but she had never seen it, so she decided to ride along with him.

Once they got to the lake, it was beautiful and not scary as the lake in Nevada (Lake Mead) was. When they saw the big lake in Nevada, they were too afraid to get out of the car.

Mr. TC got out of the car and went down to the bank with his fishing pole and the bucket he was going to put the fish he caught in. He pulled his shoes off and sat on the bank and put his feet in the water.

Chock sat in the car looking at the lake. It was beautiful, and ever so often a fish would jump up and twist about. He beckoned her to come on by waving his hand at her, so Chock got out of the car. He kept waving at her to come closer.

"Don't be scared. I won't let you fall in."

So Chock went closer to the water's edge. Chock went on down to the bank to get a closer look at the water and tried to avoid stepping in the mud.

"Go ahead, take your shoes off."

Chock took her shoes off and sat down on the bank beside him.

Chock got brave and put my feet in the water.

"If you want, you can wade around close to the bank."

Chock walked through the mud and waded around close to the bank. On her way out of the water, she slipped and fell. She was horrified for a second but laughed about getting soaking wet. Chock knew it wouldn't take long for her clothes to dry if she sat in the sun.

"I guess we should be getting back." Chock walked out of the water, but her feet got muddy again.

"You can put them in the bucket and wash the mud off since I didn't catch any fish."

Chock put her feet in the bucket, but she couldn't figure out how she was going to get back to the car without getting muddy again.

He laughed and said, "I'll just put some clean water in the bucket and you can wash your feet when we get to the car."

Once they got back in the car, Chock stuck her feet out so she could put them in the bucket, but her feet couldn't reach the bucket.

"Let me help you."

He came and lifted the bucket. He then began to wash the mud off. Chock was a little embarrassed having someone wash her feet at her age. "You have the prettiest skin. I can't stop thinking about how soft your skin is. I have never felt skin as soft as yours."

He seemed to be talking as if Chock wasn't there. Chock started pulling her foot away. Something felt unpleasant about the way he was rubbing her feet and legs; at the same time, something seemed familiar.

"Don't get scared. I just want to feel your skin."

He had stopped smiling. His voice had changed, and he looked different somehow. His hands went further up her legs.

Chock tried to pull her legs back from him. He held her legs with one hand. The other hand went under her dress, and he started feeling under her bloomers.

Chock said, "You shouldn't do that."

Chock didn't know how to tell a grown man to leave her alone. He wasn't the boy Daddy had warned them about. He was a grown man, and Chock didn't know how to tell a grown man to stop. He said,

"I'm just going to feel your skin. There is no harm in feeling your skin."

Chock took his word and stopped trying to keep her dress down and her bloomers up.

When Chock stopped struggling, he pulled her bloomers down. He was a grown man, but he was pulling her bloomers down. Chock didn't know how to tell him to stop. Chock saw him open his pants and take out his worm. Chock started screaming.

"Now this ain't going to hurt you, just be still, and stop that screaming. No one is going to hear you way out here, anyway."

Chock stopped screaming. He did hurt her, and Chock started screaming again. A white man on a tractor came up. When Chock saw him Chock was afraid, because Chock knew what white men would do. He would probably do the same thing. He said he heard screaming and came to see what was wrong.

Mr. TC said, "Aw, she just saw a snake. I just got her calmed down, and I was getting ready to take her home to her momma."

The man on the tractor said, "There are lots of rattlers around here this time of the year. Y'all better be on the lookout. I just kilt two last week." When the white man left, Mr. TC said, "You can't tell anybody about our trip. Your daddy will shoot me, and they will put him in jail. You will never see him again".

Chock knew he was right. If Chock told her Daddy, he would shoot him. Chock remembered how terrified they were when her Daddy went to jail after he had hit the white man. Mr. TC had heard the story about her Daddy being in jail in Texas and how frightened we had been when they thought they would never see him again. Chock couldn't tell her Daddy, anyway. How could Chock tell her Daddy something like that? Chock didn't know what words to use in order to tell him about it. Chock had let a man do what he had told them not to let anyone do. Chock couldn't disappoint her dad.

Chock had seen his face when her sister had told him that she was going to have a baby. Chock saw his face when her other sister sneaked off and got married.

Chock didn't want to ever see that look on his face brought on by something she had done. Chock didn't know exactly what she had done. She didn't know what was going to happen to her.

They left the lake. When they got to the little store, he stopped the car and told her to get out and walk back to the camp. Chock didn't mind getting out. Chock didn't want to go back to the camp.

The walking was painful, but Chock walked around for a long time before she went back to camp. Nothing seemed real. The sun was shining just as it had been shinning before she left the camp. Nothing had changed, but everything had changed.

Everything Chock had pulled inside and thought she could protect didn't seem to matter anymore. Everything had been smashed and made ugly. Nothing mattered, and nothing was real. Everything around her came to her from far away and had to be repeated before she was aware that it was meant for her.

When Chock got back to the camp, she was in a daze. Chock couldn't believe it. Nothing had changed. Mr. TC was there at their place just as if nothing had happened. Chock started to wonder whether she was dreaming or did she just imagine what had happened to her.

He grinned at her. Chock stared at him for a long time, wondering who he was. Chock kept asking herself, "Is he real?" Chock's mom said, "Young lady, mind your manners. Where have you been? We started to get a little worried about you. Did you get what I told you to get?"

Chock had forgotten to pick up something for her Momma at the store, but she couldn't remember what it was.

People were talking and laughing, but Chock couldn't hear what anyone was saying. When someone said something to her, they had to keep repeating what they were saying. Her Momma had to keep telling her what she wanted her to do. Chock did what she was told without saying a word.

Chock just wandered around the camp and waited to be told what to do. Chock didn't talk to anyone. Chock didn't play games anymore. She didn't laugh anymore. Chock just walked around the camp or sat and looked at everything and everyone. She was looking, but she saw nothing, and she sat looking at people she didn't know anymore.

Chock was petrified. She didn't know what was going to happen next or what she thought was going to happen to her. Was there a baby in her belly? When was she going to have it? What was she going to do? Chock just waited and waited. Her folks said that she was lonesome for her friend that had gone back to Texas.

Their whole family went to the field each day. They caught the attention of the farmer who owned the beet field. He approached her Daddy and told him about a farmer in a nearby town who needed a family to attend his farm. He had gotten hurt and needed someone to take over for him. He said if her Daddy was interested, he would call the man and have him come out and talk to her Daddy.

Chock's Daddy told the farmer he would like to talk to his relative, the farmer. His relative came to the field the next week. He and Chock's Daddy came to an agreement. Her Daddy told them they would be leaving the labor camp in Idaho.

CHAPTER 21

Their Last Labor Camp

Chock's Daddy decided to take the job offered to him by a farmer in another Idaho town. At the end of the week, on Saturday, they loaded up the truck. Chock couldn't wait to leave that camp and Mr. TC. She was sad to say good-bye to her sister and her new husband and some of the other people, but she was happy inside when they drove away from the camp. That was the last time they would see any black people, except the family, for a while.

They got to the little town in Idaho after lunch. The farmer had left directions for her Daddy to meet him at a store in town. He would show them how to get to the farm. They followed him to the farm house which was about four miles from town. The farmhouse was a four-story, run-down brick mansion. Scary wasn't the word for it. It hadn't been lived in for years. There was running water in it, but the bathroom facilities didn't work. They had an outhouse.

There was not another house around for miles. Their closest neighbor's farm was on the same road about ten miles further down the road from them. They stopped by to make their acquaintance. They were very friendly. The farm belonged to another white family. The mother was a teacher at the school they would be going to.

They had the farm all to themselves, except for the hundred heads of cattle and horses. Chock's Daddy added pigs and her Momma added chickens to the lot. It was pretty nice out there after they got over being afraid of the house.

Chock's Daddy was happy. He was a farmer again. He got to operate the big farm equipment and do the things he had been doing on his own farm. The farmer was impressed by his knowledge of what should be done on a farm. Chock guessed it was hard for him to believe that a farm worker knew that much about farming and taking care of equipment and animals.

There was also a large acreage of sugar beets on the farm. Chock's Daddy was given extra money to contract workers to work the field. Her Daddy contracted them. Before dinner, one Saturday, they were surprised to hear her Daddy talking to someone outside.

"Wuhu! Where y'all come from?"

They rushed outside to see who he was talking to. When Chock saw their visitors, her heart dropped. The last person Chock wished she would never see again, stood there with a woman. He had that grin on his face, and that laugh when he talked. He was shaking hands with her Daddy and slapping him on the back.

"I, I, huh, huh, heard you needed some help, huh, huh, so huh, huh, I decided to come to see if, huh, huh, if I could give you a hand."

Chock was saying to herself,

Please, Daddy, tell him we don't need help. Please don't let him stay here. Daddy, don't let him stay. Please, Daddy, tell him to go away.

Instead, her Daddy said,

"Sho' y'all can stay! There is plenty of work here and plenty room for y'all to stay at the house."

Everyone was happy to see another human except Chock. They hadn't seen another person outside of the family for over two months.

He introduced the woman with him as his wife. He had met her in a town. He said the name—a funny Indian name. The town was about fifty miles from their camp.

He said he and some of the other guys had heard about a town that had black people living there. One weekend, he and the guys had gone there to see for themselves.

And what do you know, there were black people living there. That was when he met his wife. He had been going to see her for over a month when they decided to get married.

That was a long speech for Mr. TC. His voice made Chock want to scream "shut up!" His voice was scratchy and the words were dragged out as if he was too tired to talk. He would stop every now and then to clarify something with his new wife.

He called her Sug, and she called him Hon. He had to add a ha-ha and a uh-huh after every other word. His voice was so irritating Chock just wanted to throw something at him to make him stop talking. Instead, Chock just got up and walked out.

Chock didn't know what to do.

Chock tried to stay outside, hoping they would leave soon. Why couldn't anyone see he wasn't a nice man?

Chock's younger sister and brother were enjoying showing him all the rooms in the house.

The woman went in the kitchen to help her elder sister and her mom with dinner.

She didn't look like any farm worker Chock had ever seen. She was dressed up in her Sundays' bests, but it didn't look as if she should go to church wearing a dress like the one she had on.

Chock saw her Daddy eyeing her.

Chock's Momma was doing her best to put on a good impression, especially after the lady mentioned how her new husband had bragged about how nice they were.

Her Momma had all of the kids bring them this and getting them that and showing them this and showing them that until it was almost dark.

When they mentioned they should try to get back to camp before dark, her Daddy suggested they should stay the night and get a start in the morning, that is, if they didn't mind sleeping in a room with kids.

Mr. TC said,

"What do you think, Sug?"

"It's up to you, Hon. I don't mind. It will be scary driving back to camp through them mountains and curves after dark."

It was settled. They would stay the night with them. Her Momma said Mr. TC and his wife would sleep in the girls' room since we had separate beds. Chock volunteered to give up her bed. But her elder sister's bed was bigger, so her Momma said they would take her bed and her sister would sleep on the living room sofa.

Chock was determined to stay up until everyone went to bed and fell asleep. She didn't have anywhere to stay. Her sister wanted her out of the front room so she could go to sleep. Chock went to her bed and tried to sit up in the corner and stay awake.

Chock didn't know when she fell asleep or how she happened to have covers on her. Chock fell asleep and had another nightmare or was it? It wasn't. It was real. He was under the covers and on top of her. His hand was over her mouth again.

He was saying, "Sheee."

When he finished hurting me, he went back to the bed where his wife was sleeping.

Was that supposed to be happening to her? Was it happening to everybody?

What was she supposed to do? Why didn't anyone know?

Chock didn't know what to do. She kept telling herself someone will come to help her and all the while she didn't want anyone to know. Chock was too ashamed for anyone to know.

Chock didn't want anyone to know she was letting some man pull her dress up and her bloomers down.

Chock was too ashamed for anyone to find out she was letting that happen to her.

Chock drifted off to sleep when she saw daylight starting to come in the room.

When Chock woke up, everyone was already gone. She was relieved.

She thought they had left. When she went into the kitchen, their visitors were at the table. Breakfast was over, and they were just sitting around talking and saying their good-byes.

Chock's Momma said, "Sleepyhead." Mr. TC said, "I thought I was going to have to wake you and say bye before I left. I told your momma maybe she should let you sleep, because you didn't get a good night's rest. You must have had a bad dream, because you were moving around and crying all night."

Chock was infuriated. He was making an excuse for her with his ha, haws and huh, huhs for sleeping late. Her Momma said,

"I hope you didn't keep our company awake all night. You should stop reading all those scary books."

Chock said, "Yes Mam."

Then Chock went to the bench at the back of the house again and stayed there until they left.

That bench was to become a constant refuge for her as the summer progressed. When they returned from the beet field for lunch on Monday, Mr. TC and his Sug had also returned.

They had all of their belongings in the car with them. They were moving in to help with the sugar beets. Chock couldn't believe it. It was going to take them about a month to finish the field. And they were going to stay with them the whole time!

Chock looked around. There was nowhere for her to go. Chock wanted to run off and hide. The only place for her to go was to the bench in the back of the house. Chock didn't want to see him, or look at him, or hear him talking. Chock would stay outside and wait for night. They had a room on the second floor of the house. Surely, he wouldn't come down those stairs and bother her at night. Chock just had to stay away from him during the day. Chock tried to stay awake.

Chock didn't know what she would do if she saw him before he was on her, but she couldn't stay awake.

It seemed as if he could tell when everyone was sleeping. Chock would feel the hand over her mouth and struggle to wake up from the awful nightmare. Then, Chock realized she wasn't having a nightmare.

Night after night, Chock would live that nightmare until she just started to pretend it was just a nightmare. She didn't know how she could stop what was happening to her when everyone was sleeping.

Chock just went to sleep and let it happen so it would be over. When the hand went over her mouth, she pretended to be asleep. If Chock was asleep, she pretended not to wake up.

As the days went by, Chock lost all interest in myself, everyone, and everything around me. Chock didn't dread going to bed anymore. She got into bed as early as she possibly could and fell asleep. She didn't want to think about what was going to happen to her after she fell asleep. She didn't want to try to stay awake waiting for her nightmare. When it was over, she would be able to sleep. When morning came, she dreaded getting up.

Chock worked extra hard when they went to work in the beet field. Chock was hoping they would hurry and finish the field so they would leave. She wanted to get the field finished as quickly as they could. She hoed twice as many rows of beets as anyone else. She didn't want to stop for anything. When someone would stop to take a break, she would get angry. They finally got the field finished. Mr. TC and his wife left when they got their money. Long after they left, Chock still didn't believe they were gone. At night she would wake up and couldn't breathe. She could feel his hand over her mouth cutting off my air. She would sit up in bed to catch her breath. Night after night the nightmare would start all over again.

Chock could never get it out of her mind that he wouldn't show up again at any time. Chock would be so afraid he would come back. Every time she heard a voice or a car, her heart would skip a beat. She was so afraid thinking it might be him. She would be too afraid to look and see who it could be, and she was too afraid not to look. Please, Lord, don't let it be him. Please, Lord, don't let him come back. *Please.*

CHAPTER 22

Chock's First School in Idaho

That summer, after they finished the field, their finances took a turn for the better. When they finished the beet field and had extra money, Chock's Daddy traded their big, long, yellow truck in and bought a car.

He bought a green and black 1949 Buick. That was nice. They could take trips into town or just go sightseeing. School was to start in a few weeks, and they needed school clothes. They went to the town the camp was located in and did their school shopping. That also gave her Daddy a chance to show off his new car and her Momma a chance to show how they had come up in the world. Chock guessed they wanted everyone to know they were worth something again.

They saw their sister who had run off and gotten married. Chock was scared for her. She was going to have a baby. Chock didn't understand why everyone seemed to be happy about it.

Her husband was laughing about it, and everyone was shaking his hand and patting him on the back. Maybe they didn't know what had happened to her. She and her husband were going back to Texas to his family before the baby was born.

Maybe my folks did know what had happened to her sister to make her run off and get married. They decided to send her other sister back to Texas to live with a relative and finish high school. That was very upsetting for Chock.

Chock would surely be then alone. On the other hand, Chock was glad for her, because the arrangement seemed to make her happy.

There was no one around them of her age. Chock guess her parents were afraid she would also run off and marry one of the older men in the camp.

The men were looking at her, and she was looking back at them and giggling.

Chock was relieved when they left the camp. They left that camp for the last time. They said Mr. TC had taken his wife to see some folks in her town and would be back that evening. Chock was happy they didn't wait around to see him. They left before he came back.

When Chock started school in Idaho, she promoted herself to seventh grade. She had spent half a year working with the sixth graders in Arizona. There weren't any records to prove that she wasn't in seventh grade, and when Chock was given another placement test, she had no problems with it. Chock was a marvel.

Chock didn't think any of the kids at that school had ever seen a black person. Chock was followed around like she was the pied piper. They kept rubbing her skin and feeling on her hair. When she talked, they would die laughing. She didn't know if they were laughing because she could talk or laughing at her southern accent.

They treated Chock like a little girl and thought she was so cute. Everyone but one girl, who made Chock think of Luzine in the second grade, didn't want to be her friend. Chock was to find out everywhere she went, there would always be one.

The kids at her school wanted her to be the head of everything. Chock must say, she was treated differently from the way she was treated when she went to the school in Arizona. She was voted homecoming queen. She was elected lead majorette in the marching band. Everyone wanted her to sing to them. Things went on like that until they hired a seminary teacher.

When Chock entered the seventh grade, the subjects were predetermined by the school. One class Chock was to take was learning about the religion practiced by the majority of that state.

That class was called seminary. Chock kept asking what they were going to do in that class. She was told they were to learn about God. *That's good,* she thought.

The class was to be held in the big church across the street. They couldn't start at the beginning of the school year because there wasn't a teacher yet. Finally, he came. He was a tall man who reminded Chock of pictures she had seen of Abraham Lincoln. He had a very soft voice and had no shoes on.

He explained to them that he had a hard time getting shoes big enough for his feet. He wore a size fifteen. Chock's Daddy had that same problem. She liked him right away.

They were on the subject of the different heavens and purgatory. Chock was told about the seven heavens. She had some misgivings about it.

Chock had been taught that there was only one heaven. She told him about what she had been taught, and he showed her in the book the names of the seven heavens. Books don't lie.

He told them they had to be good and obey the teachings of their prophets if they wanted to go to one of those heavens. If they didn't obey his teachings, they were damned to purgatory.

Then he went on to say,

"But you," pointing to Chock, "will never go to heaven, because you are black."

"Who? Me? I'm not going to heaven?" "No, you won't go to heaven." Everyone gasped.

He went on to say,

"I know you are a good girl, and you should be able to go to the last heaven before purgatory, but you are black and have no soul. Our church teaches us that you will never go to heaven, because you are cursed by the devil and have no soul. Black people are evil and will not enter into the Kingdom of Heaven."

"Are you crazy?"

"No. Black people are descendants from Cain, and they are cursed. Black people are evil. They will never enter the Kingdom of Heaven."

"Who said so?"

They had a big blowout. Chock told him he didn't know what he was talking about and ran out of class.

After that Chock was too ashamed to go back to the class. He came out to where she was sitting on the church stairs and tried to get her to come back to class.

Chock told him,

"I'll never go back in this church until you tell me that I'm going to heaven!" He never told Chock she was going to heaven, and Chock never went back inside.

The teacher telling Chock that she was not going to heaven was the worst thing that had happened to her.

It was worse than when that kid spit on her.

Not going to heaven was just too horrific to think about.

Chock was devastated. When all the kids had heard him saying she was bad, they started looking at her funny.

The girl who had wanted to be homecoming queen started spreading rumors about Chock. When the kids followed Chock, they followed her at a distance. They were then afraid of her. They were looking for her tail and her horns.

Chock stopped going to PE, because they had to shower afterward. When Chock got undressed, everyone would just stare at her trying to see where her tail and horns were.

Chock had been singing for different occasions and had competed in a singing competition. Kids from all over Idaho and from different states tried out for that competition. It was an old version of *American Idol*. The winner was to try out for the *Ted Mack Amateur Hour*, on TV, in Salt Lake City. Chock won the competition.

Chock was invited to come to Salt Lake for a tryout. Chock's accompanist was excited and made all the arrangement. She was about Chock's only friend after the so-called "no-soul" episode.

They made their way to Salt Lake. When it was her time to audition, Chock completely forgot her song. She couldn't focus. There were too many white people staring at her.

There were other people on the stage around Chock doing too many different things at the same time. She was given three tries, but each time, she couldn't remember the first word to the song. She came back to school in disgrace and gave up singing altogether.

That was the last straw. Chock was then totally miserable at that school and couldn't wait for it to be over. It seemed that at every turn something kept happening. It didn't matter where they went; things somehow kept being the same.

Why couldn't she be treated and accepted the way all the other girls were accepted? All they did was go to school. They didn't have to sing or dance or twirl a baton, and they were left alone to enjoy their life.

It seemed to Chock that when someone looked at her, they saw something in her they wanted, or something they wanted to destroy, or something they wanted to possess, or something they wanted to be a part of, or something she was doing they wished they could do.

There was something they liked about her, but they were not happy until everything they liked about her was destroyed. They tried, in their own way, to make that happen for them.

Chock kept hoping that she could find a place where she could relax and be left alone and not have to fight back, but that didn't seem to happen.

It didn't matter if they were black or white, man or woman, young or old. It didn't matter what their beliefs were; they always seemed to find something about Chock they wanted or something they needed to destroy to make them feel better.

Chock's parent were also looking for a place they could relax. They were concerned about where they were living. That past winter, there was a bad snow storm. They were snowed in for three weeks. They couldn't get out of the house, and no one could get in. For three weeks, they didn't see a soul outside of the family. They thought that they were going to starve to death.

The snow was deeper than they were tall. When it was shoveled back from the door, they couldn't see past it. Chock doesn't know how anything survived that winter.

Luckily, Chock's Daddy had killed a deer before the blizzard. After the first week, Chock hoped she would never see another deer as long as she lived. They had deer for breakfast, deer for dinner, and deer for supper. They had roast deer, fried deer, stewed deer, and deer sandwiches. That deer kept them from going hungry and maybe kept them from starving to death. Chock doesn't know what would have happened to them if they didn't have that deer.

Chock's folks decided they were not going to be caught out there alone on that farm for the coming winter. Chock's Daddy told the owner of his decision. He was understanding and told her Daddy he would keep his eyes and ears open in case he heard of anything.

Two weeks later, he came back and told Chock's Daddy he had heard of a potato farmer looking for help with his farm about thirty-five miles north of them.

They took a ride to the town to see the farmer. After about an hour of visiting with the farmer, his wife, and their four kids, they all came to a mutual agreement. They would be moving to his farm after they finished the work on the sugar beets.

CHAPTER 23

The Second School in Idaho

When her family finished the beet field the next summer they moved to a third Idaho town. The little house they moved into was the best house they had ever lived in. To the majority of the people in that town, it was considered a shack.

The house was small and unpainted, but the insides were well kept. There was no peeling paint or broken windows. The floors were covered. It had two stories. There was a working bathroom downstairs, also a bedroom, a large kitchen with a big table, and a living room. There were two bedrooms upstairs. They thought it was a grand little house.

The farmer and his wife and the three younger kids were very nice. The eldest girl, older than Chock, was the one that was a constant reminder that they were black and she was white. That should have been an indicator of how the kids would feel about Chock when she got on the school bus the first day of school.

Financially, they were doing better than they had ever done at the other places and even in Texas. Chock's sisters, which had gone to college, two were then living in Dallas, two were living in LA, and had jobs. They were always sending them money and clothes.

When Chock started school that year, she had the most beautiful clothes any girl could ask for. Where they were living was a little farming country town, and Chock had clothes from the city.

Chock's clothes were admired and envied by all the girls at that school. They liked what she was wearing, but they didn't like her.

When Chock's brother and she got on the bus, on the first day of school, Chock could hear a unanimous intake of breaths. All of the seats on the bus were occupied. Everyone just sat there not moving.

The bus driver, bless his heart, said, "What's wrong with you kids? You lost your manners or something? Now move over and let the kids sit down." They moved over, but Chock could see they weren't happy. Chock thought if her dad can face three truck loads of white men with guns, without showing fear, Chock was not going to let a bunch of kids stop her. When the kids got off the bus, they lined up by the bus door and formed a gauntlet. The kids from the other buses joined them. This was a cake walk compared to some of the things Chock had gone through. They didn't harm them physically, but they could hear some of the kids giving them a disgruntled grunt or would spit on the ground when they walked by.

Chock was relieved they hadn't spat on her.

Some of the students as well as some of the teachers would treat Chock as if she wasn't even there. Chock doesn't know if she felt better being hit or ignored. They would ignore whatever she had to say and go to the next person. Chock, however, didn't let that stop her from doing what she felt like doing.

Chock always tried to look her best every day at school. Chock doesn't know if she did that out of spite or not. The schoolwork was a little difficult for her. Chock should have been in the seventh grade, but here she was in the ninth grade.

The principal talked to Chock's parents about putting her back a grade. They said her schoolwork was fine, but she was a little too immature to be in the ninth grade. Chock didn't want to be put back. She hated going to that school and wanted to get out of there as soon as she could.

The school was larger. The kids came from the surrounding town. There was more than one ninth grade classroom. There was a teacher for each subject.

Chock had skipped a couple of grades when they moved to different schools, and it was catching up with her. Chock had to study. Little by little, some of the girls started talking to Chock. They would just compliment her clothes and ask her where she got them. They would also speak when they saw her in class or in the halls.

Basically, that was the extent of their friendship.

The girls that came from families that were well-off were the ones that would speak to Chock. They seemed to have heard of some of the places she had seen or they had seen also. They would ask her about different places, but when Chock had lunch, she ate alone. Chock walked to class alone.

At PE, Chock was chosen because she was good at sports, and they wanted their team to win. Chock tried out for the drill team and won. That was the first time the school had decided to have a drill team. They liked watching her. She was good at strutting her stuff. When Chock did her routine in front of the school's assembly, the students went mad with shouts and cheers, but when they saw Chock in the hallways they ignored her. Some of the girls on the team weren't happy about her making the team, but there was nothing they could do about it.

As a member of the drill team, Chock was a little more accepted by the students. Being on the drill team also kept her busy and gave her something to do in school. That gave her morale a boost. She decided to try out for the choir.

The choir director felt obligated to give Chock a tryout. She sang the song she had forgotten the words to when she tried out for the TV audition.

The choir director said that Chock had a beautiful voice. He never gave her a lead part during the two years she was in the choir, but Chock was a constant reminder to the girls he did give the lead parts to.

They could hear Chock in the background and always knew she was there. When they messed up, they would look at her with contempt, because they knew what everyone in the choir was thinking. Chock felt sorry for them. She knew how they felt. Sometimes anyone could mess up. At the end of Chock's first year in school, Chock knew she was not going to make it. She had not seen another black person besides the people in her family for three years.

Chock had not talked to anyone. She had not laughed with anyone. She had not danced with anyone. She had no one. She was lonely and miserable. Days, weeks, and months would pass by before anyone outside the family would say anything to her or she would say anything to anyone. She couldn't take too much of that for too much longer.

Chock wrote her parents an ominous letter and put it in a place where they could find it. Chock didn't know how to stand up and tell her parents to their face that she didn't like the people where they were living. Chock said in her letter if they didn't move, she was going to run away from home.

They found her letter but didn't mention it to Chock until after they had moved to another town. They didn't say anything to her about the letter, so Chock thought they just didn't care. Chock didn't think they cared how she felt, or how she was being treated by the kids at school, and by the people in that community.

One Sunday morning, they got up to drive to town to do the shopping for the week. They left Chock in charge of the kids and the cooking. Chock thought they just wanted to get away from them for a while. Her Momma told her what to do while they were gone and what to cook for dinner. Wow, they were going to be gone all day!

Chock was standing at the sink, cutting up the meat when she heard that voice. Chock wheeled around and there he was. All of the hatred and misery Chock had accumulated because of him and what she had been exposed to in the past years boiled up within her.

Chock heard "uh-huh huh, ha-ha" and saw the grin on his face. Chock just wanted to cut his lips off. She wanted to cut him until there was nothing left. She had heard the saying many times:

"All that don't kill you will only make you strong." Part of this saying is true, but a last part should have been added: "All that don't kill you will only make you strong enough and mad enough to kill."

When Chock turned around and saw him, Chock was strong enough and mad enough to kill, and she tried. She was still holding the butcher's knife. She swung the knife at him. He put up his hand. The knife struck his hand. Blood squirted on Chock and the wall.

When he saw the blood, his eyes got big and he backed up. Chock stepped closer to get another swipe at him. He wheeled around and headed for the door. He saw the hate in her eyes. She hated him, and if she could she was going to kill him right there where he stood.

Chock was too close to him for him to stop and get in his car. He ran past the car and down the road with Chock chasing him.

When Chock stopped chasing him, she yelled to him,

"If I ever see you again, I will kill you. Even if I have to sneak up on you in the middle of the night, like you did me, I will see you dead! You hear me? I will see you dead!"

Chock didn't know how he got to his car. Chock never saw him again. The kids told her folks that he had come by. They wondered why he hadn't stayed.

They never found out what Chock had done to him, just like they never found out what he had done to her. They just didn't talk about things like that.

A few weeks later Chock overheard her folks talking one night. They had gotten a letter telling them about Mr. TC's death. Chock heard them say how it was a shame he had to die the way he had. He was on his knees begging—begging for his life, but the man shot him anyway. It was a shame. What was this world coming to for someone to shoot a man like he was a mad dog!

They never did say what their friend had done to get himself shot like a mad dog. Chock had a feeling about what he must have done. Chock was sure it must have had something to do with his nasty ways, because they would have talked about anything else, like stealing, or killing, or cheating, or gambling, but there was only one thing they would never mention—someone had found him out.

CHAPTER 24

Going Back to Texas

During the Christmas break of Chock's second year in that Idaho school, Chock's parents decided to take a trip back to Texas for a visit. They bought a nice sized trailer to hook on to the car to put their clothes in. her Momma packed almost every stitch of clothing they owned in that trailer. They headed out.

On their trip to Texas, they had to go back through the town they had previously moved from toward Wyoming. The closer they got to the town, the more it snowed. The farther they got up into the mountains of Wyoming, everything was covered in a thick white blanket, and the snow was still coming down.

They were going through the Raton Pass, close to the Wyoming and the Colorado borders, when the car began to slip.

It was around midnight. Chock woke up when she heard her Momma calling her Daddy's name.

"Jackie, Jackie!"

Chock heard her Daddy say,

"Hush Emma, hush," in a soft voice, "before you wake up the chulluns."

Chock sat up and tried to see why her Momma sounded so scared and was calling her Daddy. Chock couldn't see a thing. Chock rubbed her eyes. There was nothing in front of them. All she could see were the beams of the car lights shining into the blackness on nothing.

Chock's Daddy said,

"Don't y'all move back there. Y'all be quiet and don't move." Chock's Momma was praying, "Lord, help us."

The car was rocking ever so light back and forth, like an invisible hand was rocking a cradle. The car had slipped off the road, and the front end of the car on her Momma's side was hanging over the canyon.

Chock's Daddy sat behind the wheel telling them to be still and not to say a word. They always did what her Daddy would tell them to do when they were in his presence. The sound of his voice told them this was another time not to question his authority.

Chock's Momma sat next to him praying, "Lord, help us."

Her Daddy said, "He's the only one that can help us now."

Chock got really scared then. That was the first time Chock had ever heard her Daddy say he couldn't fix it. She had never heard him blurt out a prayer the way her Momma did.

Her Daddy would bless the food at mealtime. He would talk to God in the morning when he got up and went outside.

The first time Chock heard him talking to God, she looked around the yard to see who he was talking to. Chock couldn't see who he was thanking for another day. She came to the conclusion it was God.

At one time or another, all of them had come upon their Daddy talking to God when he got up and went outside. They had learned he wanted that time to be alone in the morning. During that time, he would ignore them. It didn't matter what they said, or did, he would ignore them.

They sat in the car. The car sat tilted on top of the cliff and felt as if it was being rocked by this unseen hand back and forth. Her Daddy was just sitting there doing nothing to fix it.

The next time Chock's Daddy said to them, "Don't move, y'all, be quiet."

It wasn't said the way he usually said things when he wanted them to mind him and not ask questions. His voice sounded like the voice he used when he talked to God.

Then they saw bright lights coming on the road toward them. The lights were coming from both directions. Two of the biggest trucks

Chock had ever seen in her life, stopped when they saw the car off the side of the road.

Two figures got out of the trucks and came toward Chock's family.

When they got close enough to the car, Chock could see they were white men. When they came closer to the car, Chock heard one say,

"Sweet Jesus, Christ Almighty!"

The other one asked, "Y'all all right in there?" Chock's Daddy said, "Yeh, but I don't know how long we gonna hold on."

Chock didn't think they would help them. They were white men. One said,

"Y'all keep holding on. We ganna try to figure out a way to get y'all outta there."

"How many y'all in there?" Chock's Daddy said, "Eight." One of the truck drivers said, "Lord, have mercy."

In a few minutes, they started hooking chains onto the car. More trucks had stopped to see what the problem was. The highway was blocked. No one could get through. The traffic was blocked as more trucks came and stopped.

One of the men came over to the car and said, "Y'all hold on in there. I think we got something."

They started hooking and wrapping chains all around the car. They put as many chains as they could on the car to stabilize it and hold the front end up. They said they were trying to get the front of the car stable; maybe, then they would be able to get them out before the car slipped over the canyon.

When they got all the chains they could get on the car, one man gave a signal by pointing to a truck. When he gave the signal, a truck would back up. Another signal was given for the truck to stop.

One by one, all the trucks that were hooked to the car backed up just enough to tighten the chains.

He gave another signal, and they put on their emergency brakes. There were stops and starts made by the trucks, but little by little, the front end of the car got stable enough for Chock's Momma and Daddy to get out of the front seat. They gave them a rope with a loop at the end. They told them to put it around their waist when they handed it to them. One by one, they finally got all of them out of the car.

When all of them were safely out of the car, they decided to try to pull the car back from the cliff. Carefully, and slowly, the trucks would start, and then they would stop. They were trying to make sure they wouldn't be pulled over themselves. Finally, they got the car back on the road—back from the edge of the canyon.

Chock's Daddy had escaped from white men who wanted to take his life and had run into white men who saved his life and the lives of his family.

By the time they got back in the car, they were just about frozen stiff. They had to stay in the car until a snowplow came to escort them down from the pass. They put up flares and pulled the car to the opposite side of the road, away from the cliff. That was their last winter trip to Texas from Idaho.

After Chock's family were safely on their way, they had to travel two more days to get to Dallas. They were a mess when they got there, but they were thankful to have made it at all. Her sisters were happy to see them.

They stayed in Dallas and visited her two sisters and other relatives who had moved to Dallas. They were in Dallas for two days.

They left Dallas and continued on their trip. They were on their way back to the town they had left to get away from the white men. The were going back to where their lives had been changed. They were going back to their roots. They were going back to where they felt they had belonged.

They were quiet when they drove through the town where her Daddy had hit that white man. They thought about him. What would he do if he knew they were back?

They drove on through that little town and went on down to the country to their community.

They went to the place their family had lived for generations—the place they had left, almost four years ago, to get away from white men. Then they went to the house they had gone to when their house was destroyed by a tornado. They went to their Daddy's mother's house. They hadn't changed. They were still just as mean as ever.

They had all caught colds, probably from being out in the snow when their car almost fell over the canyon, but they didn't have any sympathy for them. Their rules were still the same.

Before breakfast, they had to get out of bed and make the bed. After the beds were made, they couldn't get back in them or lie down if they didn't feel well.

Chock's grandmother told her if she wanted to lie down and take a nap, she had to go to the car and not mess up her bed. It was cold in Texas. It was too cold to sit in a car.

When it's cold in Texas, it's colder than in Idaho. She left her grandmother's house and went to stay with friends. One of the friends she stayed with was a girl that lived at the last stop when her Daddy used to drive the school bus.

Due to the weather, they stayed in Texas longer than they had planned.

CHAPTER 25

Hey! What's Going On?

While Chock was in Texas, she was invited to visit the new school. The kids she had gone to school with before their escape from Texas, wanted her to see their new school. A centralized new school had been built for the black kids in their Saturday night town.

The construction of the new school was almost identical to the white school across the street.

The whites in that community had hoped to get around school integration's by building a school for black equal to the white school. They thought if they followed the separate but equal doctrine of the U.S. Constitution, they could avoid school integration.

The kids from their community were proud of the school they were going to. It even had indoor restrooms.

The kids who lived in the town, where the school was located, seemed to resent the kids from the surrounding communities who came to the school. Students, who were natives of the town, seemed to feel the school belonged to them. They thought they were more privileged and more entitled than the students who came to school from the surrounding towns.

Chock was surprised to discover this dissension between the students. She realized then, no race had a monopoly on ignorance, hatred, and fear. Her preconceptions concerning color had been completely dismantled. Ignorance, hatred, and fear were color-blind and did not distance themselves nor discriminate.

When she got off the bus, she was in another gauntlet. It was an all-black school. That gauntlet was not as hostile as the others. She did not feel the same fear she felt when she had walked the other ones. She looked at the faces around her in that gauntlet and felt sad. A strange disappointment came over her, and all of a sudden, she felt alone.

Chock wasn't too surprised when she had to walk through a gauntlet in the white schools she had attended. While she was walking through the gauntlet in that all-black school, she wondered how she would have been treated by these black students if she had been white.

She was not alone as she walked this gauntlet. After her experiences with the other schools she had attended, this gauntlet should have been a cake walk. However, that walk was one of the hardest walks she had ever taken.

She didn't know what was going to happen, but she wasn't alone. All of her relatives and friends from the community she grew up in were walking beside her. Why did they have to? Their presence said,

"She is with us."

Chock wasn't alone, but she still felt like an outsider.

She look at the faces there. The faces looking back at her were black, just like her. What was going on?

It was hard for her to believe that she was at an all-black school.

She was in an all-black school, and some of the kids were acting like white kids at the all-white schools. She felt hurt. The black kids didn't like her either; they treated her as if she wasn't one of them.

Some of the students were just curious about the visitor and wanted to see for themselves what she looked like. There weren't many visitors who had been away as long as she had and had traveled as far as she had. They had heard all the gossip about them leaving and about them coming back.

They lined the hallways looking her over. The boys made her a little nervous when she heard some of the comments they made.

"Look at them legs!" "Look at that ass!"

"Man, you see them eyes?"

Some of the girls had their arms folded across their chest. They rolled their eyes at her and then turned their heads away. Others tried to ignore and discredit her by pretending she wasn't there.

She heard a girl say,

"I don't know why she come down here thinking she better 'en the rest of us."

They tried to belittle her by making her feel that she was of little consequence to them. It didn't matter to her. Chock had heard worse, and she had been in worse, but their attitudes puzzled her.

Chock looked at the students that were looking at her. It was a different gauntlet, but it was still a gauntlet. She was still having difficulty grasping the fact that all of the kids looking at her were black. They were black kids! She had to keep reminding herself. It didn't matter where she went, people were basically the same: black or white. They had to go, see, and mark their territory and try to conquer by using the weapon of their choice: ignorance, fear, hate, and intolerance. Whites didn't have a monopoly on acting ignorant and being mean and hurtful. Narrow-mindedness and intolerance was everywhere, just waiting to be fueled. The fuel was the fear of losing what someone thought others would take away from them.

It seemed to her, the less one thought they had, the more afraid they were of losing it. Those that felt that they had nothing would go to extremes to keep it. They just wanted to keep what they thought was theirs. They wanted to keep what others thought they had that made them feel like they were worth something.

The girls who were hostile toward Chock felt that somehow she was a threat to what made them feel like they were worth something. Their physical attributes, popularity, and their good looks were their claim to fame.

They were afraid she would take away the fame that had been theirs. Some of the attention and adulation that should have been theirs was going to Chock. They had to try to invalidate her in their own way and take back what they thought would make them the biggest rock in the box.

Some of those who had failed to be the biggest rock would do anything; by any means necessary, to please the biggest rock for their own personal gains, or to get a share of the big rock's goodies. Again, Chock was reminded of Luzine when she was in the second grade. Maybe that was why, she was treated so mean in the white schools; they were afraid of losing what made them feel like they were worth something.

When Chock started school in the first grade, the kids were mean to her too, and the kids were black. When she went to the white schools, some white kid was probably glad to see someone else being picked on, and bullied by other white kids. They were glad that someone else was being made to feel as if they were worth nothing, for a change, and they were left alone.

What Chock witnessed then: the bullying, gang activities, division and bullying within races, and the separation between the races, are behaviors troubling their schools today.

During Chock's visit,she began to see things in a different light. Color has nothing to do with how people treat one another. Something has gone wrong with their beliefs. Their beliefs have been controlled by the opinions of others who need to feel like they are worth something. Along the way, they have been made to believe that what people see on the outside is all that counts toward making one feel as if they are worth something. These beliefs depend on who you are and where you are.

Chock's Daddy didn't care what others thought about him. That sometimes made him insensitive with people who cared only about what others thought. Chock's Daddy was her role model.

She thinks he had something when he told them once, "Don't pay no 'tention to them folks. They just want to feel like they worth something."

Some believe that their color makes them worth something. When they are faced with someone of another color, or someone different, they feel threatened.

They believe that their color is all they have to make them a cut above the rest, and to make them feel like they are worth something.

Chock felt hurt and felt a deep sense of loss. Why was she being treated like that? Why did they feel they were different or better than kids who were of the same color? Where did they learn to behave the way they were behaving? That was just awful!

What would they do if tomorrow came and they would have to give it all up? What would they do,if they had to leave everything behind and start over in a strange place with strangers?

They just didn't know how lucky they were to be around people that liked them. They had friends they could talk to and laugh with. They didn't know how fortunate they were to have teachers that cared about them enough to listen to what they had to say. They didn't know how fortunate they were to have a place where they could feel as if they belonged.

They were fortunate they didn't have to go through some of the things she had gone through. They were fortunate they had not been to places she had been to, and fortunate they didn't have to go back to what she had to go back to.

During Chock's visit to their school, she was still getting over the cold she had caught on her trip to Texas. She fell asleep in class one afternoon. She was awakened by someone saying,

"Nigger, shut up!"

Those were fighting words. She jumped up and looked around. Her heart was racing, and she was furious and ready for a fight. She looked around, and everyone was looking at her as if she had lost her mind. There was no one to fight. All of the faces that looked back at her were black just like her.

Chock didn't belong there. She was different because of the things she had gone through, and she was different because of some of the things she had not gone through. She was almost two years younger than most of the kids in that class, but sometimes she felt so much older.

She had gone through too much, seen too much, and too much had been done to her. Chock could never belong to any group.

They didn't believe some of the things she said she had seen. They didn't believe some of the things she said she had done, nor did she.

Sitting there and looking at all those black faces made it hard for her to believe she was not dreaming. Everything that had happened to her didn't seem real. Chock wasn't having another dream, but she was hoping she was, because something was going wrong.

They, blacks and whites, said she sounded funny, and they laughed at the way she talked. Some blacks said she talked and acted like white folks. Some, black and white, said she behaved like a little girl. She was never around kids her age. Chock never learned to be herself. She didn't know who she was supposed to be, especially then.

When she was little, she always tried to be like someone else. Someone would say she looked like this sister and acted like that sister. On the other hand, she looked like that grandmother and acted like that grandmother.

She was always someone else. She had to keep being someone else, because she thought that was all she had to make her feel like she was worth something.

Chock's social growth had stopped when she left Texas. She didn't know how to talk to the girls when she got back to Texas. She had not been around girls she could talk to about things 'GIRLS' talk about.

She didn't know how to behave around boys either, and she didn't know how boys should behave around her. She didn't know any boys besides her brothers, and they were younger than her.

In most of the classes she visited in Texas, her time was spent answering questions about the places she had been to and the people she had seen. They wanted to know about the school she was going to and how she was treated by the white kids.

Chock was too ashamed to tell them about how the white kids treated her in Arizona and how the kids treated her in Idaho. She couldn't tell them that she had no friends at school, and that she was alone.

She could not tell them that the people 'out from here' up north didn't like black people either. She could never tell anyone about the horrible, terrible, and nasty things, a black man she thought she could trust had done to her.

She couldn't tell them, but she should have told them that some of the white kids at the white schools treated her the same way as some of the black kids were treating her at that black school.

They treated her as an outsider there—the same as some of the kids were treating her as an outsider here. They treated her as if she didn't belong there at their school, and she was being treated here as if she didn't belong here at this school.

Chock didn't belong there, in Idaho, in an all-white school, and she didn't belong here in Texas, in an all-black school. She had come back to what she thought was home, but she wasn't one of them anymore.

She didn't know where she belonged and didn't know if she would ever feel that she belonged anywhere ever again. She would always be on the outside of the groups, looking in and wishing she was part of it.

CHAPTER 26

Chock Got a New Attitude

The weeks Chock had spent in Texas had made a difference in how she felt about the school she was attending in Idaho. When she got back to school in Idaho, she knew she couldn't take being in that school for too much longer. After the trip to Texas and the news about Mr. TC being dead, she began to relax a little. Her perspective had changed. She didn't think she would ever be free enough to laugh aloud again, but she decided to take more of an interest in what was happening around her.

She no longer thought of the kids as mean, inconsiderate, and bad-mannered white kids. She thought of them as just mean, inconsiderate, bad-mannered kids who had to feel like they were worth something.

The trip to Texas helped her to get through the remaining months left in the school year. When school started again, she was at peace, because she had come up with a solution to her problem. She was just going to leave home. She was going to run away.

She had formulated a plan. She would wait until her folks went shopping. She would tell them that she was sick and wanted to stay home. When they left, she would hitchhike to the main highway and just go. She had been saving her money. She would try to get to Los Angeles, or Dallas, to where her sisters were.

As it so happened, she didn't have to leave. Late one evening, during deer hunting season, they heard gunshots. They didn't dare go outside. They might shoot them.

Their dad was in the barn taking care of the animals.

They looked out of the windows to see if they could get a look at the culprit hunting on farmland. No hunting signs were posted on all of the roads leading in and out of the farm. Deer hunters would shoot anything that moved during hunting season. They were known to shoot people and farm animals. A little girl was shot while she stood waiting for the school bus.

Anyone, with any sense, should know better, and would not hunt in a residential area or near houses. Their dad went out to tell whoever was shooting that they were trespassing on private property and couldn't hunt in the area.

When he got to the car, he saw two black men. The two black men were just as surprised to see a black man on the farm.

They just stood there looking at one another like Santa and the red M&M candy, not believing the other was real. When their Daddy and the hunters finally got their voices, it was "Man, where you come from? Man, who are you?" They finally settled down and started answering one another questions. When they got acquainted, Chock's Daddy found out that they lived about thirty-five miles away from them.

The town they were talking about was the town Mr. TC's wife, Sug, was from. It was a town and not a labor camp.

Her dad brought the two men to the house to meet their Momma. Chock bet he was thinking, *Whuu, look what I found.*

The two hunters told them about the town. There were about five hundred black people living there. Some of them owned their own homes. The men worked for the railroad, telephone company, or at one of the factories nearby. There were also two churches in town and all the members were black.

Church was all their mom needed to hear. They hadn't attended church since they left Texas, except, when they attended during their visit to Texas the past Christmas.

Before the two men left, her folks vowed they were going to take a ride there next Saturday. They would do their shopping and look the town over.

They couldn't wait for Saturday to come. That day, they got up early and got dressed. They were ready to go right after breakfast. They had put on their Sunday's best.

They drove to the town. The town was huge compared to other towns they had visited—with the exception of Vegas.

There was an Albertson right on the road just before they got into town. They kept going. They wanted to see the whole town. They saw a J. C. Penney's. They saw Sears and Roebuck. They saw Woolworths and lots of other stores they hadn't heard of.

They decided to stop at Woolworths and go shopping. She was just looking at all of the things she could buy. Then she saw them. Two black women were shopping at the same store she was in.

Chock couldn't believe her eyes. She forgot all about shopping and just watched them. She was taken in by them talking and laughing together. They didn't notice her watching them. She followed the two women out of the store with an arm load of merchandise she hadn't paid for.

The clerk saw her leave the store with the unpaid items and followed her. The two women turned around when they heard the clerk asking Chock,

"Miss, do you want to pay for those items?" They thought Chock was talking to them.

The clerk came up and said,

"I'll take this stuff for you, and when you finish talking, you can come back inside and pay for it."

Chock was mortified. By then, her folks had seen what was happening and got out of the car. The clerk said she could see that she was not trying to steal anything. She seemed to have been excited about seeing friends and followed them out of the store. She had forgotten all about the things she had in her hands.

Her mom talked to the two women for a long time after they got things all straightened out. They told her about their church and invited Chock's Mom to come back and visit them. Chock's Momma said she would be at church the next Sunday. They were surprised when their Daddy said he would come, too.

When they returned from Texas, to their surprise, their dad started going to a Catholic church in the little town they were living in. There was another church in town, but he had been forbidden to attend it by his boss.

His boss said that under no circumstance were they to go to that church if they wanted to keep on working for him. He had a very strong dislike for the people that followed the teachings of that particular church. So did Chock.

Her folks weren't too thrilled at being told what church they could go to. She decided it would be a good time to tell them what she had learned in school about that church. Just the thought of someone telling her Dad what she had been told about having no soul almost made her heart stop.

She guess, almost falling over the cliff and all the other things their dad had faced made him realize it was time for him to give back. He needed to let them and others know that there was a force in the universe stronger than everybody. He did just that when he started going to church. At church, and everywhere he went, he had a story to tell, and everyone looked forward to hearing him speak.

The owner of the farm got a wild hair and decided he wanted to get out of the farming business. He sold his farm and bought a piece of land. He wanted to develop that land into a resort.

The new owner told their dad that he would be beholden to him if he would stay on and work for him. Chock thinks her dad had already decided to leave. He told the new owner that he would stay on until Christmas. During the Christmas break of Chock's sophomore year, they moved.

Chock called it a town because there were houses close together. The streets were also paved. There were churches, grocery stores, courthouses, J. C. Penney's, Woolworths, playgrounds, and many other places of business that one could go and shop.

The population of the city was posted on the sign on the outskirts of town. The sign showed the population. When they went by the sign after they had been living there for a month, Chock's Momma said it was wrong, because they hadn't added them.

The women from church had already found a house for them. The house was located in the black section of the town. It was the best house they had ever lived in so far.

The house was a huge, one-story house, with peeling white paint. Everything in the house was in working condition. There were at least four bedrooms.

It needed some repairs. Their Dad was good at fixing things. And the women from church got their husbands to help him.

During the repairs, one of the men who were on the ladder helping her Daddy, almost met with a disaster. That man was prone to telling funny stories. He told one of his funny stories while he was on a ladder fixing a ceiling light.

After the punch line, their Daddy started laughing and slapped the storyteller on his back and knocked him off the ladder. After a few minutes, he was all right.

Their Dad told him,

"Man, you ain't got no strength at oll."

The man said,

"You got too much."

The man stopped telling his stories to their Dad and was careful what he said when he was around Chock's Dad. He made sure he wouldn't be standing close to him when someone else told a funny story.

He and his family became good friends of their family, but Chock was careful not to get too close to him, but she enjoyed hearing her Daddy tease him.

Chock's daddy told him once that he was so skinny that even raindrops would miss him. He started to laugh, but he quickly stopped and put his hands up to remind her dad not to slap his back.

Chock's dad got a night job working in the grease house for the railroad.

During the day, he did the plowing and hauling on a potato farm.

By then, all of her younger brothers and sister were in school. Chock's Mom also got a job in the hospital. They were really coming up in the world.

They had been in the city for about two months when Her mom went to visit one of the church members. She saw a house that had a "For Sale" sign posted in of the front windows.

The house was an old brick two-story house, but their mother fell in love with it. She got in touch with the owner. After talking with the owner for a while, she convinced the owner to sell the house to her.

All she needed was to come up with a hundred dollars, and the mortgage would be fifty dollars a month. In the 1950s, that was still a lot of money for a family with seven kids.

Her folks came up with the down payment, and they moved to our own home. For the first time since they left Texas, they had a home of their very own again.

The house was located on a corner lot. Chock's mom planted flowers in front and her Daddy planted a garden in the back. There was also a storage shed in the backyard.

Chock's daddy didn't believe in throwing things away and was always bringing junk home that other folks had thrown away. Her Momma said she was glad he had a place to put his junk.

Every day when he came home from work; he would be out back working on something. He would be messing around with something he had found or tinkering on one of his vehicles.

For the first time in years, Chock felt that she finally had a place where she belonged. Her behavior must have conveyed her feelings. When she came home from school one day, Momma said,

"I hope you have forgotten all about running away."

She just looked at her Mom and smiled. She had read the letter.

She had probably felt the same way she had when they were moving about from place to place with nowhere to go and no one to talk to. When she saw the house, she probably wanted to buy it, not because it was so grand, but because she felt that they all needed to have a place so, they could feel we belonged somewhere again.

The lives of her family seemed to have made a turn for the better after they moved into their house. They felt good about living in their own home. They had become comfortable with their life. One of their relatives from Texas wrote to them. The letter informed her folks of the violent death that had befallen the man whom their hit. They assured them it would be safe for them to come back home to Texas.

Her parents considered moving back. They talked about moving back. They talked about the life they had left behind when they left Texas. They talked about all the moving around they had done. They talked about the life they would be leavin then if they moved again.

They also talked about the day he hit the white and how scared they were when they had come to their house with guns. They thought they were going to kill their Daddy and kill some of them.

They talked about going back, being afraid, and waiting for the day when other white men might come. When they came again, who would the men be coming for the next time?

They had four sons. Would the time come when one of their sons would have to leave home, because white men came to their house? Would their sons be fortunate enough to escape if the men came for them? Would it ever be safe to go back?

They thought about the white men and all of the moving they had done. They felt they had moved their children around too much already, so they decided they needed to stay put.

They decided they needed to stay where they felt safe. They needed to stay in that place where they had become a part of and finally felt they belonged.

They had found a home, a decent place, to finish rearing their family. They needed to stay put.

They spent the rest of their lives in that same house.

CHAPTER 27

Another School in Idaho

Before they moved to the town in Idaho, that was to be their permanent home, they had visited the town. During their visits to the town, she had seen the school she was to attend. It was across town, and it was huge. She would be walking there with some of the kids she had met in church.

There would be about five black students walking with her. That was the total number of black students who would be attending the school. They would be walking to and from school each day when the weather would permit.

There is always one. Chock had met most of the kids around her age and her brothers' at church. When she started school, the first school day after Christmas, she became acquainted with a girl she hadn't met. She was in the same grade as her. She didn't seem as friendly as the others kids they had met.

When she was introduced to her, she looked her up and down without saying a word and ignored her when she spoke to her.

She monopolized the conversation and everyone seemed eager to agree with everything she said. Her opinion and what she wanted to do was all that seemed to matter to her. Chock sensed that she must have been the queen bee of the pack.

When the kids started complimenting Chock on her clothes, or her singing in church, and other things they had seen her do on the playground, she became hostile.

On the way to school, she said,

"I'm tired of hearing about how great she is at this, and how good she is at that. She is nothing but a piece of po country trash, and you all go around treating her like she is Ms. High-and-mighty!"

She continued to say,

"I don't think we should have anything to do with her. We don't know anything about her and her family. We don't know where they came from. They could be a bunch of thieves, for all we know, just waiting to get in your house and take everything you got!"

When she finished the tirade, she stalked off angrily. No one followed her. She went a few steps and looked back. When she saw no one was with her, she threw her head up the air with a "hump," turned around, and walked to school alone. She didn't walk with them for a few days after that. When she decided to walk with them again, she was never social.

There were over fifteen hundred kids in that school. Only five of them were black. There were only two black girls in that school. The two black girls did not speak to each other. The other kids in the school seemed not to care one way or the other if she was going to school or not. They went about their own business. She was just another kid in school. She couldn't have asked for anything more than to be left alone. No one, other than that one black girl, said anything mean to her or harassed her in this school. Some of the kids, she had class with, would speak or stop to talk to her when they saw her in the hallways.

The other black girl in that school would walk by her, as the white kids had done at the other schools she had attended, and act as if she weren't even there. She thought she was doing something. She just didn't know.

The only thing that bothered her was the schoolwork. She was having trouble with Math and English. She had never had algebra and had a hard time understanding it, and she thought "pie" was something one ate.

English gave her the most trouble. She had never taken an English class. She thought English was being able to talk. Everything she handed in came back with red marks all over the page.

Chock didn't understand all of the red marks telling her what was wrong, and the teacher assumed she knew what she was referring to.

What was she supposed to do with a dangling participle or a double negative? She didn't know how to diagram a sentence, nor do the other things that were required for that class.

Chock did excel in literature. Literature was taught during the second half of the English class. Her literature grade kept her from flunking the course. She read a lot, because she was alone a lot.

The subject she should have excelled in, she was flunking that too. She flunked PE. When she found out she had to shower every day with a room full of girls, she stopped going. Also, she didn't like what all of that steam did to her hair, so she just didn't bother to go.

The Dean of Girls, her counselor, and teachers felt it would be beneficial for her if she was put back a grade. They felt that she was too young to be in the tenth grade, and she was having trouble keeping up her grades.

If she had been put back a grade, she would be going to the junior high school. She knew the kids and thought that it would be humiliating for her. They would think she was dumb.

If she had been put back; she would not have graduated from high school at sixteen. Maybe she would have had another year at growing up before she graduated. Maybe she wouldn't have graduated at all.

Maybe things happened the way they were supposed to happen. Anyway, Chock stayed on at the high school and finished the tenth grade. For the first time, her grades were just above average. She was not considered a marvel anymore. She was just normal. "Yeh."

CHAPTER 28

New Friends

Before they moved to their new home, Chock had turned fourteen that winter. She had managed to get through the last months of that school year with less problems than usual. When school was out, this would be her first summer in that town and in their new home with their new friends. Some of the kids had little jobs, but when they weren't working, they hung out together during their free time.

They would visit one another's house, play records, and dance. Sometimes they would go to the TV station and dance. A show was on that was a version of the *American Bandstand*. They would usually end up at the playground behind the church.

When they went to the playground, they would just talk or play around. When Chock became more comfortable with being in contact with boys, she would play football.

When the boys would choose a team, she was the last one chosen. At first she was not chosen because she was a girl. She was chosen last because she was so small. She was also not chosen because they didn't think she knew how to play.

They had to choose her one daybecause the teams didn't come out even. After a few games, she would be one that would be picked first. She wasn't afraid to hit, and she could take a hit. She was fast, and she could also catch.

There were two older boys on the playground who were buddies. They were the biggest kids on the playground and had to be split up for fair play. They were usually the captains and chose the teams.

They were also competing with one another on the playground. The big boy on the opposing team would always try to tackle her. She kept her eyes on them and knew what they were up to. She had managed to stay out of their way and had avoided being tackled by either one of them.

They got together and decided to play against the whole bunch of them. When the game was going good, she went out for a pass. She saw one of the boys coming at her. Chock ducked him and ran right smack-dab into the other boy. They went down. Then, the boy she had managed to avoid fell on top of them.

They had her down. They held her down and started feeling under her clothes. Why did it always have to come to an ending like that with boys?

Her team didn't realize what was going on. They thought the boys were trying to recover. Her team piled up on the two boys. When the two boys wouldn't let her up, the pileup turned into a fight and a shouting match.

Chock heard a gruff voice say,

"Y'all stop that! Stop that. Get off her and let her up!"

Chock had been rescued again. The voice carried the same authority that Daddy had in his voice.

She thought, *Who did it come from?*

She got up from the huddle. She looked around to find the owner of the voice she had heard. She saw him. He was standing there. It was Jimmy, the man she would marry. He had told someone earlier while they were watching us; she was going to be his future wife.

CHAPTER 29

Chock's Future Husband

Chock and her new friends had been playing football on the playground behind the church she attended. The two oldest and biggest boys in the group had decided to gang up on their team for the sole purpose of tackling her to cop a feel. They had managed to get her down when she heard the voice. The voice demanded that they get off her and let her up. When she got off the ground and found the owner of the voice, she was surprised. Jimmy, her future husband, was standing there looking as if he had just come from church. It wasn't church he had come from.

He had been sitting on a friend's porch across the street from the playground. He had been partying with his honky-tonk going friends. While they were drinking, they were watching the game we had going.

Chock had seen him around the neighborhood, and he seemed to be well liked by the women as well as the men.

From their house, they could see almost everything going on in the neighborhood. Every evening, he seemed to be in and out of someone's house on their street.

He was always dressed in a suit and ties with cuff links and tiepin—the whole works. His shoes were always shining, and he always had on a hat. He would walk down the street as if he was hearing a drum, and he didn't miss a beat. He had been in the military.

In the evenings after work, and on the weekends, most of their neighbors would be out in their yards or sitting on their front porches relaxing and being nosy.

He would come by with that military strut of his. He would throw up his hand and wave at everyone that was watching him. And everyone would watch.

They would stop, whatever they were doing, and watch him until he marched out of sight. Even when he was out of sight, they could still hear the echo of his shoes hitting on the pavement.

Sometimes he would stop and talk to someone. If he didn't want to stop and talk when someone would say something to him, he would walk sideways while he was talking, but he would keep walking. Whether he stopped to talk, or kept walking, he always left them laughing.

Some of the men watched him walk away with envy, while some of their women watched him with envisions. It was said he was a ladies' man, a gambler, had a way with women, and with words.

People thought he had the physical resemblances and characteristics that were displayed by the late Sammy Davis Jr. and the wit of the late Richard Prior. If Chock had been older or more mature, she would have seen the characteristics of someone else.

Her Daddy said, when he got to know her future hubby better, "That boy show can talk. He can talk the devil into giving up hell." Everyone seemed to be glad to have him around. He always knew what to do and what to say to make people laugh and draw attention to him.

He was always on stage. His stage was a bar stool or a chair around a table wherever he happened to be. Wherever he went, he was the life of the party.

He and his friends were much older than the kids she hung out with. One of the women that were sitting on the porch, drinking with him, and watching them on the playground, told her later, "We laughed at Jimmy when he said you were going to be his future wife. We told him he had better leave that little girl alone."

Jimmy started coming to the playground almost every day. He would sometimes bring a treat for the whole group. Chock was flattered when he would single her out and start talking to her.

After her future hubby started coming to the playground, whenever he came into the neighborhood, he started waving to her family. Before the week was over, he was stopping by and passing time with Chock's Dad.

Chock's Dad was always outside tinkering on his car or with some of the junk he had collected. He started courting her folks. He would drive by the house and just wave.

Then, when he drove by, he would stop where her Daddy was tinkering on his car and question him about what he was doing. Their cars were the same make and the same model-what a coincidence? He had won him over. Pretty soon, he was tinkering on Jimmy's car.

After one of those visits, she heard her Dad say to him, "Get out and sit a spell."

He did. Chock thinks her folks were in awe of him and so was she. They were flattered that a young man like him would stop and talk to them instead of visiting the other people he had been visiting in the past. It wasn't long before Chock's Daddy was inviting him to come into the house. If her mom was cooking, he would be invited to stay and have a bite to eat.

He knew just what to say to Momma to win her over. Momma was always proud of her cooking. When he complimented her and told her how good everything tasted, winning her over was a done deal. When he added that he hadn't had a home cooked meal like that since he was a boy growing up in Texas— that put the icing on the cake.

Texas was another deal breaker that put him in Momma's favor. When she found out his mother had died when he was a little boy, Momma was almost in tears.

He would tell her stories of how badly his relatives treated him after his mother died. Momma pulled out all the stops for him. She would make sure he got enough of this and make sure he tasted that. She would fix him a plate so he could take something home to eat later.

Her future hubby also liked to fish. When he went fishing, he would always bring his catch to their house. Of course, he had to stay and have dinner when the fish was fried. The first time he stayed for a fish fry he said,

"This is the best fish I ever had." He went on to say,

"When I take fish home, my aunt always cooks the little fish for me and saves the big ones for her company. You sho' is good to me."

He had a little grunt and a snuffle in his voice as if he was about to cry. Momma patted his back and told him,

"You are always welcome here. If you want me to fry fish for you, just bring it on by."

He seemed to always be around the house after school and a regular on the playground. He even started to be a regular at church.

After a church social one Sunday night, he offered to walk home with her. Her folks hadn't attended that social. He said he wanted to make sure she got home safely.

Chock was afraid to be alone with him, but she didn't know how to tell him. The other kids knew Chock's Father and didn't think it was a good idea either. She told him she had planned to go with her friends. He convinced everyone to walk her home. He realized she was not going with him but was going with her friends.

When the other kids decided to walk with them, they took the long way to her house. They walked down the street from church a block past my street. Instead of coming up the street to the front of their house, they went around the block and came up the street to the back of the house.

When they approached the back of the house, they didn't see her daddy sitting in the backyard. He was sitting in front of the storage shed smoking. They were frightened out of their wits when he said,

"Hi, y'all?"

All of them, except her future hubby, panicked and started running in every direction. She forgot where she was and ran in the opposite direction of their house. Her future hubby kept walking with his quick steps.

When Chock's dad recognized his voice, he said,

"Whuu, I didn't know it was you. What you doing out here this time of the night?"

Her future hubby said something to him, but she couldn't hear what was said, however, she could hear them laughing.

The other kids had started to get a little resentful of him. They said when he came to the playground, he was stopping the games. He always wanted someone to get out of the game and talk to him.

Most of the time he would single her out and talk to her. By the end of summer, he, her future husband, was well entrenched in their lives—on the playground and in the lives of her family.

CHAPTER 30

Chock's Junior Year

Chock was only fourteen when she began her junior year in school and would turn fifteen in a few months. She was still having issues with her teachers. They weren't exactly sure about what to do with her.

They said they couldn't make up their minds. When they thought she was too immature to be a junior, she would do or say something that would make her sound as if she was much older than all the students.

She was still having problems behaving the way others thought she should behave. When they found out she didn't fit in where they wanted her to fit in, they would get irritated with her and try to shame into behaving the way they wanted her to behave.

In some instances, older people said she was too playful. On the playground, sometimes, the kids said she was acting like an old woman. Her future husband liked the way she behaved and always gave her compliments on the way she behaved. He would often say, "Aw, you're so cute."

"That was so funny." "That was so mature."

"Whatever made you think of that?" "You act so grown-up."

That was the extent of their conversation. She was always grateful when he made the comments about her behavior in front of others. She felt that her behavior was validated, and others didn't know what they were talking about when they said she acted too young or was acting too old.

Most of the time, when they were together, he would drive around waving at people he knew. Sometimes he would stop, the way he had done when he was walking, to pass the time of day with someone. He always found something to laugh about before he drove off and would dwell on it afterward.

Some days, they would pick them up and take them to lunch. After school, he would just happen to drive by and would offer them a ride. If they accepted the ride, he would drop the others off first. When he dropped her off, he would invite himself in for a short visit and sometimes he would stay for dinner.

During her junior year, two new boys came to school. One was a senior and the other a sophomore. When they were together, they looked like Mutt and Jeff. One was tall and the other was very short. The brother, that was a sophomore, was her age. He was handsome and was built like an athlete, but he was not into sports. He was a scholar.

That young man and Chock became friends. They never thought of the girlfriend or boyfriend thing. They had someone to talk to about some of the things they were interested in. Going out together never crossed her mind.

They would talk about what they thought of this and what they thought of that. They would talk about problems they were having in school. He would help her with her schoolwork, and sometime she would help him.

After dinner one night, they heard someone knocking at their door. They were having their usual family time. Their Daddy was sitting by the door reading the Bible and Momma was in her rocking chair sewing. When he heard the knock, he said, "Come in!"

The knock came again. Without getting up to open the door or looking up to see who was there, he repeated,

"Come in!"

In came her tall friend. He came in with the arrogance of one who knew they would be welcomed anywhere. Chock was surprised to see him. She looked at her mom for help. Chock's Daddy still hadn't looked up to see who the visitor was.

He took his time to stop reading. He closed the Bible and started looking up. His eyes traveled slowly from her friend's feet to the top of his head, and then back to his eyes. Then he asked,

"What you doing here?"

My friend said, "I came to see Chock."

"You came to see Chock? Boy, you better get out from here! I heard about you."

Chock wasn't too surprised by her Daddy's reaction to her friend, but she was puzzled. She wondered what he meant when he said "I heard about you."

What had he heard? Who would know about her friend and would talk to her dad about him? She felt it was her future hubby. What did he tell Daddy? After she had become friends with the new boy at school, she didn't see too much of her future hubby. She walked home with her new friend.

Her future hubby would see them and wave. Sometimes he would ask if they wanted a lift. They took him up on it a couple of times but decided to take their time and walk home. After Daddy ran my friend off, that ended the friendship between them. From then on, he, her former friend at school, was surrounded by white girls. In his senior year, he was voted student body president.

Later that year, he was killed in a car accident. He was hit by an eighteen wheeler when he ran a stop sign.

One evening after work, Jimmy came by the house and told their Dad he wanted him to go for a ride with him. He said he had something he wanted to talk to her dad about. Their dad got his hat, and they got in her future's car and drove off.

About three hours later, when they were sitting on the front porch, they saw their Father. He was walking. His hat was sitting far back on his head. The way he was wearing his hat made them a little apprehensive. The only time their dad would wear his hat like that was when he had been taking a drink.

They turned to looked at their mom. They knew she didn't like for them to see him after he had a drink. The smell made her sick. When their Daddy had been drinking alcohol, he would go straight to the truck and sleep there.

He opened the front gate and came in the yard. He was grinning from ear to ear.

"Hi, y'all?" he said. Their mom asked, "What you doing walking?"

"That boy ain't worth nothing!"

"You know, he took me slap down yonder." He pointed.

"We went in that place, and everybody was sitting and standing round drinking whiskey out of these little bitty glasses."

Chock's Dad had never been in a bar, and when he drank, which was very seldom, he drank white lighting, or moonshine, or rot gut liquor out of a quart jar.

He went on to say,

"The next thing I knew, he put his head down on the table and went to sleep, and I couldn't wake him up. That boy can shoo sleep. I just had to put him on my back like a cotton sack and tote him to his car and drive him home."

He repeated,

"That boy ain't worth nothing."

They didn't see her future for a few days. When he finally got over his embarrassment, he came over one evening.

Chock's daddy asked,

"Boy, where you been? I been wondering what you wanted to talk to me about."

He said,

"I been a little sick. I wanted to talk to you, because I wanted to ask you if I could take Chock to lunch sometime."

"Shoo you can. Just make shoo you have her back at that school in time."

He had her folks' trust.

No one asked her what she wanted to do. It was assumed she wanted to do what everybody wanted her to do.

He would come by the school and wait by their arranged spot and take her to lunch whenever he could, or whenever he had the money or transportation.

Most of the times, he would take her to lunch at the Parker's Drive-in. They would sit in the car and eat lunch. The first time he tried to kiss her, she jumped out of the car. She started walking. He convinced me to get back in the car by saying that she would never get back to school on time if she walked. He apologized and said,

"I'm sorry. I don't know what came over me."

They kept going to lunch, and he didn't try to do anything funny. There was a drive-in movie theater on the outskirts of town.

Everyone in school was talking about a movie.

Chock knew she would never see it. She happened to mention it to him at lunch. He came up with the idea. He asked her parents to let him take her along with some other kids to see that movie. After her parents got all of the particulars, they said she could go.

He picked her up, and there was an older couple, his friends, in the backseat.

All through the movie, the couple in the backseat was drinking, giggling, hugging, and kissing. Chock was a little embarrassed by what they were doing. When they dropped them off, she mentioned it to him.

He said, "There's nothing wrong about a boy and girl showing affection when they like each other."

They went to the drive-in with that couple a few more times. Each time they went with them, her future would get just a little more friendlier and friendlier. One night, just the two of them went.

By the end of her junior year, they were an item.

CHAPTER 31

Prom Night

During her junior year, she didn't see too much of her neighborhood friends. Her future hubby was monopolizing all of her free time. At the end of the year, there was to be a junior and senior prom.

This event was the talk of the school. She wanted to go. She had mentioned this to Jimmy but she didn't see how she could go without a date. Her future husband came up with the idea of asking her parents to let him take her to the prom.

After much convincing, her folks gave him permission to take her.

She was going to the junior and senior prom that year with jimmy.

All of the girls were in a buzz about what they were going to wear and talking about who they were going with. Chock wrote her sisters and told them about the prom.

Her sisters in California sent her a dress. It was the most beautiful dress she had ever seen. It was a bluish-green lace on black taffeta with spaghetti straps. It was fitted—a size seven but had to be altered in the waist.

There was a ruffle of taffeta and lace that started above the knee. The ruffle was slit on one side, leaving the leg bare. The ruffle gradually cascaded almost to the floor on the other side. They had also sent some high-heeled, black suede, bareback shoes along with the dress. No one knew that a little girl like her could have a figure like that.

The girls asked her who she was going with. When she told them about the guy she was bringing, they were flabbergasted.

When Chock put his name on the guest list, the dean of girls called her to her office. She had to give her some information about her date.

He wasn't a student. The dean of girls asked Chock if her folks knew she was bringing him.

She said, "Yes."

She had to bring a letter from home that said he had her parents' permission to escort her to the prom. She said she didn't approve of Chock dating someone that old; he was twenty-nine, but she couldn't stop her. Her parents had given their permission.

When she went to the prom, no one knew her. They couldn't believe the change in her. They said she looked older.

When Chock went to school, she wore cute, little girl clothes, but nothing had made her look like she did on prom night. Her sisters had sent her clothes before, but the dresses had full skirts, and the sweaters and tops had sleeves and collars. That was the first time anyone at school had ever seen her in a grown-up dress.

She guess her sisters must have remembered their prom night and the disappointment they felt when they had to wear an old dress borrowed from someone. They wanted her to have something special for her prom, and it was.

The prom was a blast. Chock really enjoyed herself—for a change. They even changed partners a few times. Boys that had never spoken to her before the night of the prom, asked her for a dance.

When couples danced, she saw them hugging and stealing kisses. Her future decided he would follow their lead. She wasn't too keen on kissing. He had wet lips and slobbered on me.

After the dance, they went out to dinner. He took her to a place where he was acquainted with the owner. The place was one of the town's hot nightspots. There was a fast-food drive-in back, a restaurant on the main level, and a bar downstairs in the basement.

The owner greeted her future warmly when they entered the restaurant and slapped him on the back as he looked her over.

Chock ordered chicken. She had never been in a restaurant before. Chicken was all she recognized on the menu. Her future had a steak. Before the steak came, he had a drink. When the owner asked her if she wanted a drink, she told him that she didn't drink.

Her future said,

"Aw, come on, it won't hurt you to have one sip on a special night like tonight."

The bartender said he could make her a drink that tasted like lemonade. She wouldn't be able to taste the alcohol at all.

He went back to the bar and made her a drink. The glass was decorated with an umbrella and a cute little stick that had a cherry and an orange slice cut in half on it. He said the name of the drink was Pink Lady. It tasted good, and she couldn't tell if it had alcohol in it.

Before she knew it, she had drank the whole glass, and the bartender brought her another. By that time, other kids from the prom came in, and they had a grand old time drinking and trying to act grown-up.

When they got back in the car, her future was being really affectionate. He said,

"If you let me, I want to show you how much I love you."

He drove her to the outskirts of town to a gravel pit. He parked behind that mound of gravel and started his kissing and feeling on her again. She was feeling a little playful, and it felt pretty good by then. The next thing she knew, he had unzipped her beautiful dress. When she went to stop him he said, "You should take it off so it won't get wrinkled."

When her underwear came off, Chock got scared and told him she wanted to go home. He told her he loved her and what they were doing wasn't wrong. They were doing what people did when they were in love. She felt this had happened to her before but in a different atmosphere.

She didn't know what to do. If she had been wiser, she would have put two and two together. She would have seen the pattern of the two men who had taken off her underwear.

Chock had also liked the man before he had hurt her, but she hated him afterward. She had tried to kill him. But this was different. This was her boyfriend. He said this was what people did when they loved each other, and she believed him.

Maybe she would feel different because she thought this man was different. He said that he loved her. She'll just let it happen the way she let it happen with the other man. She'll just get it over with and go home.

When it was over, she didn't say anything. She just got dressed and sat by the window.She sat as far away from him as she could get. She didn't say anything all the way home, and she didn't feel as if she could say anything.

Chock got out of the car before he could and went inside. When she got to her room, she got into bed with her beautiful dress on and slept until she heard loud talking in the kitchen.

When she heard the voices in the kitchen, she knew he was there. He was telling her folks all about the dance. She got up and took off her dress. She hung it in the back of the closet. <u>She felt</u> she never want to see that dress again.

She went into the bathroom and took a shower, got dressed, and went into the kitchen. <u>Her folks</u> were beaming at him. While he was talking, he was complimenting Momma on her homemade biscuits and fried green tomatoes.

Chock looked at him. He didn't seem to be any different. Her folks still liked him. He was nice to me, the way Daddy was to Momma. He hadn't sneaked up on me and put his hand over my mouth, or had he?

After prom night, he practically took over all of her free time. When he came to the playground, he would park and honk for her or beckon her to come to see what he wanted.

He said that she was a young lady then, and she should not be on the playground with a bunch of kids. She wanted to behave like a grown-up, so she did what he asked her to do.

CHAPTER 32

# You Belong to Him

When Chock began her senior year, she was fifteen and would be sixteen before Christmas. After the prom night, her future husband had taken over her life. He bought her clothes that would make her look more grown-up.

She wasn't hanging out at the playground any more. She only saw the neighborhood kids when something would come up, and he couldn't pick her up.

When he did pick her up, they would hang around people his age at someone's home or at the places his crowd liked to go. She usually would sit in a corner and watch what was going on. She was ignored by him and his friends. She was an old hand at being ignored and watching others.

One day, during her senior year, their class went on a tour of the college. While she was there, she saw someone that looked familiar to her. He was a big fellow, and when he saw her, he started smiling. His smile was so wide she smiled back. Then they started laughing.

He said, "I saw you somewhere before."

She said, "Seems like it, but I can't remember where." "I haven't seen you around town before," he said.

I haven't lived here very long," she said. "I haven't seen you around town either."

"I have been here at the college almost four years," he said.

While they were walking, she saw a picture of the football team. In the same instance, they seemed to recall where they had seen one another. She remembered seeing him when she was majorette for one of the school she had gone to in Idaho. Their school band had come to the college to march at their homecoming.

Their band was leaving the field and their football team was coming on. He almost ran over her. When she saw that big black man running toward her, she was too stunned to move. He just sort of picked her up, a hand on each shoulder, and set her to one side and out of the way.

Sometime, after the field trip, she would see him at the get-together she went to with her future. He would come over and talk to her. They became good friends. Sometimes they would look at each other and just start laughing again at something they saw an thought was funny.

He finally got the nerves to ask her out. She told him she was engaged and was going to marry the guy she came to the party with.

He said, "You're too young to get married."

Chock had never thought about it, but it had been a long time since she felt young and felt like laughing. It seemed that she had stopped having fun a long time ago.

She was constantly told to stop acting like a teenager, until just sitting still and doing nothing was the only thing she felt safe doing.

On her sixteenth birthday, she was given an engagement ring. She was officially engaged. She was never asked if she wanted to get married. It was taken for granted that getting married was what she wanted to do. They went to the restaurant they had gone to on prom night to celebrate their engagement. Her future hubby thought since they were going to get married, she should celebrate by having a drink with him. Also, because they were then going to get married, they went to the next place they had gone to on her prom night—the gravel pit. They made that trip many nights after their engagement.

When spring came, she was going to have a baby. She had learned that much from their dad's sex education class and from the health class she had been taking in school.

When her friend saw her looking sadder than she usually looked one night; he kept asking her what was wrong. Chock finally told him. When she told him she was going to have a baby, he just got up and walked away.

She didn't tell anyone else until she had a bad fall during PE. The PE teacher had wanted me to sign up for track when she started her class, but she had refused. During one of their classes, she took them outside on the grass to run. It had rained and the grass they were running on had some wet spots.

She was going out for the one hundred yard dash. She had been put in the class with the school's track star, and the teacher wanted to see them run together. Chock had her beat until she hit a slick spot where water had accumulated and slipped. When she fell, she actually saw stars. She was out for a second or two. She had to be carried into the nurse's office. The school nurse started asking her questions. She asked her if she was pregnant. Chock told her she thought she was. She told the dean of girls, and they took her home. They told Chock's mom what she had told them. She couldn't tell how Momma felt about the news. She never said anything. When her future came over, her folks told him she was going to have a baby. They said they should get married as soon as possible. Her future was elated. He assured her folks about how much he loved her and told them how happy he would be to marry her.

When he left their house, he went out on the town and celebrated.

He told everyone he saw that they were going to have a baby.

Getting married was his primary concern. Her folks thought they would just go to the courthouse and get married there. But her future had other ideas.

He began to make plans. He set a wedding date. He bought a book on etiquette and gave it to her. Chock had no idea of how to go about planning a wedding. She had not attended one. He got his aunt to plan the wedding and the reception.

He took her shopping to find a wedding dress and all the other things she would need for the wedding. Everything was taken care of by him. He even rented an apartment and furnished it. She just sat back and went along with the plans and did as she was told.

Her attitude reverted back to sulkiness and indifference. She couldn't get along with anyone in her family. She had slipped back into that dark place again. She didn't feel like talking to anyone. She just did what she was told and waited. Momma said one day, "I'll be glad when you get out from here."

Chock was giving everyone too much trouble. Everything anyone did irritated her and made her angry.

She started losing weight, and she actually felt sick. She stopped going to school. Their mom lost her patience with Chock, and she became impatient and couldn't get along with anyone. She just wanted to be left alone.

When she was out of school for a month or so, the school nurse and dean of girls came to their house to see Chock's mom again. They told her they wanted her to graduate.

They said if Chock didn't graduate before she had the baby, she probably wouldn't ever graduate. They said her grade were good enough and she had enough credits. They also said she didn't have to come back to school if she didn't feel like it. They would make all of arrangements. Chock graduated one week, got married the next week, and a week after that, she lost the baby. During that time, she didn't know what was keeping her sane, and she don't know what kept her alive, but she managed to keep on going.

She was tired. There seemed to be no end to her troubles.

The only thing she remembered about her graduation was that she was in pain. She was sick and just wanted it to be over. She didn't remember where her graduation was held, or what happened during the ceremony, how she got there, what she wore, what she did while she was there, or how she got home.

PART 3

MARRIED LIFE

(FOR WORSE, MORE WORSE, AND THE WORST)

CHAPTER 33

Getting Married

She doesn't remember her graduation, but she does remember some of the things that happened the week after graduation—the week she got married.

Three days before the wedding, she had a fight with her eldest brother. She had taken all of her clothes out of the closet and the drawers. She was going through them trying to decide what she wanted to take with her and what she would leave behind. She had put clothes over all of the chairs in the front room.

Her eldest brother, but younger than her, came in and started moving her clothes. He was not only getting her confused by throwing her clothes in one chair but was wrinkling them up. She kept straightening them out and laying them back on a chair he had decided he wanted to sit in. They kept going back and forth without saying a word until she had got fed up with him.

She snapped. She went in the kitchen, and she got the biggest knife she could find and went back to the front room. When he saw the knife, he jumped up and ran out of the house.

Chock and her brother would have the same kind of fights her sisters had when her folks were gone. After she got married, they became allies. He became the protector of them—her sisters and brothers.

Chock followed behind him walking. She doesn't know why she was so angry at him. She followed him down the street. She didn't run after him. He kept running and kept looking back to see if she was still coming after him. When he saw her still in pursuit, he took off again. She kept following him.

She followed him up the street and down another. Her brother got tired of her chasing him and went to the hospital where their mother was working. She followed him in the hospital; not caring about people looking at them or what they were saying.

Someone at the hospital recognized them and found their mom. They told her what was going on. When Momma found her brother, she took him home. She hoped Chock would follow him.

When Chock got home, Chock's Mom was waiting for her with a switch. Three days before she got married, she got a whipping. Momma stopped after a few licks. She noticed she was not moving or saying anything. She just stood there. She didn't feel a thing. She didn't care about anything anymore.

She told Chock's daddy what happened and how Chock was acting. He told her she didn't have to get married if it was bothering her. She felt it was too late. She was going to go along with the plans and do what everyone had planned for her to do.

The plan was for her to get married. That was what she was going to do.

She didn't know what was going to happen next. She had to wait and find out. Everything that happened to her seemed to happen for a reason. Maybe someone else, with more problems than her, had been praying for a miracle also.

So many times, she had escaped from the bad things that could have happened to her and her family. But then, she was in another situation. She had no idea as to what she should do. So many things had happened. She didn't know what would come next.

They had escaped from the tornado.

She had escaped from mean, uncaring relatives.

She had escaped from dying with the whooping cough.

They had escaped from the white men who had come to get their Daddy. She had escaped from a school with mean, nasty kids.

She had escaped from a man who did horrible, nasty things to her.

They had escaped from falling over a cliff.

She had escaped all of those things and more. When she had escaped,she had managed to get herself into something else and had no idea what would happen to her if she tried to escape again.She couldn't keep on escaping. She just had to wait and see. Maybe, she was the miracle someone had been praying for.

Her future hubby had different groups of friends. He had friends he went to the honky-tonks and drank with. He had friends he gambled and drank with.

He had friends he had dinner and drank with at their homes.

He had friends he drank with when he went to the so-called respectable events with.

He had his liberal white friends he drank and partied with at the white bars.

All of those friends came to their wedding party. In time, and on different occasions, she got to meet all of those different friends.

She doesn't remember getting ready for the wedding. She don't remember the wedding ceremony. Everything had been planned by her hubby's aunt.

Four months before her seventeenth birthday, she was getting married. His uncle was to marry them at his church. A reception would follow the wedding.

The reception after the wedding would be held in the social hall of the church. After the reception, at the church, there would be a party at the men's club. Alcohol and food would be served.

The plans were for Chock to get dressed at her folks' for the wedding.

After the wedding reception, she was to go back there and change for the after party.

Her hubby was to go to their new apartment and change.

The apartment they were going to move into after they were married was ready. They had moved all of their belongings there before the wedding, except for the clothes she was to wear on her wedding day.

She remembers going home to change her clothes. When her hubby took her to her folk's house to change, all of her family was at the reception at the church and she was there alone. They would stay at the church to help clean up after the reception and see that all of the gifts got to their apartment.

Her hubby let her out at the front gate and told her he would be back in about half an hour. All she had to do was to pull off her wedding gown and put on the dress that he had chosen for the party. He had picked out the dress for her on one of their shopping trips.

Chock got dressed and waited. One hour passed. Two hours passed. Three hours passed before he came back to get her. While she was waiting, she fell asleep.

That was the only peace and quiet she had had before the whole thing started on prom night. She was dressed, but she didn't really care if he came back to get her or not.

She was awakened by the sound of a honking horn. She went to the car and got in. She didn't ask why he was late. He voluntarily gave me an explanation. He said he was late because there was an emergency, and he had to take care of something. She took him at his word. She had no reason not to believe him and didn't care to ask him any questions.

When they arrived at the party, it was in full swing. The men would come up to slap him on his back and make comments like:

"You ole dog, you."

"You couldn't wait to start the honeymoon."

She wasn't quite sure what they were talking about and was a little embarrassed about the way some of the party goers were looking at her. His best man showed up at the party with one of her hubby's white, drunk girlfriends. She came over to the table to give her a present. When she handed her the gift, she said, "He married you, but he spent his wedding night with me." It never dawned on her what she was referring to.

Everyone at the party was his partying friends, and acquaintances, or drinking buddies. The kids her age were too young to come where alcohol would be served. Everyone danced and drank way past midnight. Everyone was having a good time except her. She didn't feel like dancing. She didn't drink. She just sat in a corner as usual. Every once in a while, her hubby or someone else would come over to her and comment on the wedding, or the reception, or the party.

Everyone celebrated her marriage but she sat in a corner and watched them. They left the party before it ended. Her hubby had to swing around to his favorite hangout to make an appearance and to see what was going on. She stayed in the car. She didn't feel like another party. He was in there for about half an hour then they went home to their new apartment.

When they got to their apartment, she went in the bathroom to take a shower. When she came out of the bathroom, her hubby had already fallen asleep and was snoring. Their wedding night was the next morning.

The next day, her brother and his friend came to see Chock. They waited for her hubby to leave. After he left, they told her when they had come to her apartment during the reception to bring the wedding gifts, they saw her hubby's white girlfriend in her bed with her hubby. They were naked.

Overnight, her brother had become her protector. They were angry and wanted to help her pack up her things. He wanted to take her back home to her folks.

Chock always wondered why she didn't leave at that moment. She didn't see why she should be angry with her hubby for doing to that white girl what he was doing to her; she deserved it. She didn't care if he did the nasty, hurtful thing to her every night as long as he would leave her alone.

CHAPTER 34

No Baby

The day after their wedding, her pain had increased. She continued to get sicker as the days passed. She was very sick by Thursday; five days after the wedding, she started bleeding. Friday morning, her hubby's aunt, the one who had planned the wedding, came to see them to see if she could help with the thank you cards.

When she saw all of the bloody towels, she told him he should take Chock to the hospital. When Chock got to the hospital, they put her in a cubicle, and a nurse took her vitals. She said her blood pressure was dangerously low. They said she needed to stay until she saw a doctor. They put her in a room and hooked her up with tubes, and her hubby left.

When the doctor came, he said he needed to take the baby from me. He needed someone to sign the papers giving him consent. Chock was not old enough to sign.

She needed blood, and she needed a D&C. Her hubby had to give his permission before the surgery was done. They had to get in touch with her hubby and get his permission. They couldn't find him.

Chock's parents came to the hospital and signed the papers giving the doctor permission to do the procedure. When her hubby left, she didn't see him until she was checked out on Sunday.

When she got to the operating room, she was almost unconscious. She heard a nurse while she was talking to the other people in the operating room before she lost consciousness.

She commented, "A baby having a baby. What a shame!"

The doctor said that the fetus had stopped developing months ago. He said the loss could have been caused by the tumble Chock had taken in PE but that was not certain. She should have been taken to the hospital right after the fall. She asked him if it had been a boy or girl. He said the embryo had stopped developing too early to tell.

When she came home from the hospital,she weighed almost one hundred pounds. She stayed in bed a lot, while her hubby stayed gone a lot.

When she got well enough, he thought he would cheer her up. He took her fishing with him. He said he knew where a lake was and the fish were biting. Chock packed a picnic basket, and he packed his beer, and they took off.

He had a Ford then. On the way to the lake, he would sometimes drive one hundred miles an hour. They drove for about an hour. She didn't know where they were going, but when they got there, she knew where they were. They were at a lake she had wished she would never, ever, see again.

CHAPTER 35

Neighbors and Friends

Chock had been out of the hospital about a month before she started getting her strength back. She tried to adjust to married life. She was overwhelmed by all the things she didn't know about and was expected to do.

The apartment housing they lived in had about ten units and resembled the housing in the Idaho labor camp. They were the same color and the same size. There were two buildings with a sidewalk running between them.

The people who lived in those units were about his age, and some of them already had kids. There was a lot of interaction among them.

The women stayed home, and the men worked. That is where she learned some of the things she should have known about before she got married. When the women got together during the day, over coffee or playing cards, she just listened to their conversations.

All of the women that lived in the apartments were older than her. Some of the things she heard were shocking to her, but she tried them out anyway. They talked about ways to get over on a man when they didn't feel like being bothered. They also talked about what they would do, or what they had done to get even when their man messed with them. Some of the things she heard almost got her killed.

Before she got married, she had met her next-door neighbor when they were moving into the apartment. The subject came up when they were playing cards about how much pain they had been in when they had their babies. During the conversation, she found out where a baby came out from.

Chock had been under the impression that a baby comes out from the rectum. She found out that a baby comes out of the same place it went in. That was a shock.

She went next door to the apartment they were moving to. She got a mirror and looked at herself down there where the baby would be coming out. She cried for the rest of the day and on into the night until she fell asleep.

There was a couple of honky-tonks about a block from their apartment. When her folks heard about her patronizing those places, they were furious. They said those places were no place for a decent person. She shouldn't be around the kind of people that went to those places. They said she might be married, but she was only sixteen, and if she was older, she still shouldn't be going there.

She went to the honky-tonk with her hubby. She listened to the working women talk. They would give their opinion on the best way and fastest way to please men. They also talked about some of the things they had done when a man tried to mess with them.

Those women had their own little houses they did business in. They would sometimes run games from those little places and sell drinks on the side. Those little houses were known as the houses of ill-repute.

Her hubby seemed to be the gofer at those houses. He would go for this and go for that. He would bring them this and bring them that or anything they asked for. The women seemed to depend on him.

The housewives were called bitches by the working women. The working women were called hoes by the housewives.

When Chock went to talk to the working women, the housewives would say, "I heard you been talking to them hoes again. You keep on hanging around them hoes you gonna end up just like 'em."

When she was seen talking with the housewives, the working women would say, "If them sorry-assed bitches would stop giving pussy away to everybody, we could make some money. You keep hanging around them stupid bitches, you gonna get hurt. They ain't up to no good."

It was ironic. She was around two different groups of women who couldn't stand one another; but basically, they thought the same. They didn't realize they were in whatever situation they were in, because of one common factor—men.

She had learned the names of the male and female reproductive organs in PE. When she listened to the prostitutes, she learned the vulgar words and slang they used when they discussed their trade.

From the women taking care of their husbands, homes and kids, she learned things about quickies, sex, intercourse, pregnancy, sneaking around, hookers, prostitutes, and the vulgar words they used when they talked about the intimate side of their life.

Chock learned from the working women and her neighbors, but none of them told her how they felt when they tried those tricks on men. She believed all of those things they told her they had done were things women were expected to do.

She learned from both groups of women. They seemed to like telling me stuff. Besides laughing at the shock on her face, they said they were schooling her, and didn't seem to mind having her around. Both groups of women seemed to like her hubby, and her hubby seemed to like them. When she went out on the weekend and wasn't with her hubby, she went with the women from the apartments. When a man would come over and try to talk to her they would say, "She's Married, and that's her husband."

When she went with her hubby, she usually ended up sitting with one or more of the working women. When one of their paying customers tried to talk to her, they would say,

"She's married, and that's her husband."

They would often tell her, "You don't even know how pretty you are. I wished I had half your looks."

One night, Chock was sitting at a round table, in a booth, with the women she had gone to the honky-tonk with. They were talking loud and making fun of how a working woman was dressed.

She didn't like that at all. She got very scared sitting with them while they were amusing themselves at that particular woman's expense. She was a big, red woman about six feet tall and went by the name of Tex. She was from Texas.

On occasion, when she had been at the club with her hubby, she had seen her take down men and some of the working women she called her friends, because they had done something she didn't like.

Chock liked her. When they were over to her little house, she showed her all of the needle points she had done while she was locked up. She gave her a crocheted table cloth and matching napkins as a wedding present. They were beautiful. Chock also liked her because she reminded her of her eldest sister. She was no one to mess with.

She kept warning them they had better stop talking about that woman and leave her alone before someone got hurt. The other working women had told her to watch what she said around her, because she was crazy. She had been in prison for splitting a man's head open with an ax. Tex was sitting on a bar stool and seemed not to be aware of what was going on. The others in the booth were egged on by the comments one woman was making, and they were getting a little loud. She finally got up from the bar stool and came over to the booth where they were sitting. She said, "Chock, I want you to get up and come out from there."

Man, was she ever ready to get up and come out! Chock started to get up because that was not a good place to be. She didn't know if she would pull a gun from somewhere and start shooting or a knife and start cutting.

As Chock was getting up, the woman that had been doing most of the talking caught her arm and said in a voice to make her sound as if she was tough, "She don't have to get up if she don't want to."

She wanted to. She got up. Just as she left the table, she heard something scraping the floor and glass breaking and loud whacks.

The woman had pushed the table back, so none of the women could get up; she had about five women pinned in the booth while she whipped their heads with a pool cue.

Chock started screaming, "Tex! Tex!"

She was finally subdued by her man and others before anyone was seriously hurt.

She said to her later, "I heard what they were saying about me over there. I heard you trying to get them to shut up, but they just kept on. They think 'cause I walk the streets to make a living, I'm blind, dumb, and can't hear. I keep telling you, them stupid bitches gonna get you hurt one day."

CHAPTER 36

Fried Chicken vs. A Quickie

Three months after Chock got married, she agreed to take her niece home to her mother in L A. before school started. Her hubby worked for a company that offered free train travel. She could travel anywhere for free, and she wanted to get away.

When she took her niece to visit her mother, she stayed and visited with her sister for two weeks. When she got back to their apartment, there were women clothes in her closet, and some of her clothes were missing. His answer was maybe someone had come in the apartment and stolen her clothes. They never locked the doors then.

When she asked her hubby about the strange clothes hanging in the closet, he didn't know where they came from.

Chock was in the car with him late one evening and saw a new working woman walking the streets wearing her prom dress and the shoes her sisters had sent her. She had hung the dress in back of the closet and had tried to forget about it, but it was still hers.

When she went to get out of the car to get her clothes, Jimmy grabbed her. He said he didn't want her wearing those clothes after she had worn them. He went on to say he would buy her another dress and shoes better than those.

He knew more about her than he let on. He didn't want her to get out because he knew she carried a straight razor.

When Chock mentioned what the new woman on the street had done to her, the working women she was acquainted with were furious.

They didn't like he anyways; she was competition. They offered to get her clothes back for her. But she said she didn't want them.

They, and her hubby, let everybody know what she had done. They put the word out that she was a thief. Every time a man approached her, they warned him by saying, "You better hold onto your clothes. You better watch out for your wallet. She'll steal you blind."

She wasn't in town too long after that.

At lunch, her hubby would come home for what she learned was a "quickie." After work, he would come home for another quicker quickie. After his quickies, he would be gone.

One evening, when he came home for his quickie, Chock was frying chicken. He wanted her to stop. She wasn't about to stop frying her chicken. She knew he was stone out of his mind. There was nothing she liked better than some good ole fried chicken. He got angry because she wouldn't stop cooking to give him his quickie. But that day, he just had to wait.

She was turning the chicken. He shoved her away from the stove. He tried to cover it up on the pretense that he was looking for something in the drawer under the oven.

When he bent over to look in the drawer, some hot grease popped on his neck. Boy, did he get angry. He jumped up and started cussing and swearing at her, and he hit her in the face as hard as he could with his fist.

Her head snapped back, and her mind snapped with it. She wheeled around and went in the bedroom where he kept his shotgun. She got the gun and some shells and came back to the kitchen.

When she went in the bedroom, he had turned the stove off and was pulling off his belt. He thought she had gone to the bedroom to give him his quickie.

When he saw the shotgun in her hands, he took off running. He didn't know she hadn't loaded, nor could she load the gun. She had picked up the wrong shells. After Mr. TC had run out of the house, she had pledged she would not let anyone hurt her again without putting up a fight.

Chock learned from talking to other women about what to do to a man when he messes with you. She thought about how her hubby had treated her on her wedding night and about her clothes another woman was wearing. She thought about the night she had lost the baby, and he had disappeared. Then he hit her. She doesn't know if she was angry at herself for being so stupid or at him for being such a prick.

When he ran out of the apartment, she didn't know where he had gone until her dad came back with him. Jimmy had gone to her folks and told them she had lost her mind and tried to kill him for no reason. He wouldn't come into the house with her Daddy. He sent him in.

When he came in, Chock still had the gun. She had found the right ammunition by then, and it was loaded. She got a chair and put it by the door. She sat there waiting for him, just as Daddy had waited for the white men, with the gun on her lap.

When Daddy came in the house, he said, "Girl, what's wrong with you? You put that gun down."

When she finished explaining why she was going to shoot her hubby, he said, "Long as you stay in this house, I won't come back, 'cause I'll shoot him myself."

Daddy finally talked her into giving up the gun, and he took it with him.

He never came back to their apartment to see them or to see them in any of the other places they moved to. When they went to see her parents, he was cordial, but kept his distance.

Her hubby kept his hold on her mom. Momma was raised to respect the man as the head of the household. When Chock went to see her a few days after the fight, she said, "You shouldn't do thing to make your husband angry."

She advised her, "When a man and woman get married, it is the woman's duty to obey the man and do what the man tells her to do. The man is the head of the household, and he has a right to make the woman mind."

Her Momma, like her grandmother, didn't know what that man wanted her to do. Momma didn't know men like her hubby. She only knew her Daddy.

She didn't know what the man wanted her to do either. When she found out about all the things she had to do, it was too late to stop.

When her hubby came back in the apartment, he kept saying sorry over and over. He said he didn't know what came over him.

That was the first time he hit her, but it wasn't the last. He was sorry, but she still had a black eye, a swollen face for days, and a growing resentment toward him.

He was so affectionate and generous after he hit her. She just knew he wouldn't hit her again because he was so sorry and so nice. He brought her flowers and all kinds of presents. He stayed around home for a few days, and his quickies were not so quick.

They never had a genuine conversation or discussions about anything she was interested in: the kids, education, or other places and things that were happening in those other places.

She can't remember having one conversation about their future plans or what he wanted to do. All he seemed to be interested in was hanging out in bars and honky-tonks drinking, gambling, and chasing women. When he talked, it was about street life: who did this, who did that, who shot who, who had who, and who he sure would like to get a piece of. What was happening on the streets seemed to be all he was interested in—besides quickies.

CHAPTER 37

Whups! Chock Did it Again

Chock turned seventeen four months after she got married. By the first of the next year, she knew she was pregnant again. This pregnancy was different. She went to the doctor as soon as she thought she was pregnant. She was going to make sure this baby would be all right.

When she told her hubby, he wasn't as happy about it as he had been when he had found out she was pregnant the first time. He wanted her to keep it a secret for a while. He didn't want her to leave the house. She walked the three blocks to the club he hung out in one evening, when he didn't come from work. He was embarrassed for her to be seen by his friends. When he saw her he said, "What you doing here with your big belly? Nobody wanna see you looking like that!"

The man he was talking with was an older man who was childless.

He said, "I would give anything to have my wife looking like that. I have been trying to get my wife to look like that for years. Man, you don't know how lucky you are."

Then he got a chair for her.

That summer during her pregnancy, Chock's second sister and her husband came to visit her folks. The day Chock's sister and her husband arrived, she went over to her folks to see them. Her hubby said he would be over after work.

When he finally came by, he was dressed in his finest and had already had a drink or two. He was at his finest, aiming to please and leave them laughing.

When he got tired of sitting around with her family, he asked her brother-in-law if he wanted to take a run with him and get out of the house for a minute. Chock's brother-in-law thought it was a good idea and they left.

Her brother-in-law came back in a taxi. He said her hubby told him he had a short errand and left him at the club with some of his friends. When the club closed, he still hadn't returned. The club owner called him a cab.

Her sister asked their folks, "How could you let Chock marry a man like that? He is almost old enough to be her father."

Before she went back to Dallas, she was at her apartment making cakes when a guy came to get food for her hubby. When she found out about Chock taking food to her hubby at night and where he was gambling, she was livid.

She told Chock she was never to do that again. She could fall and hurt herself out there in the dark by herself. He shouldn't be leaving her home by herself anyways while he went out carousing around.

When she went back to Dallas, she must have told her eldest sister about her hubby. Before the month was over, Chock's eldest sister came out to pay her a visit and to help her out when the baby was born.

Thank God she did. The night she went into labor, she thought she was having problems with her bowels. Her stomach hurt, and she had wet the bed before she could get to the toilet. She couldn't sleep. She made several trips to the toilet.

Finally, Chock woke her up. She asked her if she knew what labor pains felt like. She asked her if she was having pains. She told her about her trips to the bathroom. She said they better get to the hospital.

They had no way to the hospital. It was three o'clock in the morning. Her hubby was still carousing around. She had no phone. How were they to get to the hospital?

She finally went to the apartment of the people who had a phone and woke them up so she could call a cab. The cab came but didn't want to take them to the hospital. He was afraid she would have the baby in the cab.

Her sister told him if he didn't take them to the hospital, he had better leave town. She would make him her lifelong mission. She would find him and make him feel like he was going to have baby. They went to the hospital.

When they got there,she was too young to sign herself in. The attendant said someone who was responsible for the hospital bill needed to sign her in.

Chock gave her sister the phone numbers of some of her hubby's friends. She told her to ask if they would call around and try to locate him to tell him that she was in the hospital. Someone finally got in touch with him. When he got there, she had already had the baby. They got everything straightened out as to who would be responsible for the bills. They took their little girl home. He was crazy about the baby. When he was home he doted on her. He bought her beautiful little dresses, and he took her everywhere to show her off.

Her sister stayed with her for two months. She doesn't know what she said to her hubby, but while she was there, he behaved himself. Chock got pregnant again when her first child was three months old. She had her second child, a son, on her daughter's Birthday. Then,she had another daughter. Her last child was another son. She had given birth to four children before her twenty-first birthday.

Her babies made her feel good inside and happy. When she was alone with them, she felt as if her heart came out of the sad place she kept it hidden when adults were around. She was another person, and nothing else mattered. Her children, the children of her friends, the neighbor hood children, and later the children in her classroom gave her a reprieve from the ugliness she felt inside. She treasured the time she spent creating games, stories, and reading to them.

Thank God for her parents, and her sisters and their husbands, and her brothers. They were role models for her and her children. They kept her on the right track.She would have treated her kids like toys or they would have been neglected or both.

Chock had so much fun with her children. Sometimes, she would forget to cook, wash, and clean house when she should. Her mother and her sisters were around to remind her.

On the other hand, she would get too involved in cooking, washing, and cleaning. She was too busy and too tired to take the time to play and just sit and hold them as much as she should have. She should have hugged them more and whipped them less.

Her parents were not the hugging and kissing type. They were afraid it would make them soft and go to their heads. If it wasn't broken, and they didn't see blood, they were OK. They had to suck it up and go on about their business.

Whenever they were seen idle, they would say, "What you doing sitting there doing nothing? If you can't find anything to do, I find something for you."

She said when she had children, she would raise them differently from the way her parents had raised her. She got so caught up in life that she forgot what she said and resorted to what she knew. She did what she saw her parents do. She knew nothing else.

When her kids got older, they would walk everywhere that was in walking distance for them. She didn't drive. As they walked, she felt so proud looking at them trying to keep up with her. As they began to get older, she felt exhausted trying to keep up with them. She would have to carry the baby until the baby was old enough to walk. She didn't even have a stroller. When her babies coughed, she took them up and ran to the doctor.

As her kids got older, she wasn't afraid to leave them at night. She became restless. They went to bed around seven. She would be alone for the rest of the night. She would sit outside on the steps and talk to some of the women, or anyone who happened to be around, but she soon got tired of that. Her younger brothers and sisters were more than happy to watch the kids for her. Almost all the kids they went to school with were on that street or close by. She started going back to the neighborhood honky-tonks.

CHAPTER 38

Secrets and Hidden lies

After a bad fight, her hubby always went through a period of being sorry and nonstop affection for about three weeks. Then his sorries would taper off gradually until everything would get back to the fighting stage.

After the first child was born, her hubby gradually went back to his old bad ways. She was too ashamed to let others know she had married a man that didn't like her.

He liked everyone else, but he hated her. All the women she thought were her friends turned out to be more than friends to him. Whenever she met someone, he made sure they ended up being his friend and not hers.

Her hubby didn't like anything she did. He said she didn't know how to provide for a man. He didn't like anything she said. He didn't like the way she dressed or combed her hair. He didn't like when she spoke to men, and he didn't like it when she didn't speak.

They would have a fight when they went out and a fight when they came back. At least once a month, when couples were doing something or it was to his benefit to show up with a wife, he would take her out. When they went in the door where the event was being held, he would be his Sammy Davis/Richard Prior acting self. She would watch him being the life of the party. As she watched him, she would think, *Is that the same man who was in a rage a few minutes ago?*

He was under the assumption that she was either trying to embarrass him by wearing the wrong thing or she had chosen to wear it to please someone other than him. She could never be right.

Damn, if she did, and damn if she didn't.

When they went out, she would watch him being the life of the party, dancing, snapping his fingers, laughing, and clapping to the music—laughing and joking with everybody but her.

He saw her looking at him one night at a party. He was going through his act, and he was looking so handsome. The women were falling all over him. No one would ever guess who he would turn into when they left the party.

On the way to the car, he started in on her.

"I bet you didn't think I saw you looking at me with them cow eyes of yours. Did you? You got your f . . . nerves looking at me like that in front of my friends!"

By the time they got in the house, he was a raving maniac. If she said anything, she was in for it. She turned around to go the bathroom. Plop! One eye closed.

Chock put her hand over her eye and went to bathroom.

"I don't know why you always make me do this to you. I'm sorry. Let me put some ice on it".

He held the ice pack on her eye while he kissed the other part of her face.

When he thought the pain had gone away, he pushed her down on the bed.

She pushed him off her. "What's wrong with you?"

"I said I was sorry, what else do you want?"

"You don't know how to appreciate a man like me. Other women would give their right eye to be with a man like me."

Chock guess it never crossed his mind that she just had.

Every time he said he was sorry and he wouldn't do it again, she thinks he believed it, and she believed it.

Things would be going along smoothly and out of the blue he would get angry about something. The venom and anger came out of him as if the devil himself had crawled into his soul.

He would get angry and start cursing and yelling at her. He would get angrier because he felt that she made him curse and yell at her. At dinner time, or before he ate, if he was yelling and cursing at her, he would stop to bless the food and start back yelling and cursing after the blessing. That put fear in her.

"Why do you always make me mad? You should be happy that I married your stupid ass, 'cause no one else would want you!"

Their next-door neighbor moved into a house down the street. They got a new neighbor. He was a single man. As he was walking by her, he said, "You shouldn't let him beat on you like that."

She looked around to see who he was talking to. He added, "You should leave or fight back."

Chock didn't know anyone could hear what was going on. She was so ashamed.

The next time he plopped her, she plopped him back. He was so taken back that he stopped yelling and cursing. He pushed her over the sink. That was a very bad place for him to push her.

She knew her kitchen, and she knew how to handle everything in it. She knew what was in the sink. She grabbed her favorite knife and swung it. He jumped back and ran in the bedroom. Just as he was closing the door,she threw the knife. It stuck right in the center of the door.

Their new phone rang. Chock picked it up. It was her girlfriend. "I can't talk to you now. I'm fighting."

She thought she was joking and started laughing. She said, "I'm not joking."

"Who you fighting with?"

When she told her it was her hubby and what he had been doing to her, she said,

"You otta be ashamed of yourself, lying 'bout that man like that. You know he wouldn't hit you. I knew him for a long time. I knew he was whorish, but I never heard of him hitting anybody."

Of course, when he got out of the bedroom, he made a beeline to her folks. Momma came back with him. She told her to go home. She didn't know what was going on, and she was tired of her taking his side. She didn't believe she had to do what the man wanted her to do if she didn't want to anymore, but she did believe in staying married. Neither one of them knew what marriage was. They never grew up. He didn't have parents to rear him, and she was still trying to find her way into adulthood.

When she started fighting back,they were like two children—you kill my dog, I'll kill your cat.

Her hubby fell back to his old tricks of getting some unattached bachelor to keep her busy while he gambled.

Chock went to the club one evening. She saw a man she thought she recognized, sitting at the table with one of the working women. He mistook her for a working woman. The woman he was with set him straight.

She told him she was married to one of the men back at the gambling table. She thought she was sitting with her so she could keep her eyes on her. She was sitting with her because she was lonely.

The man looked so familiar. She kept looking at him. He got a little irritated and asked her why she kept looking at him.She told him he looked familiar. He said he had been coming to town for years, and he had never seen her before.

The working woman said he was a regular of hers and was from out of town. Then Chock remembered who he was. He was the farmer who had sold his farm and was building a resort in the little town they had lived in before they moved here to this town.

When she called him by his name, he looked at her a little puzzled. When he realized who she was, he was happy to see her and a little embarrassed.

She asked him, "How long have you known about this town?"

He said, "My dad brought me here while I was a little boy, and I have been coming ever since."

She asked him, "Why didn't you tell us about this town?"

He said, "I thought y'all knew, and I didn't want to talk about it, because I didn't want my wife to find out about my Saturday evening trips."

Her hubby started branching out after she started bothering him at the neighborhood club. He started going to white clubs that were out of the neighborhood—places she was not familiar with and places she couldn't walk to.

Chock was becoming an inconvenience to him. She was not where he wanted her to be. He had things set up so he could move from one place to another whenever he chose, and she was interrupting his movements—cramping his style.

One night, Chock showed up at one of those places. He got an unattached man to keep her company. He needed to run an errand and would be right back. When she finished her drink, she got ready to call a taxi. He said he didn't mind giving her a ride home. She had seen him around town for a while, so she said OK. When they got in the car, he said he had to drop off something on the way before they got to the apartments.

That man drove to a house only a few blocks from the house. From the car, she could see through the window. He was trying to set her up.

He thought when he showed her what her hubby was doing, she would fall in his arms, and she would be his putty.

She could see her hubby. She could see what he was doing to that long-haired blonde that always seemed to be around.She had heard others talk about her hubby's playing around with this woman and that woman, but she had not actually caught him in the act.

They were at a house party. They had a card game going. The guys started talking about a certain woman.

Her hubby chimed in, "I have been with almost every woman I know. I can tell you anything you want to know about them. I can tell you who is good in bed, and who is bad. I can tell you who has the best and who has the worst. I can tell you whose pussy stinks. I can tell you who has the stankiest and the sweetest pussy in town."

One of his friends told him to shut up. He was just trying to start some shit.

Chock's knowledge and imagination was limited. It never dawned on her how he had come about all of that information. She couldn't perceive in her mind what others had told her about him.

His behavior with women reminded her of her grandmother's behavior when she wanted a drink. She would keep a bottle hidden in designated spots all over the house and outside.

She would make sure when she wanted a drink, a bottle was close and convenient to her. When she took the drink, she didn't seem to enjoy drinking, but it was something she had to do—like the devil made her do it.

Her hubby had this way about him. He had no boundaries, but he wanted to be in control of others. He was never happy with what he had. He would always look around to see what others had. He thought what someone else had was better than what he had and would find a way to get it.

When he was at one place, he thought he should have been at another place. They were probably having more fun there than he was having where he was.

He did everything only when he was ready.

He only had something to eat when he was good and ready. When dinner was on the table, he wouldn't stop what he was doing to eat. Sometimes he would get so hungry he would be almost sick and be forced to stop what he was doing before he would eat anything.

Or, he would wait until Chock had put everything away. When she stopped waiting on him and had started doing something else, he would demand that she set the table again just for him.

When he finally ate, he wouldn't be satisfied with what he had. While he ate, he would talk about how good something else would be if he had it.

He would talk about it and hint around until she would feel bad and get it, so he would just shut up about it.

After she saw him with that woman, every time she went out, she would see that long-haired blonde around. She would be sitting, watching, and waiting. She would always be dressed in a long black dress looking like a witch with her hair hanging almost to the floor.

One afternoon, he took the kids for a ride. They were gone all evening. She thought it was so nice of him.

The next day, when she was putting his clothes away, she saw long blonde hair all over them.

Her seven-year-old daughter saw the hair. She said, "That's that woman's hair."

Chock asked, "What woman?"

"The woman Daddy took us to see yesterday. When we went to see her, she made us some Kool-Aid and told us to go outside and drink it. When we went outside, I looked in through the window. Daddy was on top of her and was kissing her."

When she was telling on her dad, she seemed to be as angry with her dad as the story was making her. By the time she finished telling her the story, she was livid.

She started plotting what she was going to do to him. She said to herself, *I'll fix him.*

He was coming home for lunch. She made him a sandwich with that hair and mayonnaise. When he started eating his sandwich, she asked him,

"How do you like your new hairy lunch meat?"

When he got the hair out of his mouth, he jumped up and almost killed her.

After the fight, she took the kids to her folks. She walked downtown to the pawn shop and bought a gun—a .38 caliber.

The pawn shop's owner knew all about her hubby. He had been in his shop many times. He didn't want to sell her the gun. He had an idea why she wanted the gun and called around so someone would warn her hubby; to let him know she had bought a gun. He also notified the police.

The police went to her folks' and told them about Chock buying a gun. Her brother came to the house on the pretense of looking for something he had lost.

She didn't know he knew about the gun. He looked all through the house but couldn't find what he was looking for. She had the gun in her pocket. She sat on the front porch and waited for hubby to come home. She had left her kids at her folks' for the rest of that day and the next. On Monday, she took the gun back to the pawn shop. The owner gave her ten dollars more than she had paid for it. He said he was never so happy to see something come into his shop.

CHAPTER 39

Deuce and a Quarter

Before Chock took the gun back to the pawn shop, she had decided she was going to leave her hubby. When he came home, she didn't mention the beating he had given her or ask him where he had been. She said nothing to him. There was nothing more to say. When he left, she packed up the kids, got on the train, and went to Los Angeles.

She had learned from her folks that sometimes it was better to go. When she got on the train with her kids, her folks called ahead to let her sisters in LA know she was coming. She left everything behind. When she got to Los Angeles, she had ten dollars.

When she left Idaho, in a sense, it was similar to when her parents had left Texas. She left all of a sudden to save—somebody's life. She left everything behind. She was broke. She had taken her children from where they had grown-up, the only place they knew, and from the only people they knew.

Moving to LA was a cultural shock for her as well as the kids. They also had a problem fitting in. They were the new kids in the neighborhood and a target for the neighborhood bullies.

When they arrived in Los Angeles, she moved in with her fourth sister. She had four kids, and she felt more comfortable around her. She took them in and treated them as if they were her family. She lived with her until someone turned her in to the housing authority.

She lived in a housing project in East LA. Her house had the same atmosphere their houses had when they lived in the labor camps—the center of attention.

There were always people there from the village. When she came, she couldn't spend as much time and money on the get-togethers.

When she started going out with Duce, he didn't want her hanging around the people from the village either.

They knew someone didn't want her living with her sister and had tipped off the housing authority. Someone was trying to control the both of them.

When she was turned in, she had to move out within three days or she would get evicted. She didn't have any money. She was told to go to the state. She went to the state and applied for welfare. She told them her situation.

When she left, she had an apartment close to her sister's, vouchers for clothes, and a check for more money than she had ever had in her hands. They had to sneak to her sister's apartment at night because they didn't have any furniture in their apartment.

She was in LA for about a month when she went over to visit her third sister. A friend of her husband was there. They were introduced. He was a very impressive man in his appearance and conversation. He asked her out, and she accepted.

They called him Duce after the cars he liked to drive—a deuce and a quarter. He was a well-dressed man. The first time Chock went out with him, he took her to a well-known club she had heard about—the 77 Sunset Strip.

After she saw what everyone had worn to the club, she was embarrassed at her little small town attire. The clubs and places she went to with Duce were somewhat more up scale than the ones she had been patronizing.

When she went out with him, he also wanted her to look a certain way. His friends lived in Baldwin Hills, and the clubs they went to were patronized by famous people or featured famous entertainers.

He took her to see *B. B King* one night. She saw *Isaac Hayes* another night. She saw *Etta James, Roberta Flacks, The O Jays*, and many other entertainers she had heard about, or had seen on TV, and never dreamed of seeing in person.

She had noticed the sleek, sophisticated, and sometimes risqué attire worn by the women in his circle. She had also noticed how the other women at the clubs he frequented were dressed.

The women at those clubs wore furs, leather, silk suits, and coats trimmed with leather or fur. Their jewelry was real, and their boots were tall.

Before, when she had gone out, everyone thought she looked good in what she had worn, but her little small town clothes were no match for the city clothes the women wore in LA. After going out with Duce a few times, a truck backed up to the back door of her apartment. She went out to see what was going on.

Usually vendors came to the square in the apartment complex where she lived, and everyone went out to buy what they wanted.

The truck that backed up to her back door was loaded with clothes, shoes, and other accessories. The clothes and shoes happened to be just her size. She thought it was amazing. They had come to her back door. They asked her if she wanted them to bring the clothes into the apartment so she could take a better look. She said yes. She didn't usually let strangers in her house, but the clothes were gorgeous.

Chock didn't know Duce had picked out everything in the truck and had it delivered to her. Anything she chose would be fine. She didn't mind him choosing her clothes. She wanted to be properly dressed when she went out with him. She had been conditioned to do that.

Duce had assessed her wardrobe when they had gone out for a few times. In a sense, he was no different from the man she had left and had come to LA to get away from. When she went out with him, he also wanted her to look a certain way. Basically, the men she had come to know were the same. They just went about getting what they wanted but in different ways. They all want to control. Chock kept choosing the same kind of men—the next one is more sophisticated than the last but, nevertheless, the same.

Those clothes were the clothes sold in magazines and in the expensive shops for the rich in the town she had come from in Idaho. They told her she could choose anything she wanted. Chock told them she couldn't afford that. They said it had been taken care of.

Duce took care of everything. He came by the apartment every day. He gave her money for what he thought she needed for herself, the kids, and for things he thought she needed around the apartment.

When he came by, he didn't bother to call to see if she was home. When Chock wasn't home, he would question her about where she had been and who was there.

She was very busy. She worked during the day. She went to school at night. Sometimes,Chock and her kids would go for walks or catch the bus and go sightseeing.

When she moved in with her sister, she made little girls' dresses to make money to help out her sister. She didn't know about welfare.

When school started, Chock took her kids to register, and she was astounded at all of the little girls that had on the dresses she had made. It was almost as if they had on uniforms.

When Chock took her kids to register, she was asked if she wanted to apply for a job as a teacher's aide. She applied and got the job. The state didn't cut off her aid.

They had an incentive program and would give stipends for working mothers.

They also had a program that paid mothers to go to college. Chock registered at a state college. Her state aid was doubled, and she got food stamps.

After a few months, she had a large amount of cash around the house. She needed to go shopping one day. Duce took her. When he saw how much cash she had on her, he was speechless for a second.

When he recovered from the shock, he said Chock was out of her mind walking around with all that money. She was just waiting for someone to mug her or break into her apartment and rob her. He took her to the bank, and Chock opened her very own first savings and checking account.

He also started planning outings for Chock and her children. He would come by and take them on sightseeing trips and all of the other places he thought the kids and Chock would enjoy. He took them fishing.

They would go fishing on the pier, and sometimes they would get on a fishing boat and go a long way out in the ocean. The boat trip was nice. The boat had a café and other things for amusement, but the fishing was awful. There were too many people trying to fish, and their lines would always get tangled up.

Sometimes they would go out of town for the weekend. One of Chock's sisters would keep the kids. They took a trip to San Francisco, Reno, Palm Springs, and Lake Tahoe.

Whenever they went out, the men that knew him would always seek him out. The women didn't come to their table. When Chock saw them in the ladies room, they were friendly. He would go over to different tables and would sit down and socialize for a minute, but he never invited anyone to sit at their table.

They would always have a table for themselves. If a man came by to speak to him, he would get up from the table, shake his hand, and remain standing until the man left. He never introduced Chock to any of his male friends nor did he invite them to join them at their table.

One night, he took her to a night club that was featuring a group she had a record by. They were dressed to kill—figuratively and literally speaking. He wore a black suit, tie, black shoes, black top hat, and lots of jewelry.

Chock wore a three-piece gold jersey hot pant suit with the midriff out, and gold accessories with high-heeled, brown suede, lace up boots. At twenty-four, and after four kids, Chock still had an eighteen-inch waistline.

When they got to the club, there was a line outside.

Duce marched right to the front of the line, and when the doorkeeper saw him, he let them right in. He gave the doorman a bill.

Chock was impressed.

The ladies looked at him admiringly.

When they saw he was with her, they angrily rolled their eyes away from her and turn their heads away.

The men didn't do, or say, anything. They were in LA.

When they got in the club, they were seated at a table with three other people—a woman and two men. That was the first time they had ever shared a table with someone else. Chock was seated by a man. After they got acquainted, they found out the man she was sitting by was visiting his sister.

When the band went on break, Duce excused himself and left the table. When he returned, Chock had gotten involved with the out-of-town visitor and kept talking to him after Duce had returned.

Chock guess she was ignoring Duce. He excused himself again and left the table. She didn't think much of it and kept talking to the man she was sitting by.

She got a glimpse of Duce in the crowded club coming toward the table. Chock was engrossed in the conversation.

The next thing she heard was a maniacal laugh and Duce's voice.

The man Chock was talking with stopped talking. His head went back and his hands went up at the same time.

"Mother f—, you trying to steal my woman from me right under my nose?"

Chock looked up. Duce had a gun pointed at the man she had been talking to.

The man tried to explain, "Naw, man, I—" That was all he said before the gun went off.

Chock thought she had been shot. There was blood everywhere.

Mayhem broke loose. People were running and screaming all over the place.

The only reason she didn't move because she was in a daze and too scared.

The other two people at the table were screaming at Duce, and the sister was trying to help her brother. Duce just put the gun on the table and took a seat and waited for the police.

When they came, they seemed to know him. They asked him a few questions, and then took them to the police station.

When they got to the police station, they talked to him for a little while and put him in a cell to wait for his attorney.

While he was waiting for his attorney, a tough-acting, uniformed cop came up to the cell Duce was being held in. That white cop kept hitting the bars with his stick and was looking at Duce all mean as if he was going to do something with it.

He said, "If you weren't already handcuffed and locked up in there, I would beat the hell out of your black ass!"

Duce said, "If you don't get away from me, I'll bite you to death!"

The detective sitting behind the desk said, "You better get away from there and leave him alone 'cause he'll do it."

The detective asked Chock a few questions, but she didn't know any of the answers.

He said, "A little girl like you should not be mixed up with gangsters like him."

"A gangster?"

"I thought you knew. He is well known in LA."

Chock didn't know anything about Duce. She didn't know if he had a mother, father, son, daughter, or wife. She just went out with him. He seemed all right because her sister and her husband knew him.

Chock doesn't know what the outcome was in reference to the man he shot or what happened to Duce for shooting him. She didn't want to know. She never wanted to talk about it. She was afraid she would say the wrong thing to the wrong person. She didn't know what would happen to her. She was an eyewitness to a shooting, and he was a gangster.

When the detective finished talking to her, he told Chock she could go. She could call someone to come and get her or a patrol car could drive her home. Chock called her sister. It was almost morning when she came to the station to get Chock.

While she was there, she went over to talk to Duce and to tell him she was taking Chock home. When she came back, she was crying.

She said he told her when he got out, he was going to throw her over the bridge into the LA River.

After that night, Chock was terrified of Duce. When he got out of jail, he wanted to move in with her. That was the first time she said no to him. Chock had gone along with him calling all the shots up until then.

He tried everything he could think of to bribe her into letting him live with her, but Chock held her grounds. The answer was definitely a no. The more he tried, the more suspicious Chock became as to his motives. The more she said no, the more suspicious he became. He said the reason she didn't want him to move in was she had someone coming around at night to see her.

Under no circumstance would she ever allow a man to live with her while she had young children. Chock knew what could happen to a child at night after she fell asleep. That was never going to happen to any kid of hers.

His routine and behavior changed. He started coming by the apartment early in the morning before Chock got out of bed, and late at night after she got in bed, and throughout the day. She knew he was checking up on her. Any man that came by during any of those times knew not to come back.

Vendors would come to that apartment complex. A lot of people living there didn't have transportation to go shopping. And some of them had no desire to venture away from the apartments.

The vendors would drive down the streets while someone with a megaphone would advertise what they had to sell. When the meat truck came, Chock went out and bought enough meat for the week.

The next morning, she was awakened with the smell of something cooking and whatever was being cooked smelled something awful. She went downstairs. Duce was making hamburgers for breakfast. He had the door open and was swearing at the top of his lungs while trying to fan the smell away.

When he saw Chock, he asked her where in the hell had she bought that meat from. She told him about the meat truck. He finished cleaning up his mess and left.

Later that day, another truck backed up to the back door of the apartment.

Chock assumed it was the truck bringing another batch of clothes.

When she went out, she saw the meat truck. Chock told them that she didn't want any more meat from them. When they got closer, she noticed they had been in a bad fight. They had cut and knots and bruises all over their head, face, legs, and arms. She didn't know if she should be talking to them or not.

They said they came to get the meat she had bought from them the day before. They went on to explain that they had given her the wrong batch and wanted it back.

Chock gave them back all the meat except the hamburger Duce had cooked. They refunded her money. They said she could pick out anything she wanted from the truck.

Chock went in the truck. She wasn't sure she should trust them. Chock noticed that everything looked good. She decided to pick out a ham and some bacon.

Chock wanted to play it safe this time. She said that was all she wanted. They said she could have anything she wanted at no charge. "Why?"

They said Duce had sent them, and they wanted to make sure she was happy.

They started unloading everything they thought Chock needed with four kids.

When they finished, they said, "Lady, when we come here again, don't come to the truck to buy anything from us. We don't want your business."

When Duce came over that evening, he looked in the refrigerator. He said, "I see the guys brought the meat over."

Chock was more afraid of Duce than ever, but she wasn't intimidated enough to let him move in.

They had been gone for almost two years before the kids father started calling to talk to them. Duce's behavior was getting more erratic than ever.

By the time the earthquake came, Chock was ready to leave LA, but the earthquake finalized the decision for her. The bedrooms were upstairs. Chock had just put the kids to bed. She went into her room. She thought she heard planes coming. She went to the window and let it up and stuck her head out to look around to see if she could get a glimpse of the planes.

They sounded as if they might be in trouble coming in that low. The noise sounded like the noise that had been made by the planes in a movie Chock had seen. The noise sounded like the noises made when the planes were coming in and attacking Pearl Harbor.

She stood in the second-story window looking out. All the dogs in LA started barking, and every alarm on every car went off. She felt the floor vibrate, and then she felt a jolt. And everything started tumbling down around her. Chock had to hold on to the window sill to keep from being thrown through the window.

Chock heard the kids screaming. She tried to go to their room to get them. She was thrown on the floor. She couldn't stand up; the floor was moving. She had to get down and crawl to their bedroom to get them. They finally managed to get down the stairs. They were there for a while before all the rumbling and noises stopped. When she could hear nothing from outside and the rumbling and everything had stopped moving inside, she took the kids back upstairs. She told them to find their warmest clothes and hiking shoes. They were going back to their big momma and big daddy's house.

Chock got dressed in the warmest clothes she could find. She packed their backpacks with things they would need on a long hiking trip. When they were ready, she opened the door. What she saw scared her just as much as the earthquake had.

Chock saw no one. At that time of night, the village usually came alive. There would be people everywhere talking aloud, playing loud music, shooting crap, cursing, fighting, shooting guns, cars coming and going, shots, and sometimes a killing. But then, after the earthquake, there was not a sound coming from anywhere, or a word coming from anyone. The streets were completely deserted, and the cars were still and silent.

If all of those tough people were in, it was not a time for her to be out. Chock slammed the door shut. They fell asleep on the sofa. They were too scared to go upstairs because the tremors kept coming.

The next morning, they went outside to take a look and to see what had happened. When she opened the door, her neighbor came out and spoke to her for the first time since she had moved there almost two years earlier. Everyone was friendly and helpful until the aftershocks stopped. When they stopped, everyone was still a little friendlier.

Later that day, the kid's daddy called to see if they were all right. They were happy to hear from him. That was probably the best thing that could have happened to them after what they had gone through that night.

After that day, he called the kids often. After the kids talked to their dad, they would give her the phone.

"Daddy wants to talk to you."

They would look at her with those sad eyes.

Chock knew he put them up to it. After a few calls, he started to sound like the person she knew before they got married. He promised he had changed, and he wanted them to come back.

She knew she had to leave LA and go somewhere. Chock's sister was hoping she would leave too. She was also afraid of Duce. Some of the neighbor men, who were her friends or husbands of her friends, told her what he had said to them when he saw them at her apartment.

After Chock talked to the kid's dad a few more times, she decided to take them back to Idaho. She needed help. She needed someone that would go to the stores to get a bottle of aspirins, if need be, so she didn't have to leave them alone.

Chock didn't know if she would get with their dad when she got back. She just had to wait and see. Then, she knew she could take care of herself and would do what she had to do to take care of her kids. She was more afraid of staying in LA than she was of going back to Idaho. When Chock told Duce she had decided to move back to Idaho, he was furious.

He said, "All this time, I knew what was going on. You and that no-good-for-nothing husband of yours have been fucking over the telephone. Now you can't wait to get back to him."

He started to cry.

That made Chock really scared.

While he was crying, he said, "I should get rid of you right now!"

He finally calmed down and left. When he left, Chock intensified her preparations in getting the kids things ready to go.

Chock didn't have to worry about packing food. She packed two big bags and called her sister.

She brought the kids to the apartment. They packed up the car. They were out of there in record time. Chock's sister took them to the train station. She said she would pack up everything and send it to her later.

CHAPTER 40

Midnight Train to Idaho

Chock felt as if she was on a merry-go-round when she got on the train. She left California and went back to Idaho. They arrived in Idaho around noon the next day. The kid's dad had talked her folks into letting him pick them up. They were happy to see their dad when they got off the train. She was a little apprehensive.

He took them over to her folks' house. Her mom was also happy to see them. She saw her coming back as getting back with the kid's dad. She said they were welcome to stay with them while she got everything straightened out with their father. She went on to say it was her place to be with her husband, and the kids needed their dad.

They stayed with her folks for a couple of days. Chock's parents were happier to see the kid's dad than they were to see her. He dropped in whenever he felt like it. While he was there, he would plead with Chock in front of her folks, as if he was about to cry, to come home and give him another chance; he had learned his lesson, and if she would give him another chance, he would prove it.

Chock gave up, and they moved back into the same house she had left two and a half years earlier. Everything in the house was almost as she had left it.

There were a few undertones she didn't quite understand, but Chock and her kids basically went back to the life they had before they moved to California.

The only difference was Chock didn't sit at home waiting for her hubby to come home. She applied for a student loan and enrolled in college.

Chock's hubby, friends, and neighbor were not supportive. When they learned of her plans to go back to school, they laughed and said she was just wasting her time, because no one was going to hire a black teacher to teach their kids. The only ones who encouraged her to go back to school were the working women and her parents.

Chock's hubby was happy about the loan money when her loan came through, but he wasn't happy about the time she spent away from home. Before, he would always know where she would be.

Chock didn't have a car, and she didn't know how to drive. As a way to keep track of her, he would drop her off. She would always have to wait for him to pick her up. He flatly refused to teach her how to drive. When Chock tried to teach herself, he had her arrested for stealing his car. He didn't realize it was her car too.

He was losing some of his control over her, and he was not happy about it at all. Chock got into college life. She was older than the girls going to school, but some of the boys were her age and older. They were always happy to give her a ride to places they hung out.

Chock went to the fraternity parties, and on weekends and holidays, they hung out at her house. She partied so much she almost flunked out during the first semester. She wasn't at his beck and call anymore. When she was home, she spent as much time as she could with her kids. The time she had left, she spent studying. When her hubby was home, they spent that time arguing and fighting with each other.

About three months after she moved back to Idaho, their lives had digressed beyond what had made her leave him in the first place. They were thrown out of their house. They were evicted. Her hubby refused to use his money to pay rent.

He said his money was for his fun, and if there was anything left over, she could use it for the house.

After Christmas, they had to move. Chock's kids had to change schools again. They moved to a so-called white section. Their neighbors weren't too happy about them moving into their neighborhood.

The kids were called names and were chased by the neighbor's dog when they walked by on their way to school. She made that dog a special hamburger.

When Chock got accustomed to her new life of going to school and doing homework, she started venturing out with friends, attending social events, and sometimes she went out alone.

On one of those nights when she decided to go out alone, she looked in the closet to find something to wear out;she saw the three-piece hot pant outfit she had worn that night in LA. The suit was practically a two-piece swimsuit with a matching, long fitted smock. She didn't think the cleaners would be able to get the blood out, but they had.

She put the outfit on.She also put on a long Cleopatra wig. When she got to the club, no one recognized her at first.

She was at the bar talking to some of their friends when she heard her hubby come in. He always had to make a grand entrance to let everyone know he had arrived.

When he approached,Chock turned her back to him so he wouldn't see her face. She had just ordered a drink. When the drink came, he said, "Let me get that for you."

He paid for the drink.

"You don't look like you from here. You must be new in town?" Chock shook her head again.

"Wow! You don't talk much. A beautiful girl like you shouldn't be so shy."

She kept shaking he head up and down to answer his questions to prevent him from hearing her voice.

"Why don't we get a table and get better acquainted. I sure would like to get to know you better. I bet you are as beautiful with that outfit off as you are with it on."

Chock hadn't heard his voice that soft and mellow since they had gotten married.

She was amused at first, but she started to get angry. She kept playing along to see how far he would go.

After a few minutes,their friends were so tickled they couldn't hold it in anymore. They burst out laughing. "Man, you trying to pick up on your own wife!

She turned around.

He almost swallowed his cigarette but managed to say, "Oh my God!" Chock was so disgusted. She just looked at him and left the club. She was more than happy to go out alone and to attend the social events alone.She tried to leave her hubby out of her social life. She didn't wan t to go through the drama of what she was wearing, or who she talked to, or how she talked to someone. She went out alone, came home alone, slept alone except for the wee hours of the morning when he did come home.

Their kids talked her into planning a surprise birthday party for their dad. Chock should have known better, but they had their hearts set on giving him a party. If it wasn't his idea, it wasn't a good idea.

On Christmas Eve, Chock would always have an open house. Since she had started teaching, she invited the faculty, those that didn't feel like hanging her from the flagpole, to stop by.

Four of her coworkers and some of their friends showed up. The house was beautifully decorated. The table was set with silver and crystals; a fire was burning in the fire place, and the food was to die for.

Chock had a real Christmas tree decorated with presents all around it. Everyone was having a good time eating, laughing, and drinking, listening to Christmas carols, and just relaxing. About nine o'clock, her ex came home drunk and started yelling at the kids and cursing at her. She asked him to please keep his voice down as they had company.

He grabbed the Christmas tree, decorations and all, still plugged up and threw it out the front door in the snow. Somehow, that seemed to short circuit the lights. All the lights in the house went out. There we were sitting in the dark. Chock knew her coworkers were frightened out of their minds.

The kids thought it was funny. She could hear them giggling in the dark. They were always laughing at some of the antics their dad and Chock were pulling on each other. She always felt badly about some of the things she did to get back at him. Her parents had taught her better, but she felt she had to fight back.

They finally got the lights back on, but the party was spoiled. Everyone politely excused themselves and left. Chock made a vow never to bring her work home with her and never take her home to work. At one of the kid's parties, their dad had mentioned he had never had a birthday party. They made plans, and they told everyone about the party. Everyone who wanted to come was welcome. Chock spent two days cooking and planning for his surprise party. Almost everyone they knew came but the birthday boy.

He showed up the next morning. When he got home, she was dressed and ready to go. He tried to explain saying he was with all the friends, who were at his party, in a big poker game, and the next thing he knew, it was day outside.

He was relieved Chock was going out. He was too tired to be bothered trying to answer her questions. He was so relieved to see her go he volunteered to stay with the kids until she got back.

Chock went and got a room at a close by motel and spent the night. When she got home, he was too mad. He was puffing on a cigarette and blowing smoke like a bull. She could see the muscles in his face contracting.

"Where you been?"

"Out with my friends," she said sweetly.

"What could you and your friends be doing up until now?" "Doing the same things you were doing with your friends when you were out." Chock got almost another killing.

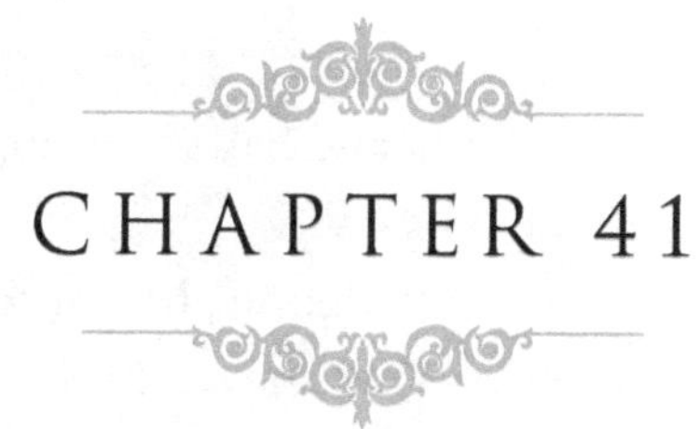

CHAPTER 41

You Got to Love Somebody

Chock was married, but she was lonely. Almost everything she did, if it didn't involve the kids or school, she did it alone.

The college student she had met while she was in high school was also going to those events alone. He was hanging around her hubby and her hubby's different set of friends.

They were thrown together by coincidence and on demand. When her hubby was out and something needed to be done at home, he would send this guy to take care of it, so he wouldn't have to come home. One night, Chock went out alone. When she got ready to go home, her friend offered to give her a ride. That was a routine until one night,they didn't want to be apart. They didn't want to go home and leave the other. They had grown together. They had a number of common interests and were comfortable being together.

They just knew what the other was thinking. Both of them were married, but their spouses had different interests. When they attended any function, they attended alone.They talked about what being together would do to their families. They thought the best thing to do was to tell their spouses and stop sneaking around.

The night Chock told her spouse about them was not the night she was supposed to tell him. What happened after she told him was not what she had anticipated at all.

Whenever she went out, she was always managed to get home before he got home. That night when she got home, he was already home. He had lost all of his money gambling and had come home to get the money he had left for her to pay the bills.

When he saw that Chock wasn't home, he stayed home until she got there. When she walked in the door, she could tell whatever was going to happen would not be good. He was smoking. Smoke was coming out of his nostrils.

Chock had so many boundaries put around her about what was right and what was wrong. She just got tired of trying to lie herself out of the situation. She also got angry. He had his nerves after all the women and stunts he had pulled.

She told him, "I want a divorce." "Is there someone else?"

"Yes."

"Who?"

"You can tell me. I won't get mad. Go ahead, tell me."

He finally convinced her that it was safe to tell him who the man was. After his constant questions, Chock, like a fool, gave him the name of the man she was involved with and told him they were in love and wanted to be together.

"In love? You gonna sit there and tell me you in love? I knew you were seeing somebody, but I thought you were doing it for money, and you gonna tell me you in love!"

If she thought he was angry before, it was nothing compared to his reaction when she gave him her friend's name and told him she was in love.

Chock doesn't think her hubby and she were ever in love. They loved each other and they loved their kids. They loved each other for what they saw and what others saw on the outside.

They never grew up enough to learn about the inside. They didn't know how being in love made one feel about the other. He wasn't taught, and she hadn't learned.

Maybe he knew about love when he was young, before his mother died. Maybe he prayed for someone to love him the way he had been loved and should have been loved.

Maybe, their children were the answer to his prayer. Maybe, through Chock, his prayers were answered. They had given him unconditional love, but he didn't realize it. He was still going from place to place searching.

Chock had the love of her parents and family. And she loved her children. She never knew love between a man and a woman, not even when the man put his hand over her mouth and said he loved her. She could never put love and sex in the same sentence before she started seeing her friend.

When she told him she was in love with someone other than him, he knew he had lost all of his control on her. Then he lost all of his control. He picked up the phone and called the man's wife and told her about her husband and Chock. He woke their kids up and told them about her in the most derogative terms he could think off. Then he called her folks to tell them what she had done to him, but they were out of town. He destroyed the phones when he finished his calls.

He loaded his shotgun and went to the kitchen and put a knife in each back pocket. He went outside, got in his car, and speed away. When he left home, Chock got the kids dressed, and they ran to my niece's house, which was in another part of town.

He went to all the bars he patronized. He told everyone why he had a gun and two knives.

He went to the neighborhood bar after he left the other bars. By then, he was drunk from all the pity drinks his friends had bought him.

Chock's friend was there shooting pool.

Chock's hubby went in hollering and cursing him. He pointed the gun at him while he was doing all of that talking.

She got the details from a friend that was there with her husband. "I'm going to blow your m—f—head off."

Her friend wasn't aware she had told her hubby about them. He replied, "What for?"

"You know what for, you mf!"

Someone managed to talk him out of pulling the trigger.

The police came and took him home and told him to sleep it off.

He started attacking my niece's house the next morning. The noise he was making, trying to get inside, made her think about the tornado that had destroyed their house when she was a little girl.

They didn't go out, and they didn't let him in. Chock had to keep the kids inside. She was afraid he would take them and use them as a leverage to make her come outside. He finally gave up and went home.

He came back that night; he had a robe on over his underwear.

They called the police again. This time, a policeman riding a bike came. He tried to talk to her hubby in a civil manner, but her hubby was having no part of it.

"Mister, you need to leave or I will have to take you in."

"You go tell me you gonna arrest me for just wanting to talking to my wife?"

"Your wife called and said you were being disruptive. If you don't leave, I will have to take you in."

"How you go take me in, m—f—? On that motorcycle?"

Click, click. The officer put the handcuffs on him. He led him to the motorcycle, put him on the back, and took off.

They just had to laugh while watching them ride away. It was such a funny sight watching the two of them ride off on the motorcycle, and her hubby's robe flying in the air behind them.

The next day, Chock knew she had to leave. Her niece's house wasn't equipped for another adult and four kids. They had nothing left in the house to eat, and there were not enough beds for the kids.

Chock decided to take the kids over to her folks. She knew they were still out of town, but they never locked their doors.

When she got to her folks' house, shew as exhausted. She hadn't slept for more than a few minutes all the time she was at her niece's house.

Chock felt safe at her folks' house. She didn't think he would come in her folks' house and bother her. She fell asleep. The kids must have felt comfortable too. They went outside to play with their cousins who were visiting and staying with her eldest sister across the street.

While they were outside, her hubby sneaked in the house.

Chock felt a blow to her head, and everything got blurry. She tried to defend herself, but she was too groggy. He pulled her off the bed and started stomping her.

One of the working women told her later that he was drunk when he came in the bar and had been in the bar drinking since it opened. All of his friends, men and women, were there buying him drinks. Some of the women were consoling him, and others were egging him on saying what their husbands would do to them if they did something like that. She said, "I told you them sorry bitches were going to get you hurt one day.

"He was breaking things and knocking things over. The kids must have heard the commotion coming from the house. They went across the street to get Chock's sister. She saw her come into the room. She grabbed her hubby and threw him against the wall as if he was a rag doll.

The police came. They asked Chock what happened. She couldn't talk at first. When she was able to talk, she couldn't remember anything. She didn't know her own name.

They told her sister she should take Chock to the hospital. They said Chock needed to be looked at.

When Chock got to the hospital, they asked her what had happened to her. Chock told them she was attacked by a dog.

When Chock was released from the hospital, she went to her folks' to get the kids. Her hubby had taken them home with him. She felt she had no choice, but to go home and be with her kids.

She went home. He behaved as if nothing had happened.

When Chock's folks got home, he went over and told them the whole story of how she made him lose his temper. He cried on Chock's mom's shoulder until she got angry with her. She came to the house and said she had embarrassed her again and that she would never forgive her for what she had done to her.

Chock talked to her friend a few times, but they didn't see each other again. After a while, he left town. He felt that it was the best thing to do before someone got hurt. He had become an outcast among her hubby and his friends.

She was an outcast among her friends. Chock's married friends' husbands had forbidden them to have anything to do with her. They said she was a bad influence on their wives.

The wives were angry because their husbands were watching them like hawks. They couldn't get out of their house. When they did get out, their husbands went with them.

Chock's hubby stayed around home a little more for about three months. When he felt he was in control again, and it was safe for him to leave her home, he continued his street life.

When her friend left town, her hubby went back into his street life with full speed. Then, he felt entitled after what she had done to him. Chock was sorry for the pain and embarrassment she had caused her kids. She concentrated on trying to make it up to them. She had a year left in school, and when they went to bed, she stayed home and studied.

Things went along smoothly. She just let her hubby do as he pleased and didn't bother to ask questions.

CHAPTER 42

Going Rogue

After three years of cramming and getting her brains bashed in at the same time, Chock finally finished school. She hadn't planned on marching in the graduation exercise. She just wanted her diploma so she could get a job.

Chock's hubby, her kids, and her mom and dad talked her into marching so they could come to see her graduate. She went along and made all of the arrangements.

On the day of the ceremony, she had to be there two hours early to line up.

Chock's hubby took her and went back home for the kids.

After she marched out, she waited by the prearranged door for them to come out. No family ever came out of the doors.

Maybe they had gone to the wrong door. She walked to the side of the building to see if they were at any of the other entrances. Not a soul.

Chock went in and called home. Her daughter told her that when she got her diploma, their dad took them home. He told them that the ceremony would take hours, and he didn't want to stay until it ended. He took them home and said he was going back to get her later.

It was a hot day. Chock didn't have anything on but her underwear, the cap, gown, and high-heeled shoes.

Her feet were killing her, so she had taken off the shoes. She could have walked home. She had walked to school when the weather would permit, but with comfortable shoes.

Someone from the cleaning crew came out and told Chock if she needed to use the phone again, she had better do it then, because they were ready to leave.

Chock called home again. The kids said their dad hadn't made it back. She told them to call around to the bars and leave a message for him telling him to pick her up.

The cleaning crew left. She was there outside all alone. She finally got tired of standing and sat down on the curb.

When she had the chance, she should have called someone else, but she kept thinking he would be there any minute.

The ceremony was over before two thirty. When he finally picked her up, it was almost seven o'clock.

Chock didn't say a word. She just got in the car and rode home in silence.

When she got home, her kids had planned a little party for her. They had a cake and other goodies, and their presents were on the dining room table.

She snatched everything off the table and threw it in the garbage.

Then, she went in the bedroom and locked the door.

When she calmed down she knew it wasn't their fault that she had been stranded. She took everything out of the garbage and apologized to them for being angry.

They were also upset with their dad, but he was nowhere around. She guess he had gone back to finish what he had been doing before he picked her up.

They had their little celebration, and Chock never ask her hubby where he had been. She never talked to him about it.

When their anniversary came around the next month, he planned for them to spend some time together.

Her mom agreed to keep the kids. He went to the meat market and had two steaks cut for their dinner. She was to have everything ready, and when he got home, he would fix the steaks.

Chock had the potatoes in the stove. The salad in the refrigerator, and the asparagus were ready to be steamed.

The wine was chilling and the table was set with candles, crystals, the best china and silver, and fancy folded napkins.

Chock had taken a class while she was in college for self-improvement. She had been inspired by her Momma's homemaking skills to take the class. Momma always believed in setting the table and making it look good. Chock wanted everything to be just right. Maybe this dinner was just what they needed to get them back on track.

She put on her best lingerie and waited. He should have been home by five. She waited until about seven, and he still wasn't home.

By eight, she had gotten dressed and went to look for him.

Chock got in the car and drove to his nearest hang-outs. Then she drove over town. Just as she was pulling in the entrance to the parking lot from the back, she saw his car leaving the parking lot by the front exit. That was also the parking for one of his favorite bars.

It was still light enough for her to recognize their little station wagon. Chock went closer to the car. There was a blonde sitting so close to him she didn't see her at first. There was another woman in the backseat.

He had his arm around the woman in the front seat and was kissing her. He was so engrossed with her that he wasn't aware Chock was right behind him.

He pulled out in the street and headed up the main street of the town. He was taking his dear time.

Chock followed him. He drove for about ten minutes more before she was fed up.

When he stopped at a red light, Chock bumped him. He got out and looked at the back of his car. He was never looking at the driver of the other car instead he waved to indicate no damage was done.

He got back in his car and continued on his merry way hugging and kissing on the woman in the front seat with him.

Chock followed behind him as he continued to drive up the town's favorite strip.

Before they got to the next light, a police car had cruised up in the right-hand lane with the traffic.

When Jimmy stopped at the second red light, Chock really slammed into him. She caught his eye in the mirror. When he recognized Chock, he stepped on the gas.

The police car put on the siren. They were racing up the strip and being chased by a police car.

When they got to the third light, another patrol car had blocked the lanes.

They had to stop.

When Jimmy stopped his car, Chock pulled up on the medium beside his car. He jumped out of his car and started running. He was tackled by one of the cops.

When he jumped out of his car and ran, Chock went to the door he had left opened. She grabbed the woman by her blonde hair and dragged her out of the car.

When the other officer came up, he told Chock to let her go. He said,

"What the hell's going on here? "Y'all crazy or something?"

The other officer came back with her hubby. They knew each other well and seemed to be having a friendly conversation.

The officer called him by his first name and told Jimmy to get in his car and leave.

The policeman said he was going to give him a ten-minute head start before he let She Chock go.

They put the girls in the backseat of the other squad car. Then Chock was told to get in her car and go home.

Chock went home and got dressed to kill. She put her favorite knife in her purse. She drove to the bar where she had seen her hubby leaving with the two women.

When she got to the club, Chock sat in a booth where she had a good view of everything and waited for him. knew he was going to show up. All of the booths had bubble bowl candles lit and sitting in the middle of the tables. was there about an hour before he showed up.

He had gone home and changed. When he came in, he didn't make his usual grand entrance. The only indication of how he felt was the way he was puffing on a cigarette and blowing smoke like a bull. Otherwise, he was acting cool.

Just by looking at them, no one would have ever guessed what they had been up to about an hour earlier.

He saw Chock sitting in a booth while he was walking downstairs.

She was alone and was waiting for him to start something.

He went to the bar. He saw one of his friends there talking to a big blonde.

He went to join his friend and ordered a drink.

When the blonde saw him, she came and stood by the other side of him. She was known as an AAA woman—anywhere, anytime, anybody's woman.

Chock's hubby started flirting with her. She could see he was looking in the mirror behind the bar watching her.

They kept getting a little too friendly with each other as if she wasn't even there. His flirting kept getting a little bit bolder.

Chock should have left. If she left, he would follow. She did not want him to get to her when she was alone. When he got her alone, he would make her pay for what she had done to him in public.

Chock was still boiling mad about what he had done to her. He had her planning an evening with him at home, and he had no intention of showing up. It was just another way of keeping her busy at home.

After a couple of drinks, Chock had reached her breaking point. She picked up the candle from the table and aimed it at the back of his head. He turned to say something to his friend when the candle hit the side of his head, and the wax splattered out and ran down his face.

The friend standing beside him told everyone when he heard her hubby yowling; he turned around and saw a waxed sculpture.

Jimmy went to the bathroom and cleaned himself up. Chock knew when he came out of the bathroom she would have to fight. She was ready.

When he came out of the bathroom, he was laughing with his friend.

He looked at Chock. His look told her, "I'll take care of you later."

His moment came when Chock saw a familiar face coming down the stairs. She hadn't seen him for years. He was the most gorgeous man she had ever seen, barring none.

Chock watched as he made his self-assured entrance. He was glancing around as if he was looking for someone.

When he saw her looking at him, he started smiling. He was making his way over to Chock's table when her hubby greeted him.

Her hubby was standing close to the table where Chock was sitting. He ordered a drink and stood talking to her hubby. She didn't know they were acquainted.

He was still looking at Chock while he was talking to her hubby. Her hubby noticed him looking at her and said, "Man, you know my wife?"

He said, "Your wife? We were in school together. I didn't know she was who you married. I'll just over and say hi."

Vic came over and sat down. Patrick Swayze, Brad Pitt, and Robert Redford had to be rolled into one to get an idea of how Chock felt about that guy.

He had a band when they were in school. He would play at the assemblies and school dances. The girls would go crazy. They would scream and cry as if he was Elvis. In school, he was a skinny, unkept looking kid, with long blond hair.

He was about Elvis's size but he was blond.

He played in a few of the lounges around town before he started traveling. He said he was between gigs and came to visit his family. He had a couple of hours to kill before he had to go to the airport.

They had never spent any time alone together, but when he saw Chock at school, he would always smile, and sometime he would stop to speak.

Chock happened to run into him a few times at the clubs where his band was playing, and he always find time to stop by her table. Several times he had asked her to come up on the stage to do a number with him. By then, both of them had gotten married. One night, he asked Chock why she never wanted to talk to him when they were in school.

She really didn't know why, except, her future hubby was monopolizing all of her time, and she wasn't into trying to talk to boys she wasn't familiar with.

They were older now. He was divorced, and Chock was not happy. She enjoyed watching him on stage and hearing him sing. That boy knew how to walk. He knew how to talk, and he knew all the dances. When she saw him coming down the stairs, she forgot all about her troubles. They had a good time drinking and laughing about old times.

They talked for about thirty minutes. He said he had to go before he missed his plane.

Chock had let her guard down. She was still basking in the glow of Vic's visit when she felt a lick upside of her head.

Immediately after her friend left, Chock's hubby came over and hit her. He turned away quickly before she could react, and walked away as if he had done nothing.

When her attention was on the person talking to her, he would come over and hit her. He did that every time she would take her eyes off him. He hit her about three times.

He was standing with his cousin. They were looking at Chock with that "what you gonna do about it" look. He wanted her to come up and do something. Then everyone would think she had started a fight for nothing.

Chock turned to her hubby and said, "You better not do that again."

Then Chock said to his cousin, "You better not be standing by him if he hits me again."

Chock turned away and pretended she wasn't watching him. She saw him come up and raise his fist; when he did, Chock swung at him with the knife. The blade caught him across his forehead.

Blood squirted out of the cut onto his cousin.

His cousin started yelling, "She cut me. She cut me!"

Chock's hubby ran out of the bar with blood running down his face.

A few minutes later, Chock got a call from the hospital. He gave the nurse the number to the club to call her. She called the club and asked for Chock.

The nurse in the emergency room knew them by their first names. Chock had been at the hospital several times with the kids and getting patched up from their fights. When the kids happened to get hurt, she would call Chock and let her know if she should come to the hospital.

When Chock got to the phone, the nurse told her she should come to the hospital. Her husband was there, and he was hysterical and was asking for Chock. They couldn't tell what was wrong with him. He said he wouldn't let them touch him until Chock got to the hospital. They needed to see what was wrong with him so they could stop the bleeding. Chock told her she wasn't coming.

Next, a friend of theirs called. He was at the hospital. He said Chock needed to come because her hubby was in bad shape. He might lose an eye.

Chock drove to the hospital. When he saw her, he reached his hand out and grabbed on to her like a drowning man. Chock thought she had really hurt him. He was crying that fake cry while he clung onto her hand.

He had to get two stitches. Chock drove him home.

The next time she saw her dad, he told Chock, "Gurl, you can't go around fussing and fighting to make people see things your way. When you have to fuss and fight about something, you already lost, 'cause you forget what you fighting bout and do everything you can just to win." Chock had forgotten about what she was fighting about. She was trying to top what had been done to her and didn't think about what she was doing to her kids.

Chock had to leave or she had to play the hand she had been dealt. She just stayed and took the beatings. When she couldn't take it, and if she felt like it, she would fight back. Chock fought back until the kids tried to intervene and were put in harm's way trying to stop their dad from shooting her.

Chock didn't realize what she was doing to her kids. She was determined to stay with their dad until all of them graduated. She almost made it.

CHAPTER 43

Hey! Hey! Good-Bye

Chock tried to live up to the deadline she had given herself, but their life at home was becoming unbearable. The final straw came when she was attacked by one of her hubby's girlfriends and her mother.

She decided to go out one night. The kids were out, and she was alone. Chock got dressed and went to one of the clubs where she knew some of their acquaintances would be. Her hubby was there. After a few guys made a fuss over her outfit and how she looked, her hubby decided to come over and mark his territory.

After a drink, he suggested that she go home and he would meet Chock there.

Like a fool, Chock believed him again. She got in the car and started home.

Chock decided to take a shortcut and drive through their old neighborhood. When she got to one of the hole-in-the-walls in their neighborhood, his car was parked out in front. Chock got out and went in to see what was going on. There he was, hugged up, with one of his girlfriends.

They had a few words, and he left. The girl and her mother were not too happy about Chock being there and him leaving. She turned around to leave, and she was hit over the head with a beer bottle. The blow knocked her down. Then the two of them attacked her. When the two women finished kicking and stumping her, they pushed her out the door and locked it. She was left lying outside on the ground.

Chock managed to get up, get in the car, and drive home. When her kids saw the condition she was in, they asked her what happened. She told them about the beating. Their dad was home, but after they heard the story her kids told her, "Momma, you need to leave Dad." On Monday of the following week, Chock found a lawyer and filed for a divorce.

Chock had told him many times before that she was going to get a divorce, and many times she had changed her mind and didn't go through with it.

And this time was no different. When Chock told him she had filed for a divorce, he didn't believe her. When he was served with the divorce papers, he went to the kids and tried his pity tricks. He opened up his floodgate and told them she didn't want him around anymore. His next stop was to her folks.

Momma came to give her the "a woman's place" talk. She said, "He'll come around directly. If the streets didn't slow him down, Father Time would."

This time Chock wanted out. She didn't want to sit around and wait for Father Time.

He was served the divorce papers but would not leave. In his words, he thought the kids and her mom would bring her to Chock's senses, and she would call it off like before.

He had time to leave the house on his own. He refused, and Chock had to call law enforcement to escort him out of the house.

When the police came, he tried his pity tricks on the kids again. "See what your mother is doing to me?"

"You'll be next. She'll get tired of you too, and she won't stop until she gets rid of you too."

The kids didn't say a word.

Chock felt their pain as they watched their dad being escorted out of the house by the police.

The police had been at their house many times. That was the first time they had told him he had to leave. Before, they would tell him to walk around the block and cool off. Even when he had threatened to shoot Chock, they had just come, taken the gun, and walked him down the street.

Chock don't know when he decided to get an apartment. He could have had one all along. After he was escorted out by the police, he moved into his apartment. Some white woman moved in with him.

He would come by whenever he felt like coming by. His excuse was he missed the kids. He had been away longer when he lived with them, and sometimes would not see them for days.

A court date had been set. When Chock and her attorney showed up for the hearing, he showed up without an attorney.

He gave the judge his hard luck and pity story. The judge gave him an extension to give him time to get legal representation.

He thought by the time the other hearing came around, Chock would have changed her mind.

He didn't bother to show up at the next hearing. She was given an uncontested divorce.

CHAPTER 44

Oh My Goodness

When Jimmy, now her ex, heard he was divorced, he was outraged.

He said, "Why didn't you call and remind me that I had to be in court?"

The divorce didn't stop him from coming by whenever he had the urge. Again, he would use the kids as an excuse for coming by whenever he felt like stopping by. He went overboard with treats and presents. He would take them out to get something to eat and would bring something back home for her.

Pretty soon, they started asking Chock to go with them. Pretty soon, she did. Pretty soon, she started going out when the kids were busy doing other things. When she went out with him, he was the person she had met on the playground.

He tried to be affectionate, but Chock couldn't get all of his meanness out of her head. Chock never stopped to think he was up to his old tricks again and was trying to get her under his control.

There was a good chance he would have succeeded and worn her down. He was not successful because divine intervention stepped in.

Chock's high school friend showed up. Vic looked even more gorgeous than the last time she had seen him.

He found out that Chock was divorced and came to see how she was getting along.

After a short time, she was doing just fine.

Chock had known him for years. She was surprised by how comfortable they were together. He was in that 'all you need is love' time period and love was all she needed at the time.

She always thought he was divine, but she had never thought she would get romantically involved with him.

When he came by, they talked for a while, and he invited her out to dinner. He said, "You need to get out of this house and have some fun. Why don't you come with me and have dinner?"

Chock was a little weary about going out. She was afraid they would run into her ex.

He said they could go where none of her ex's crowd hung out. She agreed to go.

They drove out of town and had dinner at the airport.

They had a good time. They thought the sensation they created was amusing.

He had movie star qualities, and she had been told on several occasions that Chock was easy on the eyes.

It was still early in the evening when they finished dinner. He asked if she would like to stop by his room for a drink, then they could listen to some of his music.

Chock said, "It sounds like a good idea."

They had a few more drinks and listened to some music. Both of them loved music and singing. They started singing along, and then they danced. The dancing led to kissing. The kissing led to trying to rip of each other's clothes.

Chock had seen all the movies and heard all of the talk about ripping off someone's clothes, but she had never thought she would feel like it. She had never put desire, enjoyment, excitement, or any of these words, and sex in the same sentence.

That was the first time Chock felt the urgency to be with a man so strongly that she felt like ripping off his clothes. When she got his clothes off, she started laughing.

"What's so funny?" He started laughing at Chock laughing at him. She was hysterical and couldn't stop.

Chock pointed at his manhood. "What's wrong with it?" The joke was on her.

She had listened and laughed about the jokes told about white men. None of them were true.

Chock finally calmed down enough to tell him why she was laughing.

He said, "That's just a myth. Just as the myth white people have about black men. It's such a myth that some men won't go after the women they would like to be with. They are too ashamed to let the woman they want see them if they don't think they are as well endowed as they should be."

Vic was like that. Chock could talk about anything with him. Every now and again, she would feel him just looking at her. Chock had slip off into space. Images of the past would sneak into her thought. She would sit, in almost a comatose state starring into space, watching these images.

He would put his arms around her and say softly, "What happened to you? You can tell me."

Chock would smile but she never did tell. There were some things she didn't think she could ever tell anyone.

They were together whenever he was in town. His visits seemed to be more often and longer.

When he saw her ex out and occupied, he would come by the house to see her. Sometimes, they would sit on the steps and talk. If she was busy in the yard, he would help her with her yard work.

He wanted Chock to go out with him. She cringed at the thought of being seen together at a bar by her ex. She convinced him that they could not let anyone know they were seeing each other. Vic would hear of a band playing in a nearby town. They would go there to hear them. They completely avoided the clubs in the town they lived in. She wasn't ready for the fallout.

Chock's ex was still around. They would see each other every once in a while. She was afraid he would react as he had before when she had told him she was seeing someone.

He still referred Chock as his wife. She had changed the locks of the house, but her ex seemed to get in whenever he felt like it.

Whenever Vic went on tour, Chock's life would come to a standstill.

CHAPTER 45

What Shall Chock Do Now?

Vic was gone for almost a year. Chock's kids were gone. All of her so-called friends had put her down. She was alone. Chock started buying liquor and started drinking herself to sleep. Chock's drinking came to a screeching halt when she suffered a heart failure.

She was in the hospital for seven days. When she got home, her ex started coming by. The more she tried to keep him away, the more clinging and agreeable he became.

Chock told him she didn't like him coming in the house whenever he felt like it without any warning. He said it was still his house, and he would come in whenever he felt like it.

Chock didn't know he harbored resentment against her for getting sole possession of the house.

He said, "You should sign the house back over to me."

She told him, "Before I let you and your girlfriend have my house, I will burn it to the ground."

She felt the house was rightfully hers. She had scrimped and saved for the down payment. When she fell short,she had called her sisters and they had helped her out. He had constantly drained her bank accounts. When she stop putting money into the accounts, he would search around the house until he found her hiding place.

After Chock told him how she felt about the house, he added, "You know you have cancer and you gonna die. Why don't you just kill yourself and get it over with?"

What was he talking about? Was he trying to find a way to get rid of her?

He was talking to somebody, probably, the same women that beat her up.

Chock told him to get out of her house and stay out.

She finally got better.She would go out alone. If she happened to run into him, he would monopolize all of her time. He would make a point to let everyone know Chock still belonged to him and to keep away.

When they were married, it was the opposite. When other men came over to their table, he would invite them to sit down so they would buy the drinks or to keep her occupied while he was busy elsewhere.

There weren't many available men that she was acquainted with.

The ones she was acquainted with were also acquainted with her ex.

They wanted no part of either one of them. They were afraid of their mouths. They were afraid of her ex opening his big mouth and afraid she wouldn't keep her big mouth shut.

On her way home from work, Chock stopped by to see her girlfriend. She was mourning the death of her boyfriend. She had been living with him for years before he died. She talked Chock into going to a club with her. She tried to get out of going because it was a school night. Chock could tell she was lonesome, so she decided to go along.

Before they left, Chock told her she didn't have any cash on her. She said it would be her treat. They went to the club which had been a favorite of theirs. When they got to the lounge, the band she wanted to see was on stage.

The waitress seated them and took their orders. She ordered a drink and a huge platter of hot wings. That was something new, and she said Chock just had to have some. Chock also ordered a drink.

Before the order came, a friend of hers saw her and came over to talk to her. The band saw her and played her favorite song, and she just had to dance.

While she was on the dance floor, the order came. The platter of wings was so huge,Chock felt embarrassed sitting alone at the table, with them in front of her. Chock found enough money in her purse to pay for the order. When she paid for the order, the band went on break.

Her friend came back to the table when the band went on break. The musicians stopped by the table. When the wings were gone, and the drinks were gone, the band went back on stage. Her girlfriend went back on the dance floor. Chock ordered another drink. When the drink came, she had written a check so she would have some cash on her. She said she would have to go to the bar to cash it.

Chock went to the bar to cash her check.

While Chock was at the bar waiting for her check to be cashed, she felt someone touch her shoulders.

She froze and her heart dropped. *Oh no,* she thought, *he is about to get on my last nerve. I can't turn for him.*

Chock turned around to give him a piece of her mind, but it wasn't her ex.

The man she saw standing there could have been a stand-in for the popular soul singer, Black Moses.

He said, "You don't have to cash a check to pay for the drinks. I'll pay for them."

Chock looked at him and asked, "Why are you sounding like that?" He had a heavy accent.

He said, "Like what?"

"Like you trying to be cute."

"That the way people sound where I come from." "Where do you come from?"

"Trinidad."

Chock kept giving him the third degree. His name was Isaac. Isaac said he had been sent to Idaho by his union. He was a welder, and welders were needed at one of the plants in a little town nearby.

He said he was surprised to see her. He wasn't aware black people lived in this town.

They kept talking. He said he had stopped in with a friend of his, and he was on his way home.

He asked if she would care to meet him one day for a drink. Chock said she would think about it. He asked for her phone number. He called her the next day.

They talked on the phone every day for about a week before she decided to have a drink with him. Chock said she would meet him at the same club.

Chock had misgivings about meeting a strange man. She told her sister and her girlfriend where she would be before she left.

She met Isaac back at the club; the band was so loud they couldn't hear one another. They had a drink. After she finished the drink, he asked her if she wanted another. She said, "No, I only have one drink when I drive."

He asked her if she would see him again. Chock agreed, and they set a date.

She told him they could have a drink at her house, and she wouldn't have to worry about driving.

He said he would bring the drinks.

He asked Chock what she would like for him to bring. She gave him the names of wines she liked.

He showed up, as scheduled, with two different wines.

When they drank one bottle, he wanted to see what the other one tasted like.

They drank the other bottle. One thing led to another. They saw each other often.

Later, he told one of her daughters, she was easy.

Chock told her sister she had met a nice man. She said, "You know, your ex is going to kill you when he finds out."

Chock lost her eldest sister two days later. She *was devastated.*

Her ex took advantage of her family's bereavement and simulated himself into every aspect of their life. He made himself indispensable. Everyone forgot they were no longer married and thought of them as a couple.

Before her sister passed away, she had told her ex of her intentions. Chock told him he was no longer welcome to come by her home whenever he felt like it, and she told him she was seeing someone else and wanted her privacy.

Chock didn't think it would be a problem. He had girlfriends all over town, and one was living with him. She didn't go where he lived and she felt he shouldn't come to where she lived.

She had changed the locks again, but she could sense that he was gaining entrance somehow. She told her family of her suspicions; they said it was a figment of her imaginations.

Everyone left after her sister's funeral, but her ex kept coming around. He thought they had reconciled. Chock had to tell him again that she had not changed her mind about being back with him and that she was still seeing someone else. He said he couldn't see how she felt that way after all he had done for them.

Chock told him that she appreciated what he had done for her family in their time of need, but what he did was for the family, and it was his choice, and was not for her.

Chock added, she would always respect him as the father of their kids, but she would never trust him enough to ever let him back into her life.

He started his pity speech about they were all the family he had with that fake crying of his. She told him he had said that speech one time too many. She didn't believe him anymore and never would again. She told him he had to leave or she would call the police. He left in his company's truck.

Chock would see him drive by several times a day. Everywhere she went, she would see his truck parked someplace. She went to the police and told them she was being followed and someone was coming in her house. They said they would look into it. But they never did.

Her ex knew where she was going and what time she would be there. They had things taken from their dwellings. Someone was eating their food and drinking their drinks. She started to get scared.

They went to the police again, but that didn't stop whoever was bothering them. They knew who the guilty party was and told the police. They said they didn't have any proof.

Sugar was put into Isaac's gas tank. They just happened to notice something white on the ground by the gas tank. All of the tires on Isaac and Chock's cars were flattened.

One night, Chock's ex and two bad boys mistook Isaac's brother for him. They told Isaac's brother if he didn't leave her alone, something bad would happen to him.

When Isaac's brother told him about the threats, he got angry. He wasn't frightened away like the other guys were.

When Chock went over to his apartment after work, he was sitting in a chair sharpening a machete that was about four feet long.

He said, "Chock, you call your ex and tell him I said if he don't leave us alone, somebody was going to die."

When he finished sharpening the blade, he took the machete and put it in his car. The next morning, it was gone.

They never considered living together. He lived with three other guys in a basement apartment. Chock moved in with him. He refused to move in with her. She was very uncomfortable, but she was too afraid to stay in her own home that had four bedrooms.

When she got up in the morning, Chock had to go home to take a shower and go to work.

They knew this arrangement was inconvenient and they could not keep this up much longer. Chock wanted to stay in her own home and sleep in her own bed. She wasn't getting a good night's sleep, and she was exhausted. When she left his apartment, she had to go home and take shower and go to work. After work, she went home and stayed until almost dark. Then Chock would go back to his apartment for the night.

He put padlocks on the inside of every door in his apartment and in her house, but someone was still coming in while they were at work. When Chock stayed home, she locked herself in and barricaded the doors when she went to bed. One night, she felt someone standing over her while she was asleep. She woke up and saw her ex. He was standing by her bed and looking down at her. Chock started screaming. He ran. They were harassed all summer and after school started.

Sometimes,they would see him peeping in the window or parked around the corner when they came home, but the police didn't believe them. They knew him.

One night, they decided to go out. They went to the same place they had met. They hadn't been out for a while, and the same band was back in town.They were there for a couple of hours before they heard her ex make his grand entrance.They decided to leave to avoid trouble.

On the way to her house,they stopped by the store and bought a bottle of wine. They watched TV for a while, and went to bed.

CHAPTER 46

My Ex's Last Stand

Chock doesn't know why Isaac wanted to keep seeing her after all the drama. They were harassed everyday and every night whether they were together or alone. They tried to avoid trouble by not going out in public. When they saw him come in the club, the night they went out, they left the club in order to avoid an altercation. They decided to finish the night at her house. No one was there. They would have a quiet evening together for a change.

After they had gone to bed, they were awaken by someone fumbling around at the front door. She had changed the locks. They knew it was him, but didn't think he would come in while they were there. They heard the screen open, and then the big door opened, and they heard footsteps coming toward the bedroom.

Isaac said, "Close your eyes."

Was he crazy? Chock wasn't about to close her eyes. She started to get up, but he held her arm. All of a sudden, the lights came on. When the lights came on, all she saw was red. She was as blind as the proverbial bat.

Chock heard her ex say, "What you doing in bed with my wife?" Isaac had gotten out of bed and was standing between them.

He said, "She your wife?"

"She tell me, you divorce long time now." Chock's ex left the room.

When he left, Chock locked the door. She told Isaac to get his clothes, and they headed for the window, but the window wouldn't open.

After a short time, her ex started hacking on the door to break the lock.

They kept struggling with the window.

Chock's ex finally managed to break the lock. When he got in the bedroom, he had a knife in each hand. A meat cleaver was in one hand and her deboning knife was in the other.

Isaac went to meet him, but Chock was standing between them and the closest to her ex.

He grabbed her and put the deboning knife, the sharpest knife in her kitchen, to Chock's throat.

"If you come any closer, I will slit her f—ing throat!" "OK, OK, mon, just let she be."

"I'll let her go if you leave right now!" "I go. You do no ting to she?"

"No, just get the hell out!"

"OK, OK, mon. I go. Just put tee knife down."

He moved Chock so Isaac could pass and wouldn't come too close to him.

When Isaac left, her ex started working himself into fervor pitch. He was going on and on about how Chock had made him look.

He was saying he had done everything he could for her and that was how she had paid him—by going behind his back and sleeping with another man.

Chock wasn't sure what he was talking about. He seemed to have lost touch with reality.

They had been divorced for three years.

The phone rang. Her ex picked it up. Chock heard him say, "You got your mother fucking nerves calling my wife!"

He jerked the phone from the wall and started chopping it with the meat cleaver.

"That was your boyfriend calling to see if you were all right! That goddam fucking son of a bitch!"

He went through the house and jerked all the phones out of the walls and chopped them up with the meat cleaver.

Chock edged toward the front door.

He grabbed Chock and pulled her back into the bedroom and pushed her onto the bed and closed the door.

He started breaking and slashing everything in the room. Then he turned on her.

Chock wrapped the thick comforter around her and rolled to the far side of the bed.

He was in a frenzy trying to slash her with the knives—one and then the other. Chock kept rolling and kicking at him.

She couldn't feel it, but she knew she had been cut. She could feel blood running down her face and saw it all over the bed.

He struck out at Chock with the meat cleaver again and again. His attack on her seemed to go forever.

Chock rolled and felt his hand and the handle of the meat cleaver hit her ear.

Her head seemed to explode, and she heard a roaring sound. There was so much blood she could barely see him.

She knew she had to think to save her life because she couldn't fight him off much longer.

Chock rolled to the far side of the bed again. When he came around to get her, she rolled back to the other side as fast as she could and jumped off the bed.

She ran to the bathroom and locked the door. She knew the door wouldn't hold him for long. Then she thought about the drawers in the linen closet.

The linen closet was right by the door, and when a drawer was open, the bathroom door couldn't be opened.

Chock opened all four drawers and pulled them out to reinforce the door.

She knew the door couldn't be opened when one drawer wasn't closed. She knew four would surely keep him out.

Chock heard him cussing and breaking things in the front room.

Then he came to the bathroom door.

He tried to break in. When he couldn't break down the door, he started chopping at the locks. He broke the lock, but the opened drawers kept the door from opening.

When he couldn't break the door down, he tried to bully her into letting him in.

"If you don't open this door and come out, it's gonna be worse for you when I get you out!"

Chock went to the window and opened it as much as she could. It wouldn't go up enough for her to get out.

Her neighbor's bedroom was about ten feet away. She tried to scream, but no sound came out.

Was she having a dream? Chock tried again, and she still couldn't make a sound.

Chock turned from the window and saw her reflection in the mirror.

She was horrified at the face looking back at her.

She would have screamed if she could.

She had a big gash in her head. Her hair was matted with blood. Her face was bruised and swollen and covered with blood. There was a big, open gash, under one eye.

Her eyes were swollen almost shut. It was difficult for her to hear with the loud, roaring noise in her ear.

She was shaking uncontrollable as she sat down on the toilet lid. Chock could hear him chopping at the door.

He started calling her name. She didn't try to answer.

He kept yelling at her to open the door. Chock just sat on the toilet stool and listened. Finally, he seemed to calm down.

She didn't know if he had calmed down because he had given up trying to trick her into opening the door or he had left.

She couldn't hear any movement on the other side of the door. He had stopped moving and stopped talking.

After a few minutes, he started calling her again.

The insane anger in his voice seemed to have dissipated. He kept calling. He didn't know she had lost her voice. She just sat there.

"You in there?" he kept on calling her name and asking. Maybe he thought she had somehow gotten out of the window. "If you come out, I won't hurt you."

Chock didn't believe him. She knew she couldn't trust him to keep his word.

She thought if she didn't come out, she was going to bleed to death. She saw a trail of blood running down the floor and under the door. He must have seen the blood.

"Oh my God! Come out before you bleed to death. I'm sorry. I didn't mean to hurt you! Come out, I'm sorry, I won't hurt you." He kept saying I'm sorry over and over.

Chock decided to take her chances before she bled to death. She pushed the drawers back in the linen closet and opened the door.

When he saw me, she think he went into shock.

He stood there with is mouth open just looking at Chock. His arm was raised and frozen in midair with a knife in his hand ready to strike.

Chock started walking to the front door. She was going to the car to drive herself to the hospital, but she was too weak. She fell.

She kept trying to talk, and finally she got her voice back.

Chock managed to get up from the floor and begged him to take her to the hospital.

She told him if he took her to the hospital, she wouldn't tell anyone what he had done to her—just like all the other times.

He believed her and drove her to the hospital.

CHAPTER 47

Citizen's Arrest

All the way to the hospital, Chock kept hearing about how ungrateful she had been to him for all the things he had done for her. He said she had paid him back by sleeping around with other men. He believed, if she had just appreciated him more and stayed with him, all that would have never happened. This was her entire fault. When she got to the hospital, Chock recognized the nurse who had been on duty when she had been there before, but she didn't recognize her. When she asked her what had happened, Chock told her she had been attacked by that dog again.

They admitted Chock and put her in a cubicle. Her ex insisted on going with her.

The doctor came who had treated Chock before. He didn't ask any questions about how she had gotten all banged up and cut up.

He told her ex he had to wait out in the waiting room.

Her ex said, "That's my wife, and I have a right to be here." The doctor said, "I won't treat her until you leave."

"When I am finished, you can come back in."

When her ex left, the doctor said, "I wanted him to leave, because I could tell that you have been battered. Did he do this to you?"

Chock said, "Yes."

"Do you want me to call the police?"

Chock said she was afraid of what he would do if he saw the police.

"I'll send you to x-ray. I'll tell them to come in through the back entrance so he won't see them."

"OK." Chock was taken to the x-ray room. Two police officers came to question her. She told them what had happened. The older of the two seemed upset and was sympathetic.

He said, "I wondered how long you were going to stay in that situation before someone was seriously hurt."

The other officer, who was younger, didn't seem to share his sentiments. His attitude was uncaring, and he seemed to think Chock got what was coming to her.

The elder officer told Chock they couldn't arrest her ex, but she could.

"Me?"

Chock would have to place him under citizen's arrest then they could take him to jail.

"How can I do that?"

"You will have to tell him you are placing him under citizen's arrest."
"We will escort you back to emergency."

"You will have to say his name, and then say, 'I am placing you under citizen's arrest for assault, for holding me against my will, and attempted murder."

They escorted her back to the emergency room.

When Chock repeated what they told her she had to say.

Her ex looked shocked that she would say he had done all those things to her.

He said, "Me? You must be out of your mind. I never laid a hand on you. All I did was try to help you, and you show your appreciation by accusing me of something I didn't do?"

The elder officer said, "You are under arrest." He handcuffed her ex and took him away.

When they took him away, Chock was still being treated. She had a broken nose, a busted eardrum. She had a gash in my head, a deep gash under one eye, and her lips were busted, and there were other bruises over her body.

The elder officer had come back to the hospital.

While the doctor was putting stitches in the gash under her eye, Chock glimpsed her ex standing at the door.

Chock started screaming.

The officer that had been standing by the emergency door entrance came in with his gun drawn. He told her ex to leave.

Her ex said, "I have a right to be here. I am here to take my wife home." "She is not your wife. You don't have a right to be here, and you are not going to take her anywhere. Now leave or go to jail again. And I guarantee you that you won't be getting out any time soon." Chock's ex left.

The officer said, "I had a feeling he would show up here at the hospital. That's why I came back when I found out he had made bail."

The doctor said Chock would be in a lot of pain when she left the hospital.

He said she was too traumatized to go home by herself. Chock would be in too much pain, and because of her injuries, she wouldn't be able to take care of herself.

He also said he could commit her to the hospital.

Chock had to have surgery on her ear as soon as he could schedule it, but he couldn't guarantee she would be safe from her ex, if he happened to come back.

He asked me, "Is there any place you could go until you have recuperated?"

Chock couldn't think of any place she could go where her ex would not be coming around whenever he felt like it.

The police officer said he knew a place for battered women, if she wanted to go there and it would be safe.

He would take her there, and she could talk to the woman in charge.

If Chock didn't want to stay, she didn't have to.

She agreed to go with him. He drove around to make sure no one was following him. She was finally taken to the shelter for battered women.

CHAPTER 48

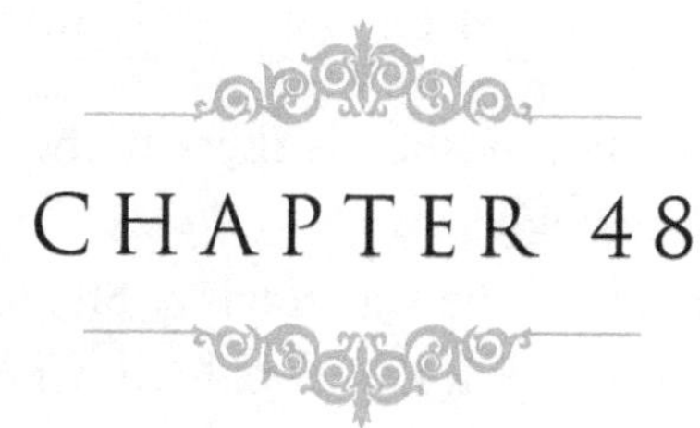

Deaf! Blind! and Dumb, Too?

Chock was in the shelter for two weeks before she got in touch with anyone. When she entered the shelter, she was unable to see, hear, and could barely walk. The officer volunteered to let her folks and Isaac know that she was in a safe place.

After two weeks, she felt well enough to go home to get some personal items she needed and to check on her house.

Chock couldn't leave the shelter without a police escort. The young officer who was at the hospital was assigned to take her wherever she wanted to go and to bring her back to the shelter. He was told not to let her out of his sight.

Her first stop was at her folks'. The officer didn't come in with her; he just waved her on.

Chock thought her folks would be glad to see her.

Only her mom was home. She said, "Well, I see you decided to show your face and pay us a visit. You ought to be ashamed of how you are treating your husband. You know, he didn't do all those things that you accused him of to you."

Chock knew there was no way she could convince her mom that her ex was not the man she believed him to be.

Chock was hurt that she still took his side. The only man she knew was her dad.

Their mother thought all men were like him and had raised her seven daughters to think the same.

They were to treat their husbands the way she treated their dad.

The man was always right.

She asked Chock where she was staying. She told her she couldn't tell her. Chock knew if she did, she would tell her ex.

She told her she had stopped by to see how the were and to let them know she was all right. Chock told her she wasn't going home and a policeman was waiting to take her back to where she had been staying. Chock's next stop was at her house. From the police car window, the house looked very sinister. It looked as if anything could be hiding in there.

The officer sat in the car and looked around to see if they were followed. He said for Chock to get her things together, and he would wait in the car.

Chock told him she wasn't going in without him. He gave a grunt and turned off the engine. He got out of the car and walked ahead of her to the front door. She gave him the key to open the door.

When the door opened, he jumped back saying, "Good Lord!"

He put his hand on his gun and told Chock to stay back. He pulled his gun and walked in a little further and beckoned for her. Chock couldn't believe what she saw. She didn't remember all of the blood and damage. The house was a horror scene.

She had refurnished the house after she had gotten a divorce. All of the new furniture had been cut up. The lamps were broken and chairs smashed. She had two huge Texas watermelons in the front room. They had been chopped up, and they were running all over her beige carpet mixed in with the bloody tracks.

Chock's bedroom was also in shambles. All of the bedding and her clothes had been cut to shreds. Blood was on the bed, walls, ceiling, and all through the hallway from the bedroom to the bathroom. When he finished checking out the upstairs, he said he would check the basement, and she was to stay by the door as watch out and let him know if she saw anyone. He went down the stairs walking sideways against the wall with his gun drawn. Chock could hear him walking from room to room. She had a storage space under the stairs.

When he opened one door, the air caused the storage door to slam shut.

He couldn't see the door from where he was. He started yelling, "Lady, lady, lady!"

Chock told him it was just the suction from the door he opened that caused the door to close.

He came back upstairs and said, "Lady, you hurry and get your things together so we can get the hell out of here. Whoever did this is crazy!"

On the way back to the shelter, he was more alert. Before he let her out at the shelter, he made sure he hadn't been followed. Then he got out and walked her to the door.

"When I got to the door, he said," If you need anything else, call the station."

Chock thanked him, and he left.

She was in the shelter another week before she had surgery on her ear. The doctor said she would lose about 25 percent of her hearing and would gradually lose the sight in the eye the gash was under.

When she woke up the next morning, after her ear surgery, there was a huge plant on the table from her ex.

Chock asked the nurse how the plant had gotten there. She said she didn't know but would find out. She asked around and was told her husband had brought it when he came to visit. They were told under no circumstance Chock was to have visitors.

Her room was off limits to all visitors. A sign was also posted on the door.

When the doctor came in, she told him she wanted to go back to the shelter as soon as he could dismiss her.

Chock went back to the shelter and stayed for another two weeks.

CHAPTER 49

Beyond Belief

Chock had been in touch with Isaac while she was at the shelter. When she told him what had happened after he had left the house that morning, he was furious. He said he had called back to the house to see if she was all right, but her ex had cursed him out and hung up on him. He said he then drove back to the house. When he saw her ex's car gone, he rang the doorbell several times before he decided to leave and go to work.

After she left the shelter, she stayed with Isaac. It was an inconvenience to him, his brother, and his two friends, but they didn't want her going back to her house. They said she would be safer if she stayed with them. There would always be someone there with her.

Chock's ex had stopped trying to hide the fact that he was coming in to where they lived when they were away.

He would leave the drawers open and things out.

He would take food out of the refrigerators. If he saw something he wanted to eat, he ate it or just left it sitting out to spoil.

If he decided to have something to drink, he had a drink.

They were afraid to eat and drink at their own homes. They didn't know if he had poisoned their food or not.

While Chock was living with Isaac, they got calls from him threatening to bomb the place if Isaac didn't leave town.

When Isaac was at her place, they got calls from him threatening to burn the place down if Isaac didn't get out of his house.

They went to the police, but they said nothing could be done. Their hands were tied until they had proof that her ex was behind all of their accusations.

Then she got a call from him one morning telling her if she didn't leave that man and come to his apartment right then, he was going to kill himself.

Chock called the fire department and reported the threat to them. They took the threat seriously and went to his apartment. She could hear the fire engines from Isaac's apartment. They practically had apartments on the same street but on the opposite side of town.

When the fire department got to his apartment, they could not get him to answer the door. One of her ex's neighbors told the firemen that her ex was in the apartment, because he had seen him go in a few minutes earlier.

When they couldn't get a response, they broke in.

Her ex had passed out from one of his all-night drinking and gambling party.

That had happened many times while they were together. He would come home after being gone for more than twenty-four hours. He would ask for something to eat but would usually pass out before he had a chance to eat, or he would pass out while he was eating.

The medics couldn't revive him when they got into his room. When they couldn't revive him, they took him to the hospital thinking he might have overdosed.

He was committed to the mental ward of the hospital because of his threat to kill himself.

They pumped his stomach but couldn't detect what he might have taken.

Chock's girlfriend heard about her ex being in the hospital and went to see him. She called Chock and told her he was in a coma, and they couldn't find what was wrong with him.

The hospital also called Chock. They told her he was in a coma, and they couldn't revive him.

Chock decided to go to the hospital; after all, he was the father of their children.

When she got to the hospital, he was still out and in a private room.

While she was there, he opened his eyes and looked around. When he saw all of the monitors in the room and tubes hooked up to him, he started screaming.

He became so agitated they had to give him a shot to calm him down.

He told the psychologist why he had been unconscious to try to convince them that he wasn't trying to kill himself. He said he wasn't crazy. He wanted to get out of the mental ward and go home. He said he was only playing a trick on her.

They decided to keep him another day for observation—just in case.

That was the last threat they got from him saying he was going to kill himself.

Chock didn't have many of her personal items and clothes with her while she was staying with Isaac. She had deserted a four-bedroom home. She had gone through a lot of expense to make her home comfortable. Now, she was sleeping on a mattress on the floor of a basement walk-in apartment and had four guys for roommates.

Sooner or later, she had to go home.

Chock decided before she went home, she would buy a gun. She went to a gun shop and bought a .38 caliber automatic and hollow point bullets.

By the time Chock had purchased the gun, school had started. On the surface, it seemed that everything was quiet.

Her folks convinced her to drop the charges against her ex.

Her ex had convinced them that he was really sorry about what had happened to Chock but he didn't remember doing what she had accused him of doing. That was also the story he told the police. No one that knew him could phantom him doing what he had done to her.

They put Isaac under suspicion. Chock's ex promised he would not go near her.

She also put a restraining order on him.

She would see him drive by in his company truck. She knew he was still going in her house, and Isaac knew he was coming in theirs.

They found out later from one of his girlfriends who told her other friend and the friend told her.

That friend had grown up with Chock's kids and didn't want to see her getting hurt anymore. When her ex offered money to guys to plant drugs in their cars to get them arrested, he thought he should let her know what her ex was up to. He told Chock her ex had been coming into the school where she worked. He would go in her room when she was outside with the kids, get her keys and make copies of them and get them back before she missed them.

She remember when she once thought she had misplaced her keys and had to make a report. All the locks in the building had to be changed.

This friend also told Chock her ex had changed all the windows in the house to open from the outside.

That's why they never could keep him out and why they couldn't open the windows to get out the night he attacked her.

Each day, Chock found something missing. Her folks had stopped listening to her. She was told he had also put a tap on her telephone. He was in the bars laughing about what he was doing to them and what he was going to do.

Chock got the gun and put it in a designated spot where Isaac and her would have access to it if need be.

They were harassed and stalked for months. It kept on until about Thanksgiving.

CHAPTER 50

Whups! Too late! "Stop!"

After Chock bought the gun, she started staying at her own house. Upon entering her home after work one evening, she reached for the gun she had left in hiding, by the door. It wasn't there. There were several places, by the door, she could have hidden the gun for immediate access when she entered the house. She wanted the gun in her hands when she opened the front door.

Her first thought was the gun had been stolen. So many other things had come up missing lately. To make sure she wasn't making a mistake, she looked in other places she could have put the gun.

Chock put her hand in a coat pocket, and she felt the barrel. She knew she hadn't placed the gun in the coat pocket that way. When she felt the barrel, she moved her hand back carefully. Something was not right.

Chock had been taught to never grab a gun by the barrel. If she had pulled the gun out of the pocket, the very least that would have happened was she would haveTbelowxnt her hand off.

She looked around the coat rack and saw plastic fishing line. The gun had been rigged with plastic fishing line. She cut the line. When she took the gun out of the coat pocket, the fishing line was tied to the trigger.

Chock couldn't fathom-her ex's thinking. She didn't want to leave the gun home anymore. She couldn't take it to work. She couldn't leave it in her car because the locks had been busted.

The only place to leave the gun was at Isaac's apartment. His job was finished, and he would be home, or he could take the gun with him if he had to leave.

After she removed the gun from the coat pocket, she carefully cut the fishing line that was tied to the gun. She took the gun to the bedroom with her and barricaded herself in.

Chock made a place to sleep on the floor, in the corner, on the far side of the bed, away from the door, and windows. She was adamant; if he was foolish enough to come into her bedroom tonight, he would die. She would shoot without giving him any warning and wouldn't stop until he was dead.

She was fed up. She had been pushed as far as she was going to go. She had to turn around and fight back if she wanted to come out of that situation alive.

Nothing happened that night. He was probably close by listening for a gunshot. When he didn't hear a shot, he probably surmised she had the gun and was waiting for him.

When Chock got ready for work, she took the gun to Isaac's apartment. She let herself in. She went into the bedroom. He was sitting up in bed reading. At first, she couldn't see him when she entered into the room because the room was so dark. There was a little entrance way blocking him from view.

He had a reading lamp on. The room was so dark Chock could only see the light shining on the page he was reading. Once her eyes got customized to the darkness, she could see him. The basement apartment was almost pitching black.

She had already told him about what had happened and her decision to leave the gun with him. She was running late. She spoke to him and asked him what he was reading.

He said he was reading a book some people left there. Chock asked him what he wanted to do with the gun. He told her to put it on the table.

She put the gun on the nightstand and left. She went to work across town.

At about ten o'clock, the secretary came to her room. She was looking a little flushed. She said, "There is a detective in the office who wants to talk to you. I'll stay with the kids while you talk to him."

On her way to the office, Chock was thinking they were finally doing something about the complaints they had made concerning the problems they had been having with her ex.

When she got to the office, the detective asked for her name. She told him.

He said, "I'm a detective. There was a shooting this morning. Your husband was involved. He was shot."

"I don't have a husband."

"The victim said he is married to you. He told us how to get in touch with you."

"We were married. I divorced him three years ago."

"We need you to come to the station and identify the shooter."
"Who is the shooter?"

"He goes by the name of Isaac. He say he knows you, and the gun is registered in your name. We need to know how the gun got to his apartment. I can give you a ride to the station and have you back to work in a few minutes."

"No, no. Thank you. I'll drive myself."

Chock went to the room and told the secretary she needed a sub for the rest of the day.

She went to the police station which was about three blocks from the school right and in the middle of the black neighborhood.

She could tell the word had spread. People were out being nosy while they pretended to work in their lawns.

She was directed to the detective's office. When she got there, Isaac was there. He was pacing around the room and acting as if he was getting ready for a fight.

When he saw Chock, he started talking. She told him he should stop talking.

Chock told the detective she wanted to speak to Isaac alone. The detective said he would leave, and they could use his office. When she asked him if the room was bugged, he said she had seen too many TV shows.

When the detective left, Chock asked Isaac to tell her what had happened, but she warned him to keep his voice down.

He said when he had taken his van to be serviced later that morning, he had forgotten all about the gun. He said he left it on the nightstand where Chock had put it.

When he left the van at the shop; he left the keys to the padlock he had installed in his apartment in the van. He walked back to the apartment. He didn't realize he had locked himself out of his apartment until he got to the door.

When he couldn't get in the door of his apartment, he had to go upstairs and ask the landlord to let him go through their apartment to get downstairs to his apartment.

He said when he got in his apartment, he went to his room and fell asleep.

He said he heard someone come in and thought it was one of his roommates. They all had keys to the locks he had installed. He heard someone come into his room. When they didn't say anything, he looked up to see which of the guys had come home. He said he recognized Chock's ex standing at the door with what looked like a shotgun in his hand.

The object Isaac thought was a shot gun was the huge wire cutter her ex used to cut the padlock to get into Isaac's apartment. Isaac said he picked up the gun from the nightstand and started firing.

He didn't know he had hit her ex until he turned on the lights and went to the front door of the apartment. Her ex had managed to get out the door and to the bottom step before he went down.

Isaac said, "You know what that fucker said? He said the steps were hard and hurt his head. He asked me to bring him a pillow.

I (Isaac) told him, "You don't need a pillow because you gonna died."

Chock had assumed her ex was already dead. When she realized he was still alive,she felt like hitting Isaac. Her ex was still around, and he would continue to making her life a living hell. She turned on Isaac. She yelled,

"You mean he is still alive?"

The detective came in and said he was taking Isaac to jail, and he would be held there for further investigation.

Chock told the detective, "This could have been avoided if you had bothered to investigate months ago. Instead, you gave my ex a free pass to terrorize us and do whatever he felt like doing to us whenever he felt like it.

How many times had they come to you for help before today? You kept telling them your hands were tied and that there was nothing you could do.

When her ex gets himself shot for breaking in a man's house, you arrest the other man for trying to defend himself and take him to jail? "Now, after everything that has happened to us, and after all of the times we have come to you for help, you are going to investigate. Now you are going to arrest a man for trying to defend himself when he thought someone, who had been terrorizing him for months, was trying to kill him?"

The jail was in another building. When they put Isaac in the squad carto take him to the jailhouse, the whole neighborhood was still watching—her folks included as their house was in sight of the jailhouse. They saw the whole thing, too.

Chock's girlfriend came to the jailhouse. She said her ex had called her. He told her that he had been shot and wanted her to come to the hospital to see him.

She said, "He's at the hospital screaming and calling your name. He said he won't let anyone touch him until he sees you."

Yea, Chock thought. She had fallen for that trick before. She agreed to go to the hospital with her.

When she got to the hospital emergency room, she could hear him. "I don't want to die! Don't let me die! Somebody help me! Call my wife!"

When Chock went in the emergency room, he was lying on his stomach, with a sheet covering his rear end where he had been shot.

When he saw Chock, he started reaching for her. She moved out of his reach.

"Can't you see what he did to me? He shot me! He shot me! He shot me!"

Chock was so enraged. He was trying to play the sympathy card again. She said, "He didn't do a good job. Did he? It's your lucky day. If I had been the one holding the gun, I wouldn't have stopped shooting until I knew you were good and dead!"

He stopped screaming and looked at her in disbelief. The hospital staff was also shocked. She said,

"This is the dog that has been attacking me for twenty-five years." "If he doesn't want you to treat him, I don't care if you let him die!" The doctor said they needed a responsible party to sign for him. "It won't be me. I'm not that responsible party. He is not my

responsibility anymore." The doctor that was attending him was the same doctor who had stitched me up a few weeks ago.

When he recognized Chock, he said he understood how she felt.

Chock left the hospital and got an attorney for Isaac. The attorney said they could hold him for twenty-four hours without charging him.

While her ex was in the hospital, he had gotten in touch with most of the people who had influence in the black community. They were also siding with her ex. Isaac was an outsider, and she had caused the problems.Her ex had suddenly become a model citizen, a hardworking man, and a good father and husband who had been wronged by an unfaithful wife.

They called and wrote letters to the company he worked for to keep him from being fired.

The man, Chock's ex, was on company time. He used the company's wire cutters to gain entrance into Isaac's apartment.

The company's truck her ex had used to get to Isaac's house was still parked out in front of his house, and they were still saying her ex had good cause to do what he did.

One fact had been left out in all of what had been going on. Everyone had forgotten one thing. She wasn't that man's wife. She had been divorced from him three years.

Before Isaac went to jail, he wanted Chock to go to the apartment to get his valuables. When she got there, the newspaper and the TV crews were still there interviewing people.

The news media was still talking to Isaac's neighbors and her ex's friends who happened to be upon the scene.

Chock went in and got his jewelry and the roll of money he had been saving for his trip and left. No one even bothered to look at her. She went in and out of the apartment unnoticed.

That evening, there was a picture of her ex in the paper and on TV being loaded into the ambulance. He had finally made the big time.

Isaac got out of jail the next day. He came to her house and stayed until he was ready to leave. The news media and onlookers were still poking around his apartment.

When Isaac got out of jail, detectives and lawyers showed up at her house.

The detectives wanted him to come to the station and press charges against her ex for breaking and entry and other things he had done.

The attorneys wanted to represent Isaac if he decided to sue the company Chock's ex worked for. They said he had a good case against the company and the city for the way they had handled the whole matter.

They kept bothering Isaac until he got irritated with them and lost his patience.

He said, "You arrested the wrong nigger. Now you want to use another nigger to help you out of the mess you made. Mon, get the fuck out of my face. Its over."

Isaac left that weekend, but before he left, Chock went to the police station and got her gun.

CHAPTER 51

It's Not Over Till—

When Isaac drove away from Chock's house, Chock stood in the doorway and watched until his van drove out of sight. Then she went inside and locked all the doors and put the gun on the table and placed a towel over it.

She didn't know why she was afraid. Her ex was in the hospital.

When he got out, he wouldn't be able to walk for a while.

When he got out of the hospital, his friends who is a married couple, took him in until he would be able to care for himself.

Chock wasn't taking any chances. At night, she would put the loaded gun on the nightstand by the bed. She was still frightened by the least little noise. Upon hearing any noise that would awake her, she would grab the gun.

She had been in constant contact with Isaac in Houston. He wanted her to come for a visit during the Christmas holidays. Chock told him her kids were coming for Christmas, but she would be happy to make the trip for the New Year.

Chock went to Houston for two weeks. When she got back to Idaho and got off the plane, her ex was there. One of her sons was also there. He said his dad told him he was going to pick her up. He told his dad that it wasn't a good idea, but her ex didn't listen and was there anyways. He was angry because Chock wouldn't let him give her a ride home.

She couldn't see how he would ever think she would get in a car with him after all she had gone through with him.

When she got to her room, Chock could tell things were a little off, but her two sons were there, and they could have been in her room. She asked them about it. They said their dad had come over to see them while she was gone, but they didn't see him go into her bedroom.

Chock let it pass, thinking her ex couldn't have been up to his old tricks. He still had problems getting around and her two sons were in the house. Her eldest son had told him once after a fight, if he ever put his hands on me again, he would kill him.

Before her kids went back on duty, they had given her some pointers on how to protect herself from intruders. They told her to never go looking for someone if she thought her house had been broken into. She was also given a hunter's knife in a pouch. She put the knife under her pillow.

They told her if someone came in the house, Chock should find a corner and put her back in the corner and wait for them to come to her and not go looking for them. They said the intruder could be hiding anywhere waiting for her. She was also told to let them have anything they wanted as long as they didn't come into the room she was in.

One night while she was sleeping, she got an eerie feeling someone was standing over her bed watching her. She opened her eyes. She recognized who it was.

Chock grabbed the gun; she didn't have time to aim. She started firing. She could hear the dragging sound made by the person. He was having trouble moving fast and running.

She waited a few minutes to make sure it was safe to get out of bed before she called the police.

They told her to stay on the line. A few minutes later, Chock got out of the corner and went to the front door. A hand grabbed her and pulled her off the steps. Chock thought it was her ex, but it was a policeman. They were waiting around the front steps.

They asked Chock if she was alone. She told them she was. They came inside with their guns still drawn. She guess they had been told about her ex getting his butt shot off.

They asked her where her weapon was. Chock pointed to the table. An officer went to the table, picked it up, and smelled it. He said it had been fired recently.

Chock told him she had fired it twice at the figure standing by her bed.

He asked her if she could identify the person she thought she saw.

She told him it was her ex.

They checked the door and said they couldn't see how anyone got in. Chock told them what had happened before to the windows.

They went outside and checked the windows. They came back inside and told her the windows couldn't be opened from the outside.

An officer went and checked the patio doors. Chock had patio doors in front and back. He lifted up on the door, lifted it off the run, and opened it in two seconds. She had seen the doors off the run, but she never thought they could be opened by just lifting up on them.

They told her how to prevent that from happening. She was to put a rod in the run over the door so it couldn't be lifted up high enough to be opened.

The officer, her ex's friend, still wasn't convinced that anyone ever came into the house. They left.

After they left, Chock called her ex. He didn't answer the phone so she left a message which was a mistake.

She told him, "If he didn't stay out of my house and leave me alone, he was going to get himself shot again."

The next morning before she got out of bed, Chock heard a knock at her door. When she opened it, a policeman was there. He said he had a warrant for her arrest.

She asked him, "For what?"

He said, "For discharging a firearm within the city limit."

He said he would give Chock a chance to turn herself in. She was to come to the station as soon as she got dressed or they would have to arrest her.

When Chock got dressed, she went to the police station. She had to talk to a detective.

She tried to explain why she had fired the gun.

He said she did not have any proof that someone had been in the house.

He also informed Chock that her ex brought a tape to the station. He said she had threatened him and he was afraid for his life. He said her ex had proof he was with someone else at the time of the shooting. Chock knew they didn't believe her just as before. She felt they still carried a little resentment because of the way Isaac had talked to them when they had asked him to sign a complaint against her ex.

They were still in the position where they could be sued for how they handled the situation between Chock and her ex earlier.

They refused to drop the charges and gave Chock a court date.

She got an attorney. She pleaded not guilty. She was given another court date. She had to pay seventy-five dollars as a fine and attorney fees.

That was fine by her. Now her ex knew she would shoot him if he kept bothering her.

Chock told Isaac about the incident when she talked to him. He said she needed to leave that town before someone killed her or she had to kill someone.

He called Chock later and said he had been assigned to a big job in LA and would probably be there for years. He said if she wanted to come out there, they could find a place together. If it didn't work out, they could go their separate ways.

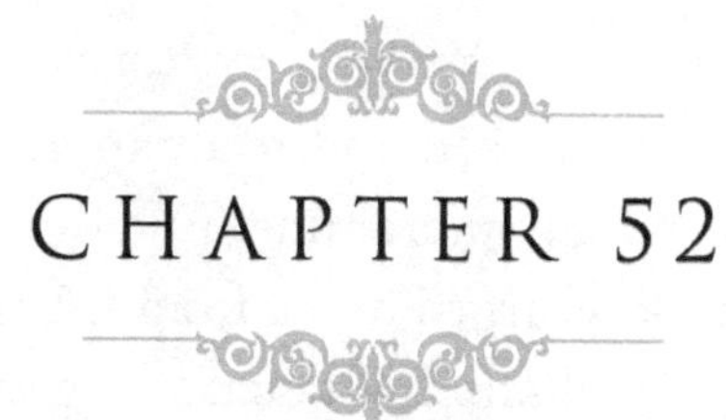

CHAPTER 52

He's Back

Isaac and Chock hadn't planned on having a long-term relationship. When they met, they made their intentions known; neither one of them wanted to be in a relationship where they had to make a commitment.

He told her he may be there today and gone tomorrow. His home was in Trinidad. He had a family in Houston, New York and other places where he had lived. He said he was a bum and liked traveling around whenever he felt the urge.

Chock told him she didn't want to become beholden to anyone. She didn't ever want to be in a situation where she felt obliged to stay. She didn't want to ever be in a relationship that would give anyone the impression they could control her.

They were pushed together by her ex.

Isaac offered to come back to Idaho to help Chock move to LA. She told him she would think about it. She had been planning to move to Texas. She had already escaped from Idaho to LA and from LA back to Idaho.

When school was out, Chock went to LA to see him and to check out the living arrangements. He had a nice apartment, and they had fun together, so she decided that going back to LA and living with Isaac wouldn't be a bad idea. He said he would come to Idaho during the July 4 weekend.

He wanted her to be packed and ready to go when he got there. He didn't want to spend any more time in Idaho than was absolutely necessary. When Chock returned home from LA, she started packing.

Chock had a huge yard sale and practically gave things away.

She put a deposit down on the largest U-Haul the company offered. He arrived early on Saturday morning, and they immediately went to pick up the trailer.

When they got to the U-Haul rental office, the clerk said he didn't have a trailer for them. He had rented the tailor out to someone else, and Chock could have her deposit back.

Chock thought that it was strange; them not to have a u-haul for them. She could see several on the lot. She called the company and told them of the problem she was having with that particular worker. They talked to him. When he got off the phone, he said a trailer had just come in.

They went out to take a look at the trailer. He wanted to take a look at Isaac's van. He said they didn't have the right trailer hitch for the trailer, and he didn't have any in stock. He said he wouldn't let them have the trailer until they got the proper hitch. Isaac asked him to show them a picture of the hitch he wanted them to have. He said it wouldn't do any good because they were the only ones who carried that type of hitch.

Isaac insisted, and the clerk showed him a picture of the hitch they needed. Isaac looked at the picture for a while and told the clerk he would be back to get the trailer. He paid the balance for the trailer and they left. He went to see the friend—the one that was with him the night they met. That friend was also a welder. They were certified to weld in any country, anything, anywhere, under water or above ground. He told his friend about his situation. His friend said,

"Man, that's no problem. We could make that hitch in no time."

They went into his shop. About two hours later, Isaac walked out with a trailer hitch that looked exactly like the one the clerk had shown him.

They went back to pick up the trailer. When he showed the clerk the trailer hitch, the clerk seemed irritated. He still had objections about letting them have the trailer. By that time, they had already figured out who was behind all of the confusion surrounding the trailer.

Chock's ex was keeping constant surveillance of her house and knew what was going on. He worked for a company that had a strong influence. Almost everyone knew him. There were other people in the office when Isaac showed the hitch to the clerk. An eighteen-wheeler truck driver was there and he admired the hitch and asked Isaac where he had gotten it. He said he had never seen anything like it before. He said it could pull anything.

After more comments and discussions from the customers in the store, they finally got the trailer. The clerk had to add a few buts, if this, if that, they wouldn't be responsible.

They finally got the trailer to her house. They packed everything they could pack in the trailer. All of the things she couldn't pack, she left behind. They finished packing around ten o'clock that night.

While they were packing, they saw her ex and several other vehicles driving by several times. They felt he was waiting for a chance to do something awful, but they were not going to wait around to see what it would be.

When they finished packing, they locked the doors to her house, got in the van, and drove away without looking back.

They were exhausted, hungry, dirty, and tired. They drove two and a half hours to Salt Lake City. When they got there, they stopped at the first motel they saw and rented a room.

When they got to the room, she put her gun on the nightstand by the bed. Isaac opened his little bag and put it on the other nightstand. They fell on the bed with the clothes on they had been wearing all that day.

It was almost noon when they woke up the following day. They took a shower, got dressed, had breakfast, and then they got in the van and drove on in to LA.

CONCLUSION

When Isaac and Chock left her house in Idaho; they made it to LA without any incidents. Isaac and Chock lived happily in LA for ten years. After this time,her parent's health began to fail. When her mother passed away,her dad suffered a heart attack which was followed by a series of strokes. They had been married for sixty-five years.

When her dad was well enough to live at home, Chock decided to move back to Idaho to care for him. Isaac also thought this was the right thing to do. He had become fond of her day and agreed to move back with her. Chock was proud, but it was also painful as she watched her dad struggle to regain his in-dependency.

Her ex husband still lived in that town and continued to drive by the house several times a day. Isaac wasn't comfortable living there under these circumstances and decided to return to LA. When he moved back to LA their relationship began to crumble as time went by.

Chock cared for her dad six years before he passed away. When he passed away,she moved to Texas to be closer to family and to make visiting them easier. She now reside in Texas.

She still hear from Isaac. Whenever there is a crisis in her family; somehow, he seems to know. Chock would get a phone call and it will be him, or a knock at the door. When she open it, he would be standing there grinning, "Gul, what 'appen to you?"

www.ingramcontent.com/pod-product-compliance
Lightning Source LLC
Chambersburg PA
CBHW051649180726
48284CB00006B/1925